Thank God for Mississippi

BY TARA COWAN

Thank God for Mississippi

ISBN-13: 978-1-7332922-6-9 (paperback)
ISBN-13: 978-1-7332922-7-6 (ebook)

Book cover and interior design by TeaBerryCreative.com

Chapter One

It was about four o'clock on a Wednesday afternoon when the Crown Prince rolled into Hammondsville. Noses were pressed to windows, spectators stepped out onto sidewalks, and Fanny Barksdale smashed a cake into the wall of her bakery.

Did I mention that he was good-looking? Or so some thought.

Mary, the secretary in our office, remarked that he looked different from his profile picture, while Melissa, one of the assistant district attorneys, thought he looked something like his mother. Paul, the other ADA, lifted his head, glanced out the window momentarily, and went back to his papers.

I hovered near Melissa's desk after laying her copies down for her, watching with my arms crossed a good distance from the office window. He drove a Jeep. I hadn't ever really considered what I thought entitled pricks from New York City should drive, but this choice might not have topped the list.

I should probably pause and give you some background. I'm Mississippi Whitson, the respectable daughter of a welder (now deceased) and his homemaker wife (now eating bon bons from Fanny's bakery). The town is Hammondsville (population ten thousand) in Tennessee, home indiscriminately to rednecks and social climbers. Among the non-rednecks, you are either a Town Person or a County Person. The Whitsons were County People, which means we are Not Our Kind, Dear. "Our Kind" involves frequenting the crappy Country Club and vacationing in the most expensive cities in Florida.

There were a few Old Money types—not many, but the late district attorney had been one of them. Henry Cane, who had died six months ago: a kind heart, a saint, and a grandfather figure to me. He had been blind for the past ten years and had needed a driver, reader, caretaker, and general factotum. Enter *moi.* I had been in his employ for eight years—geez, how old was I? Twenty-eight. As my mother reminded me daily. Biological clock ticking.

Back to Hammondsville. The high school was brutal, the restaurant scene non-existent, and the meth rampant. The town had never really recovered from the War (if you don't know which war I'm talking about, you're probably not from the South), and while there *were* mansions, most sat in a decrepit state, half lived-in or unlivable. There were still signs of the Great Depression, too: money hoarders with boxes buried in their back lawns, cracked statuary downtown (political correctness status: questionable), and a dam on the river for which no one could remember a purpose. Then there was the Great Recession, during which all of the shops and factories had gone out, the buildings left sitting empty and ugly. The town was only just beginning to limp back to life now. In a word, Hammondsville was *dank*. Economic opportunity: low; competition: jungle-level.

I mentioned that my former employer had been Old Money. I'm pretty sure that the Cane Plantation had burned sometime after the War, but the family had owned a large estate outside of town for two or three generations. It was painted white and eerie and falling all to pieces, and I lived in a cottage on the grounds. Or at least, I would continue to do so for the next month or so.

Mr. Cane had held his position as district attorney for about a hundred years. He had been mostly self-sufficient, but he had needed someone within calling distance because of the blindness. I had started out just as his typist and reader at work. When his housekeeper had retired and he had offered me the cottage rent-free as a sort of raise (and my mother was killing me at home), I had moved in and become more. I was his driver, plant-waterer, keeper of the German shepherds, maker of scrambled eggs, and agitator when he wanted to do unhealthy things old people want to do (like eating country ham or canceling the cleaning service).

He was still the DA when he had died, and, like England, Hammondsville had known no other queen (or king, as the case might be). How old was he, you might ask? Ninety-four. I'm guessing you just gasped. But if Elizabeth II could rock it, why not? He was in pretty good physical health and excellent mental health, right up until a heart attack had taken him suddenly.

During a town meeting in which the district's suggestion to the State for his temporary replacement was discussed, I had sat with Paul, Melissa, and Mary, my arms crossed in anger at the world in general and the Suits at the front of the room in particular. They had been nominating their sons for town roles (usually paid positions) for decades, and I swear, if any of them had been lawyers there might have been a fighting match to determine who it would be. But none were, and they paced the floor of City Hall, shoulders thrown back in remarkable confidence, as they considered the dilemma.

They were likely wondering who the scowling girl with the brown hair was, though she had graced the cover of the *Hammondsville Herold* more than once during her successful high school academic career, thank you very much. Oh, but they recalled so-in-so's daddy, who had been on the board of blah-blah-blah, and wasn't one of the *Riley* boys a lawyer? You know, the *Bank Rileys*.

It turned out that literally no one who met the residency requirements was willing to take on the job. No one. I can't say that I was surprised, or that I blamed any of the attorneys who valued things like their sanity. However, it did create a situation where we were literally having to try to recruit someone.

The mayor, a diminutive soul, sniffed. "I think it only right to offer the position to the only grandson of our Late, Dearly-Departed Pillar. And I happen to know for a fact that he is indeed an attorney."

It was like a lightbulb went off. All of the Suits' faces glowed. Of *course*, they said. How could they not remember?

The kid had spent every summer in Hammondsville. He was one of their own. How they would love to embrace him again!

My ire growing by the minute, my head finally exploded (figuratively), and I stood up, a scrappy, skinny, brown-haired unknown, and spouted, "He practices law in New York State! You have to take the Tennessee Bar, for crying out loud. Which you have to *pass* to *practice law* in *Tennessee*!"

The mayor squinted at me. "What is your name, Miss?"

Oh, I was *this close* to popping him. Like his daughter hadn't hit my car in the high school parking lot. Like he hadn't put the valedictorian's stole on my shoulders at graduation. Like I hadn't been in the room a thousand times when he had met with Mr. Cane. And the sad thing was, he actually *didn't* know who I was. "I am Mississippi Whitson," I said, my twang exacerbated by emotion. "And this whole meeting is useless. The State is going to appoint whoever the heck they want to appoint."

"Miss Whitwell, if you will just–" *Whitson, you blood-sucking mosquito—*

The strongest threat to the Crown Prince (my sarcastic moniker for the grandson) getting the job had been when Pearl Fitts had brought up the fact that she had looked on his Facebook account. It *appeared*, she said, from her investigation that he had a *live-in girlfriend* in New York.

This was true. I had been on that Facebook account a few times myself out of sheer curiosity when I had been working for Mr. Cane. The girlfriend was a successful and beautiful art curator, apparently very popular with a huge circle of friends, Asian American, and he was a corporate counsel at some Fortune 500. They were extremely glamorous, looking like an ad in *Harper's Bazaar* every time they chanced to be on the right side of the camera. Their apartment was pristine, though I would, personally, have made a few stylistic changes. Mr. Cane and I had taken bets on whether they would get engaged soon. (He thought no; I thought yes.) It had been a pretty long-term relationship, from the look of things.

And then she hadn't come to the funeral with him, despite the fact that half of the people in the chapel were there just to see her in person. I had known then that there must be trouble in paradise, if paradise it had been. The next time I had social media-stalked him, his relationship status, which had once read *In a Relationship*, had been turned off altogether. So...I'm guessing there was a break-up.

An alderman had sniffed loudly, calling us all to order. "It is only fitting, it is only proper, that we offer this position to the grandson of the late Henry Cane." Oh, my gosh, the freaking Gettysburg Address.

A recommendation was made to the Governor, a residency waiver was filed, a few signatures here and there, and *voila!*: the Governor made the appointment. Apparently, the State had been afraid not to offer the position to someone within the Cane bloodline. Apparently, after graduating from law school Joseph Cane-Steinem had flown down to Tennessee to take the Bar two days after sitting for the New York Bar. And passed both. Talk about making me feel like a loser as I cleaned up German shepherd poop in the yard.

And here we were, staring out the window. If this had been the old days, His Royal Highness would have been greeted at the train station (sadly now burned) with banners and musicians and screaming women.

Now, there are some things you should know about our new DA. His name, as I have mentioned, is Joseph Cane-Steinem. You may have noticed that this is hyphenated. We are usually not this cool in Tennessee. To give you the story on that, I am going to have to back up a bit to what was, according to my mother, one of the Biggest Pieces of News ever to startle Drake County.

Henry and Mariella Cane had only had one daughter: Lillette. She had been 5'10" with blonde hair, unusual eyes, and a stunning (but not classically pretty) face. She had won every stinking beauty competition in the State of Tennessee before she was seventeen and, instead of going the Miss America route, she had signed with a modeling agency before graduation. She was a supermodel by twenty, appearing in *Vogue* ads, on runways, and in cosmetic commercials on TV. She wore Chanel on catwalks, was a perfume sex-goddess, and soon had her *own* feature on the cover of *Vogue*. Later on, she was a designer, too.

This global success was pretty much the biggest thing to hit Hammondsville since the tornado of 1929. She, frankly, didn't wear enough clothes to be respectable around here, and the church ladies tittered behind their fans regarding her lifestyle and poor taste to live in Paris. Her story was followed closely, but no piece of news had ever been as big as when she had, at thirty, gotten pregnant by an eighteen-year-old from a prominent Jewish family in New York. Hence, Joseph Cane-Steinem.

She seemed to have pursued a pretty interesting course from there, ending up getting killed in a skiing avalanche with an oil tycoon boyfriend about fifteen years later, and I *swear* Princess Diana's death hadn't caused more of a buzz in Hammondsville. I remember when that had happened, for I had come onto the stage about six years after her Love Child, as he was known in these parts.

I'd seen him a few times when he had come to stay with his grandparents during the summer, but I never met him then. Now I wondered what his game was. Why a big corporate counsel from a big New York company would quit his job and move to Middle of Nowhere, Tennessee. Oh, the fact that the job was temporary didn't really enter my thinking. We all knew it was *his,* if he so wished until he, too, died in his cereal at ninety-four. So, I couldn't think he had any other plans than to make a go of it, to finish his special term and then run for office.

The funny thing about it was, I thought as I watched him drive in, I wasn't sure he knew everyone was watching him. Maybe he was just a good actor. Or maybe he just didn't understand Hammondsville at all. He seemed to be in casual clothes, and he lifted his ballcap to smooth his hand over his straight, fair hair like he was tired and feeling a bit grungy. Understandable, I admitted grudgingly. It was a long drive. But I don't think he did it for the benefit of any onlookers, because he reached down and did something in his cupholder just after that, glancing up at the road and then back down.

His obliviousness did little to allay my suspicions. Most of these qualms, I realized, were on behalf of the office, among whom I had been an honorary family member for years. Was he going to act entitled, throwing all of his work off on Paul and Melissa? He'd hear a piece of my mind, if that were the case.

I flinched.

I wouldn't be there, would I? I had received a salary from Mr. Cane's estate to stay on and keep things running at the house until the estate settled, and to smooth the transition for the new DA, whomever he or she might be.

But the new DA was here. He happened to be the new owner of Cane House as well. And I had nothing left to do but hand the leashes of Fritz and Frieda off to their new owner.

Shit. Shit, shit, shit. I jammed the unlock function on my key fob fiercely, then swung open the door of my Accord (Ruby), and got in. Why hadn't I thought of this? The last thing I wanted to do was see His Entitled Highness, but I was, unfortunately, the keeper of the keys. I didn't leave one lying around outside Cane House because it had seemed like that was asking for it. And I hadn't even thought about how he would get in until Melissa had said in one of her mild muses, "I hope he doesn't mind boxes stacked to heaven with piles of paperwork from the 1970s..." The house. He would have to get in.

I had his phone number. But I didn't want to call him. That would be a little too personal, too familiar, I reflected as I turned down the tree-lined drive and headed toward the white Greek Revival mansion. I hoped the dogs hadn't broken out of their pen in excitement. It was hard to convince them that not everyone who pulled up A) wanted to kill me and them or B) had bacon. Depending on how they assessed Mr. Cane-Steinem's demeanor, he would be either worshipped or eaten. Either way he would be attacked.

I braked to a halt. What the *heck*? There were like a hundred cars sitting in the drive. You'd think someone had just died in there. I parked, eyebrows lowered, got out, and then I saw. Women. Old ones and young ones, pretty ones and plain ones. All approaching him with casseroles.

Most of them were grannies who were terrified a male-person would go a day without a homecooked meal. Can I tell you just how much this irritated me? Do you think a single one of them would've been here if he had been a woman? No! But he was entitled to their special attention because he was, well...a *man*, as my grandma would tell me, looking at me like I needed to get with the program. Granted, a couple of the women had on push-up bras and obviously had other goals. *What* was Hetty Gibson doing here? She was married with two kids!

"Excuse me!" I called, bringing this circus to order. Everyone looked at me, and I suddenly felt a little embarrassed. Clearing my throat and recovering, I said, "Um, hi. Mr. Cane-Steinem, I forgot to leave the key for you."

Before he could even answer, Loretta Harrison attacked him with a covered dish. I watched while he thanked her in baffled bemusement. He was cute, sure. Thirty-four, but he looked younger. Kind of petite, in an extremely proportional, pretty way. Maybe about 5'10". Straight golden hair. Extremely pale blue eyes. He did favor his mother: I had seen plenty of pictures in Cane House. There may have been something of his father in his features, too, though. And he wore his clothes well—one of those people who always looked good.

All right, I'd had enough. I started to break up the mob when Pearl Fitts (Town Busybody, Grandmother Extraordinaire, Mouth of the South) touched my arm. "Do you really think this is all *proper*, Mississippi?"

"No, I do not."

She gave me the side-eye. "I was speaking of you living on the property with him."

I blinked in astonishment, though I wasn't astonished, really. This was exactly the sort of thing my mom and grandma sat around talking about. But for crying out loud! "We're not even living in the same house, Mrs. Fitts. And besides, I'm moving out by next month, at latest."

She sniffed. "Couldn't you go live with your mother for the time being?"

"I could. But I'm not going to. Thank you, Pearl, if that is all...? Fanny! Honestly, you're going to spill it on him!"

Fanny looked over her shoulder, smiling, her blonde hair in a perfect blowout over her shoulders. "Oh, hi, Mississippi!"

"Hi, everyone. I'm sure Mr. Cane-Steinem appreciates your thoughtfulness. He would probably like to get settled." I said, glancing at him. He looked at me like I was his savior.

"Mississippi, honestly," Hetty hissed, as if I were trying to eliminate the competition, which just about made me see red.

Before I could even respond, everyone moved closer to him, Pearl Fitts offering her casserole and a spot at her dinner table any time, Hetty asking whether he had found a barber yet, and Fanny questioning whether he liked sweet potato casserole—all at the same time. Yeah, he was a goner. I had, against my better judgment, done all I could to save him, and I would just have to leave him to his own devices. I slipped up to the porch, stuck the keys in the doorknob, and retreated.

Chapter Two

I decided to keep the dogs. Well, not forever, but he was trying to get settled in, and it was the least I could do. Nonsense, I had already done enough. The truth was, they had kind of been my babies since Mr. Cane had acquired them as guide dogs two years ago. They had come to us fully trained, but they fell in love with the Cane House grounds and—not to be immodest—*me.*

A week passed. He (and you'd know who *he* was if you were within a thirty-mile radius of Hammondsville) had told Paul during a phone conversation that he was starting on the 14th of April. So I went about my business, awkwardly driving past the big house out to my cottage, not approaching him. I took care of the dogs, paid the bills for Cane House, helped out at the office...

The thing was, I needed to get on with my life. I needed to find another job, another house, and, if my mother were to be believed, a man. Scratch the last, my mother would get grandkids when she stopped nagging me.

A job, though… It wasn't like opportunity sprang up from geysers in Hammondsville. There were two banks, the mall, a small factory, a few restaurants, the post office, and the courthouse where nepotism ran rampant. Nothing had come knocking. Legal Row, the street where old houses had been turned into law offices, had several attorneys. One of them (Whalen Ritten) groomed me repeatedly in the courtroom with shoulder rubs and knee presses. So that was out. Mr. Baker had an employee already. No one was hiring.

So, what then? Move to Nashville or Chattanooga? Not really in my budget. I could look for a good job in a moderate-sized town, but I was afraid I would get stuck in the practicality of it and veer off my ultimate focus of school. I had always wanted to work somewhere on the Gulf, just briefly, for the experience (and the tips). I could get a job as a waitress in Destin during the summer season and go from there. Temporary, exciting, and lucrative. Okay, so there was my plan.

The snag was that it would kill my mother. Southerners don't like their children to live farther away from them than the house next door than an hour's drive. She would ask me what she had done wrong as a mother to make me want to get as far away from her as possible. What if I *met* someone there, and never came home again? What if I *needed* something and couldn't call her? Did I want her to spend her old age (she was fifty-three) alone? I could hear it all now. She would call my grandma, and they would weigh me down with the pressure of the disastrous course I was about to pursue.

Sigh. It would be *extremely* unpleasant, laced with the knowledge that I knew the best course, laced with the incorrect but annoyingly unshakeable conviction that my mother was *always* right. But maybe if I told her my ultimate goal was to go back to college...? She would definitely go for that. It was a plan, then.

I was driving along a lane, questionably paved and lined with trees, toward town, when I realized that today was his first day. Some spidey instinct within had me wanting to change my course from the supermarket toward Legal Row. I glanced down at my phone and saw a text from Mary.

Help! Jepp Lewis and *Whalen Ritten are in here! So embarrassing! Whalen is already groping him!!!*

Looking back at the road, I thought this through. I hated it for Mary, who was sensitive, but that's what the new DA bargained for, buddy, said the *heh, heh, heh* side of my brain. He had breezed into the job as if it were his by divine right, and there were consequences to accepting a position under such terms. I wouldn't go in there. I was no longer truly an employee. I had never *been* an employee of the State but instead had been paid privately by Mr. Cane and under confidentiality agreements with the State. And yes, if my duties as personal secretary had occasionally led me to help with legal matters, that was because I was a busybody who knew how to get stuff done. If the office was having trouble transitioning without me, that was only natural, and they would learn to adapt.

Crap. I couldn't ignore a cry for help. I turned toward Legal Row.

Paul's Camry was out front, as was Melissa's van and Mary's hatchback. There were three other vehicles also, making the gravel lot tight. I pulled into my usual place and got out, going up the steps onto the porch and opening the door without hesitation.

Mary hadn't lied. The place was swarming.

"Mississippi!" Mary whispered in gratitude, and immediately started filling me in. "Mr. Ritten has left, thank God, but he may have to have some therapy, don't you think?"

"Mr. Cane-Steinem?"

"Yes."

"The first time is always the hardest," I acknowledged. "But he'll probably pull through. What else?"

"Well, the whole freaking town council was here this morning ass-kissing. You would have puked, Mississippi, so I'm glad you weren't here. They acted like they had raised him or something."

Puke, indeed.

"And *then*, Jepp Lewis came in here *again,* wanting him to take out a warrant to arrest his neighbor for a gas line encroachment, or something, and, Mississippi, *can* he do that?"

"Arrest Mr. Howell? No."

"Well, that's what I thought!" She took a deep breath, brushing back her brown bangs and adjusting her cute dress. She spent half her paycheck on her wardrobe. Not a bad idea, I thought, looking down at my own drab apparel. Geez. I needed to step it up.

The door was cracked to the big office, and I heard the voice of the amiable but frustrating Jepp Lewis, world's greatest handyman, father of seven, Hammondsville's top moonshiner, and a rebel to the core on every issue, public or private, which arose.

"I said to the wife, I said, 'Merla! They're gonna encroach!' I seen it when they was diggin' the ditch, and I seen it when they was finished!"

"He's told him this is a property law matter fifty times," Mary intoned.

Melissa, who bore a striking resemblance to Phyllis on *The Office*, was looking nervous. Paul was deadpanning as usual, but I could tell he was agitated. This would be because neither had wanted the big job. Both were incredibly shy by nature. Melissa had blanched at the very idea of taking over before the mayor had hit upon the Crown Prince, while Paul's IBS had acted up, I was pretty sure. So they absolutely did not want the man to leave his new job.

Geez. Down to me, as usual. I walked forward stridently, knocking on the door.

"Yes, come in," called a hopeful voice.

I opened the door. Whew. Pretty eyes. They met mine, like a sucker punch to the gut. Never mind, whatever. To my surprise, he didn't look frustrated or even overwhelmed. There was repressed humor sparkling in his eyes, but I was fairly certain by the sound of his voice that he wanted deliverance. "Jepp, good to see you," I said.

"Mississippi," the other man said with grace, inclining his head.

"I think I saw Mr. Howell passing by the office—"

Before I could even get the sentence out, he was up, grasping for his hat and peering out the window. "That son of a gun! I knew it! Wife's been saying he's sick every time I go over there!"

And he was out, the bells on the door jangling behind him. I looked back at his victim, whose lips twitched in acknowledgement at what I had done, but he didn't say anything. I wish I was naturally that classy, but I pretty much said what I thought, as if I believed it to be compulsory to do so. "Listen, you can't let Jepp in here," I said.

"I didn't," he replied mildly.

This was probably true. However: "I *swear* it's just because Mr. Howell started intruding on his moonshining territory, and we don't have time for this. You could've taken steps to stop him, and I'm telling you, you're going to have to."

"All right, you try stopping a freight train," he responded.

I thought he was offended, but his lips were twitching again. "Mr. Cane-Steinem," I said.

"Call me Joseph," he interposed.

I cleared my throat. "Joseph." I cleared my throat again. "There's a lot about Hammondsville that you don't know," I began. Why was I doing this? I hated his type: entitled, rich, prone to the fawning affection of Big Men. Did I mention rich? I knew because I was the Executrix of his grandfather's Will.

Something you need to understand about Mr. Cane: he never spent a dime in his entire life. He had still driven his *extremely* old Volvo up until he couldn't drive anymore, and he refused to buy a new suit except when I'd haul him down to JCPenney for Easter Sunday.

Despite his extreme frugality, he *had* been charitable. And he was too kind to me, honestly. He had me drive him to a car lot last year and told me that it was time for me to drive him in something other than the Volvo. I had looked at him in awe, wondering if I should go have him checked for a brain tumor. This was right after my fifteen-year-old Ford had utterly collapsed.

He had subtly asked me over the past few weeks before what kind of car I would buy if I had a cool thirty thousand to spare. When he told the dealer that he wanted a reddish/maroon Honda Accord, I had hissed, "Henry!" When the dealer had walked off, he had patted my arm, saying, "What does it matter to me what you drive me in? You might as well like it." I had nearly cried. He paid cash, of course, and walked away with the title. I didn't know until I had found the car title tucked behind his Final Will that he had titled the car in my name. And then I had cried, sinking down into his desk chair, feeling his loss heavily.

That had been four months ago.

Where was I? Oh, the grandson had gotten every cent his grandfather had ever saved. So yeah, he was rich. And he had been raised rich, too. His mother had probably left him with millions in her own right. So again, *why* was he here instead of on a yacht on the Long Island Sound? Why would you drag yourself to work every day if you didn't have to? Suspicious, or admirable? The fact was, either way, his type grated on me. Remind me why was I exerting myself here?

For those people out there who were nervous about this transition, I told myself bracingly.

"People will come in here demanding to speak with you, and you'll slowly lose your mind if you don't curb it. Shut your door and lock it. I'm not kidding, they will blow past the secretary and try the door. Speak softly if you are on the phone. If they get a whiff that you're back here, they won't leave until you come out. Now, the tricky part is to protect yourself from an onslaught of complaints while still being accessible. Your grandfather did this by being seen out in the community, returning phone calls, and sending letters."

His eyes had been smiling in amusement, but at the mention of his grandfather, the light dimmed slightly. Crap, I had forgotten. The two might not have been spatially close; they might even have gone a whole year sometimes without seeing one another. There was a bond of affection, not spoken of very often, so I didn't really know its intricacies. But there had definitely been something there when I had called him to tell him the sad news about his grandfather. Loss. I knew that feeling very well.

He cleared his throat. "Thank you for your advice," he said.

I looked up, eyes narrowed. Was he being ironic? No, it didn't appear so. I took a stabilizing breath. "Look, it's time for you to take the dogs."

For the first time, he looked overwhelmed. "They, um... weren't fond of me the last time I visited."

"They will grow accustomed," I said stiffly.

"I was thinking... Perhaps we might donate them to a guide dog foundation so they could help another—"

My face must have shown my utter shock and revulsion at the idea because he broke off, looking startled. "This—is—their—home!" I exclaimed.

"Okay," he said, holding his hands up. "I'll pick them up tonight, if that's okay?"

"Yep!" I said, suddenly embarrassed at my outburst and general dispersal of advice. "Okay, then. Well." I tucked my hair behind my ear. "I need groceries, so... Bye!"

I felt him watching me as I left. He probably thought I was half-mad.

Chapter Three

He didn't get home until late. I had cleaned up my cottage for no reason in particular and put some tea on to boil. I decided to wait about my shower until he had stopped by because, you know, healthy, young males and inappropriate attire did not mix, according to my mother. She had imparted this proverb during our phone call, during which I had made the disastrous mistake of telling her he was dropping by.

Young ladies did not greet gentlemen at the door in their pajamas. Lest you think this opinion was confined to her generation, my best friend, Imani, had reminded me to keep my bra on, and if I *was* in my pajamas, I needed to wear a robe. As I had been forced to pull the phone away from my ear and rub said appendage after she had screamed, "DeShawn, if you throw darts at your brother's butt one more time, it's *over*!" I wasn't sure whether this advice would make much of an impression on me.

Whatever the impression, my womenfolk had certainly gotten me hyped up. Before I had called either of them, I had simply made neat boxes of the dogs' things and not thought much more about it. Now, I was on-edge and jumped like a cat when I heard the knock on my door.

I took a second to gather myself, cleared my throat, and hopped from one foot to the other. *Oh, for heaven's sake.* I strode firmly forward, stopping in front of the old door and pulling it toward me.

He looked like he had been mauled by a bobcat. The crisp gray coat I had seen that morning was nowhere in sight, his tie hung loosely, and the top two buttons of his Calvin Klein (yes, I could spot it, whatever the state of my own wardrobe) shirt were undone. A tuft of his golden hair was standing on end, his eyes were red, and he looked skinnier. Maybe I imagined the last part.

"Hey," I said, looking him over. His shirt was still tucked neatly into his pants, revealing a trim waist and a good belt.

"Hey." His voice croaked. He cleared his throat.

"You, um, okay?"

"Um, that was...rough."

Despite myself, I looked at him sympathetically. Of course it was rough. Like facing jungle animals or a firing squad or a tank of piranhas was rough. There were *a lot* of personalities in Hammondsville. I swung the door wider, stepping back. "Would you like to come in?"

He crossed the threshold but stayed in the little foyer part, looking like he was thinking deeply.

"Have you had supper?" I asked.

He looked up at me like he hadn't even thought of it and was a little stunned by that realization.

"I think I have a pizza in the freezer," I said, like the Southern woman in front of an unfed man that I was. Sue me. I took a step toward my little kitchen.

"No, that's fine. I have like fifteen casseroles in the freezer."

Geez. "Do you know how to heat them up?"

He considered this. "I have a list of instructions."

"Good. Don't leave the Saran wrap on the dish."

"Got it." He cracked a small smile. I, metaphorically speaking, fell at his feet. That smile was dangerous. A woman would do very well to be cautious in its presence.

"So the dogs—"

"Listen, Mississippi, I need—"

We started to speak at the same time. I inclined my head regally and motioned for him to continue. But at the mention of the dogs, he looked up into my living room. I tried to see it as he would. My little couch looked shabby. Well, it *was* shabby. There was quite a bit of fur on it. Not my choice, but hey, that was life. A cute lamp I had used in my dorm during my one year at college graced a side table that my mom had cast off. *Vogue* magazines littered the coffee table my Uncle Dan had made for me. A basket of toys for when I kept DeShawn and Marcus was shoved in the corner by the T.V. And emerging from the once-cute, now-hairy, rug were two pairs of creepy eyes, advancing.

"Oh, God," the newcomer said, although, to give him credit, he didn't budge.

"Fritz, Frieda, stop," I said calmly. They did so. Fritz's tongue lolled as he panted due to the fact it was sixty-nine degrees in the cottage, while Frieda stood without blinking an eye, her mouth closed, her eyes fixed on The Male. She looked like a warrior goddess, and I smiled lovingly. "Good girl. Yes, that's my baby."

"I think she's going to kill me."

Oh, yeah. I saw it now. "No, Frieda, he's a nice man. Who's a good girl?"

Frieda advanced, never taking her eyes from him. As she slowly drew nearer, he said, obviously nervous, but with a touch of humor, "Are noncupative wills allowed in Tennessee?"

"What are those?" I asked, watching her. Good heavens. What if she pounced? She *was* extremely protective of me.

"Verbal wills spoken in times of extreme danger under the threat of imminent death."

"Ah. Well, have at it," I said nervously, moving forward, deciding to cut her off at the pass. I knelt down, taking her face in my hands. "Sweetie, we can't eat the nice man, okay? He's your new daddy. You are in charge of *his* protection now, okay? That's a good girl." She gave me a glance that said she would bring under her protection whomever she deigned to bring under her protection, thank you very much.

Meanwhile, Fritz moved forward amiably, bending his body to encircle Joseph's legs. Joseph looked down at him in alarm, as if fearing he was about to be knocked to the floor or squeezed in an anaconda-vice. "He's hugging you," I called over my shoulder.

"Ah, well, if you're sure then. Don't mind me."

When Frieda showed no indication of surrendering her ground, I rose to my feet, frustrated with my children. "Of all the... Fritz, Frieda! Come!" I commanded. Frieda came to my side. Fritz continued to encircle his new father. I grabbed his collar and escorted them out the back door to the little fenced in area. "I will be back in five minutes, and you will behave yourselves with more decorum upon my return!" I said firmly, heading back toward the door.

I closed it, seeing the newcomer craning his neck to look at us. I walked back to where he was standing.

Gently, he said, "Why don't you keep them? You guys obviously have a telepathic thing going."

I shook my head. "I can't afford them," I stated frankly.

"If I paid you child support...?" he asked.

I smiled, looking up at him with dancing eyes, despite myself. But I said, "Cane House—this property—is their home. That's very important to German shepherds. I'm probably moving to Florida soon, and who knows whether my apartment will allow them? Besides, those two need far more exercise than the thirty minutes before and after work I would be able to give them."

Something had changed in his expression. "You're leaving?"

"Probably, yes." Why I had crossed my arms, I'm not sure. I felt him studying me.

"Can I ask you something?"

A beat of silence. "Sure."

He cleared his throat. "You've lived here your whole life, right?"

"Yep. Except for one year at the University of the South."

Blue eyes searched me. After just a moment, he said, "I want this to work. My job, staying here... Do you think it will always be like it was today?"

"Listen, about the groping—"

"No, I mean..." He hesitated. "Everything."

Making a mental apology to Paul and Melissa, I answered, "Yes."

He nodded, looking like he had already known that. He drew a hand through his hair. "Do you think I can adjust? Learn how to handle it? What to say to people?"

After having lived half his life in France, the other in New York City, and worked in a pristine corporate office? It was a different world down here. And there was no handbook. Reluctantly, I said, "Not without help."

He looked like he had known that, too. He had probably ruffled a hundred feathers, had his own feathers ruffled, felt like his head was going to explode, and at the same time felt overwhelmed by the gagging (I considered it) welcome he had received. The pressure in his chest was probably intense. I had felt it before when dealing with the public. That was probably the same everywhere, and for everyone.

What was not the same was that this was Hammondsville, or the South more generally, where there were a thousand little unwritten social cues. And it wasn't like the job itself was exactly an easy one either.

"I was hoping... Well, anyway, I was going to ask you..." He looked up, wincing as he met my eyes. "To stay on. Kind of in the same job you had with my grandfather, only you would really be showing me the ropes, helping me hang onto my sanity..."

"You mean like a cultural coach?" He needed one.

He smiled. "Sort of. Just...to help out at the office with public relations, go to court with me, assist with the daily hurdles that arise. Obviously, I didn't know you had a job lined up, and I wouldn't want to get in the way of that. I know that you have handled the estate really well and pay attention to details... I just thought it would be a shame for my grandfather's death to have left you at loose ends when I need the help anyway."

"I don't have a job lined up yet. I was going to look for one. But I'm thinking about going back to college, and the tips at a Gulf beach town during the summer could float my first semester pretty nicely."

"I would give you a three percent raise over what my grandfather paid, and it would only be for a few months until the transition is made at the office."

"I think the tips would still pay better."

"You're forgetting the child support."

I smiled. The truth was, it wasn't a terrible idea. My mom would say it was the smart one, something to help me over the hurdle from unemployment to employment. One of her maxims was never to leave a job until you have another job lined up. My family had never had the luxury of fat bank accounts to cover lean times. This would help me in my own transition. If I could stay with him a couple of months, line up a job for the beginning of July, and still make peak season... Surely a college kid waiting tables would have partied out and there would be a job opening by then?

And I liked neatness and order. I was having a hard time envisioning leaving the office in chaos. The truth was, I loved those people. I wanted them to be happy. And that meant having a good work environment and a boss who didn't want to rip his hair out.

And I thought about Henry.

I had just started working for him when I found myself helping him pack for New York when Joseph was graduating from NYU School of Law. And he had said, with real joy in his eyes, "Just *think* about it! With his upbringing, I should be paying for him to go to rehab instead of watching him graduate from law school. And I didn't even have to pay for that!"

It would mean something to him, having his grandson here in Hammondsville. And he had meant something to me.

So I said *yes*.

Chapter Four

His first lesson was that, no, we did not need to drive into town together to save gas and the Earth. People would talk.

He stared at me uncomprehendingly. "About what?"

"About us."

"*Riding* together in my car?"

"To the office, yes."

"In what regards?"

Geez, he really was clueless.

"Listen, everyone knows," I said, taking a deep breath, "that you had a live-in girlfriend."

His eyes widened. "A what...?"

"It means that you *live in* the same house," I explained.

He looked bewildered. It was worse than I thought. He didn't even get the significance of it.

"*In sin*," I clarified.

His expression changed. Surprise overtook his features. His eyes started to dance. He did that thing where he didn't speak, just looked at me with blue eyes twinkling—keeping his mouth shut throughout.

"Shut up, and get in your car," I said, walking determinedly toward my own.

"Your district covers two counties: Drake and Cullman," I lectured, pointing at the district map on the wall in his office. We had locked ourselves in there. Mary was doing her level best to beat away the vultures at the door, to prepare Paul's files to go to Traffic Court at one o'clock, and not to cry when people said hateful things to her on the phone.

"You go up to Berry—that's the county seat of Cullman—the last Tuesday of every month. The people at the courthouse are nice, but the terrain is rough, and the people are... untrusting. You will need to ingratiate yourself before you are accepted. Do you understand?"

"Yes."

"Good. This is The Hill," I said, pointing to the geographic rise on the map. "This takes you to the top of the mountain, where Berry is situated. If you're going out of Hammondsville, you call it Berry Hill, but if you're in Berry, you call it Hammondsville Hill." He choked. I continued. "If you get confused, just say The Hill so you don't make a gaffe." I cleared my throat, moving on. "You must never go up the mountain at night, Simba. Good people for the most part, but Mountain

People, and you need to be careful." I wondered if he would get the *Lion King* reference to a young, inexperienced cub, but I couldn't worry with such trivialities. It was how I thought of him, and we had no time to waste.

He looked skeptical, like I was being prejudiced. Oh, geez, maybe I *was* generalizing. But I said in exasperation, "Listen, your grandpa pissed off a lot of rednecks. You'll abide by my rules, or I'm out. I won't have your blood on my hands."

"Okay," he replied mildly. "What did he do?"

"Oh, you know, things like busting meth labs, prosecuting arson, the usual stuff."

He pinched the bridge of his nose. "How big *is* the meth problem here?"

"It's been huge in the past. We've got a good sheriff who's cracking down on it, so heroin's moving in."

His lips twitched.

"You, Melissa, and Paul split the work up by category. Melissa handles all of the juvenile and domestic stuff, and Paul covers traffic and DUI. You've got drugs, rape, and murder, which is technically a lesser case load, but, of course, you're ultimately responsible for every case that comes through the door, including Melissa's and Paul's. So if one of them has a particularly sticky trial, you'll need to be there and be apprised of the details. Also, you'll handle the general direction of the office, and the media if there is a hyped-up case. There is a button under your desk which you can discreetly push that will alert the police if someone is in here threatening you or brandishing a gun. That's never had to be used; people only get really upset about property issues around here."

I lifted my eyes heavenward in thought. *What else, what else?* "If you hear people say, 'Thank God for Mississippi,' they're not talking about me." I clicked my tongue in thought. Was there anything more to cover? There was so much, but he was already looking overwhelmed. "Okay, I'm going to go do some filing, but call me if you need anything. And *lock the door* behind me."

Today, he didn't hesitate. I heard the latch execute a satisfying click as soon as I shut the door.

I entered the courthouse doors, arms loaded with files, to the sight of a court officer giving a man a pat-down and ultimately confiscating a pocketknife. The line for court snaked back several yards, and the officers were running everyone through the security checks at a creeping pace. The lawyers and their secretaries were allowed to slip through the mayhem, which was a good thing because my young protégé looked rather startled at some of the sights. The smell of lingering cigarette smoke alone was enough to knock you down.

A woman with spiked blue hair screamed, "How come they get to go through?"

Simba stopped, looking like he was about to try to be egalitarian or something, and I stuck my hand in his back forcefully and ordered lowly, "Keep moving!"

Once we were on the elevator, he said, "I hate things like that."

"You and me both. A freaking circus every Monday."

His lips twitched. "I meant that I would have preferred to wait in line with everyone else."

"You'll need to get over that. You are a licensed member of the bar, and you haven't been summoned to court. None of your hippie frou-frou equality here, or you won't make it very long, do you understand?"

He sighed.

Moving on, I said, "I'll show you to our table. Paul and Melissa should be here soon. Do you understand the procedure?"

His eyes twinkled. "I think so."

I eyed him, but we didn't have time for further conversation. We entered the doors of the courtroom between two officers standing at attention like sentries.

My flats proceeded softly across the floor which groaned miserably under the slightest weight. We walked down the aisle and slipped into the area for attorneys up front. Mr. Cane-Steinem was at once captured by a couple of big wig attorneys, and I put our folders down on the prosecution table.

Immediately, I felt a hand slide onto my shoulder and a voice say in a silky-creepy accent, "Mississippi..."

I looked over my shoulder with dread to see Whalen Ritten. Having been raised in the illusion that he was The Stuff, he smiled in a way that let me know that he understood that I was honored by his attention. "It has been too long."

The hand was moving to my back. I shuddered out of his vicinity. "Better get to work, Whalen," I said forcefully.

He smiled. "You're looking very well, Mississippi."

"Thank you. Goodbye." I walked away quickly, going to talk to his secretary, who was, I hope, too old to have been an object of his exuberance. She must nonetheless be traumatized by his endless social climbing.

"All rise!"

Judge Harvey was early today. I skittered back to my area and waited while court was called into session, before sitting between Melissa and Mr. Cane-Steinem. (I was still having a hard time calling him *Joseph* in my head.)

Said Joseph leaned toward me. "So...Whalen Ritten is bi-sexual?" he whispered.

"That is an insult to bi-sexual people. Why, did he hit you up again?"

He hesitated before nodding once. "I thought he was married."

"He *is* married, with kids. Don't be naïve!"

"I'm not naïve. I'm confused." His eyes hinted at amusement.

"He's just *sexual*, okay?" I hissed. "He hits on everything that moves."

"State of Tennessee versus John Anthony Tonneau!" Adrenaline shot through me at hearing one of our cases being blared.

Joseph stood. "Your honor, Mr. Tonneau is charged with possession of a Schedule I Controlled Substance—" My brain inserted: *BZP, heroin, or LSD* while he continued talking. This was interesting. Tony Tonneau, as he was known, was (how shall we say?) *hot* in high school. We hadn't been close, but I remembered that. Long dark hair, rippling muscles, tall frame, brown brooding eyes... He was quiet in that mysterious sort of way that drove girls crazy. I didn't know which drug he was supposed to have had on him, but he didn't look like a typical user. In fact, he was still hot.

Interestingly, though, he plead *nolo contendere* and was given judicial diversion. That meant if he completed the probation program, his charges would be dismissed. They only offered that to first-time offenders, so it must have been a recent thing that he had gotten off on drugs. I still remembered a party at his parents' mansion on Social Climbing Avenue that I had gotten invited to somehow. Whew, what a house. I had gotten lost going to the bathroom.

I was so immersed down this benign rabbit trail that I didn't consider until he sat down that Joseph had handled the situation well, with grace and compassion.

I handed him his next file while Paul got up to handle a DUI charge. The morning passed without much of an incident, except that a woman in an orange jumpsuit got away from the court officers and lapped the courtroom about three times before they tackled her. But that was pretty much par for the course.

At the end, the judge commended Joseph from the bench on his first day, expressing his pleasure that he had come to live in Hammondsville and, beaming, conveyed how proud his grandfather would have been.

Puke.

Glancing at me and apparently catching sight of my face, Joseph looked back at the judge, grinning and saying something schmoosy, soaking up the adulation around him. For heaven's sake, were they *clapping*?

"Teacher's pet," I said dryly when he sat down.

His eyes twinkled with barely suppressed humor. "It annoys you," he said mournfully.

"Yes! I've lived here my whole life, performed invaluable community service, and saved several cats from trees. Have I ever received even a meritorious mention? No! But *you* have the right bloodline, so you step right into universal acceptance. Well! As long as we take care of our boys, I say. I'm telling you, Joseph, you have no idea what kind of town you've moved to. Butt kissers."

Eyes wide with delight, he said, "Don't hold back."

"You can be sure I won't."

The week progressed in an excruciatingly long fashion. All of us at the office were exhausted at the sheer volume of people who came through the doors. Add to that a full moon during which so many crimes were committed that the police basically set up a tent in our parking lot, and we had a bad stew on our hands.

Mary hyperventilated several times and demanded that I be truthful with her: *did I think she needed therapy?* Paul cleared his throat eight thousand times. Melissa's eyes darted nervously from person to person. They all reached a consensus: Joseph Cane-Steinem would be leaving soon. I constantly reminded them that he wouldn't have hired me if he hadn't meant to give it a shot.

Anyway, there were a lot of hysterics, and when Saturday morning finally rolled around, I slept in until ten o'clock, when Fritz and Freida, who had humored me long enough, pulled back my blankets in unison with their teeth.

"Guys, honestly."

Fritz licked my face in a well-intentioned burst of enthusiasm, forgetting my rule on that, and Freida barked as if to remind us both the reason they had come to get me. "Yeah, okay, okay," I said, getting up and feeding them. They had a flap at the door which led onto the little fenced in area, so they had already taken care of the necessities.

They ate voraciously. I stumbled back to my bathroom, where I ran my fingers through my hair, which was limp and matted. I washed my face, brushed my teeth, and changed into my comfy Saturday clothes. By the time I had a bowl of oatmeal, I no longer hated anyone, and I was ready to start a load of laundry.

That taken care of, I washed the dishes which had been piling up during the week. Wiping down the counters after that, I glanced out the window up toward the big house. I could see his car in the drive, so he was home. I hadn't seen any movement yet, but I wouldn't unless he came outside. Not that it mattered.

"Okay, cooking shows, kids?" I asked, finishing up and going to plop down on the couch. Fritz was a huge fan of cooking shows. He boisterously jumped up beside me, tucking himself against me as if he were the size of a cat. "Fritz!" I exclaimed, shifting him. Fritz panted merrily. Freida, licking her paws on the rug across the room, flicked her eyes up with disdain.

We got through two episodes of *Barefoot Contessa*, and it was soothing to sit here, running my hand continuously over Fritz's head and letting the pressures of the week roll off.

Around lunchtime, I got up and leashed the dogs. Slipping on my boots, I exited the house and took them to the field where they loved to romp. I clipped their leashes off and stood back at the fence, watching them have the time of their lives as they chased scents and birds.

I heard a squeak and then the slap of an old screen door. My head turned, and I saw Joseph Cane-Steinem come out onto the side porch, lifting a hand.

"Hey," I said.

"Hey." His eyes scanned the field, and he smiled when he saw our children. "They look happy."

"Yeah, they are."

"Would you...be interested in a casserole?" He winced guiltily.

I lifted my eyebrows.

"It was very nice, but...I'm just going to be honest: I usually eat a little differently from this, and I need some freezer space."

I almost laughed, picturing him at all the little healthy cafés I'm sure New York was covered up with. Our Velveeta-based diet was probably a bit of a clash. "Well, that depends. Do you have anything made by Fanny Barksdale?"

His eyes cast up as he considered. "I'm not sure."

"I'll come look. I know her stoneware. I'll take anything that woman offered."

He laughed. "I might have to keep it, in that case."

"Too late," I responded. I didn't start for the house, realizing I had just invited myself in and wondering how to get out of this social gaffe. He was dressed, wearing jeans and a long sleeve shirt, but he might not be ready for someone to invade his domain.

"Come on in," he said, nodding with his head toward the door. "Will the dogs be okay?"

"Oh, yeah, there are acres and acres, and they know not to go too far," I answered, walking up the yard in my muck boots. Since there was no step up to this side porch, he reached down, helping me up. He was quite strong to be so (attractively, proportionally) compact. And still a good six inches taller than me, I thought bitterly, but no one was counting.

He opened the door for me, and I started toward the kitchen. I passed down the hall, seeing his grandfather's bedroom door closed, and two other bedrooms still piled with the same stuff as always. The guest room that I had always made Henry keep free of clutter seemed to be where Joseph was sleeping, as I saw a couple of his dress shirts and tons of boxes lying here and there. I felt my face warm, feeling intrusive. I turned my head away.

The grand, beautiful dining room was still piled high with boxes of old legal documents, tax records, bills, and such. We needed to get one of those massive shredding trucks out here in the worst possible way.

He needed it. I kept forgetting.

The kitchen was the same as always—old countertops and cabinets, 1960s fridge, and a battered table where Henry and his wife had always had breakfast, he had once told me.

I opened the freezer and spotted Fanny's dish immediately. *Come to Mama.* "You are going to regret this," I said, popping it out. "I'll return the dish once I'm finished so you can give it to Fanny."

"Want a couple more?" he pleaded, standing by the table.

I was supposed to be starting a fitness regimen soon. "Better not." I looked at him. Geez, he was kind of beautiful. Thick, silky hair, flawless nose, those eyes—just the faintest laugh lines around them—and (let's be honest) a great smile. I bet he had been *all* the rage at his elite high school. He just had that look about him. His whole face was expressive but especially his eyes, which *loved* to twinkle. I had seen that even during the extremely difficult week we had just experienced. He could find the humor in almost anything.

All that was to say that the ladies of town weren't going to leave him alone, of course. Which was all that I had meant by that examination. Nothing more.

His phone, lying on the kitchen table, started buzzing. I looked down in time to see *Dad* flash across the screen and then looked away, feeling intrusive for the second time.

His brows drew together. "Do you care if I take this?" he asked. "Unusual for him to call."

"Sure," I said. That must be nice. My mom had already sent me the obligatory text checking to make sure that I hadn't died in my sleep, and if she didn't call me at least three times today, I would be surprised. His father calling was an interesting development, however.

After Lillette Cane had died in Paris, the town had assumed her fifteen-year-old son would be coming to live in

Hammondsville. No one had even thought of the father, having believed from the beginning that he, at his age, had probably played little-to-no role. Who was to say what a teenager would do after the end of his relationship with a much older supermodel? You tell me. We didn't see something like that every day in Hammondsville.

But the Canes, a bit baffled, had told someone that there was no question of Joseph living with them: he was going to New York to live with his father, of course. This, among the swirl of news and startling events reported upon in Hammondsville at that time, had stunned everyone.

The father must have gotten along well enough with the Canes because Joseph had continued to come to Tennessee every summer until he graduated high school. I had never heard Henry say anything bad about his daughter's erstwhile lover. But Henry hadn't been one to talk much about his personal life at all.

Mr. Steinem had attended Henry's funeral with his son. He looked too young to have a son who was in his thirties, of course. He had a protective stance, always standing or sitting beside Joseph. His build was very similar to Joseph's, and there was some traceable likeness, but Joseph's hair and eyes had been more like his mother's.

Joseph came back into the room, pocketing his phone. "Everything okay?" I imagined someone asking me that every time my mom called and almost laughed darkly.

"Yeah, he..." He looked at me, almost as though weighing whether we were close enough for confidences. The truth was, he knew me about as well as he knew anyone here, except maybe a few friends he had made during his summers. "He thinks I'm making a mistake with all of this," he said, slipping his hands into his pockets.

I tucked my hair behind my ears. "Coming to Tennessee?"

He inclined his head once. "He thinks it's a reaction to..." He flushed, looking up. He regretted coming this far in the conversation, I could tell, but he had gone too far to back out. "I was in the middle of a break-up when you called and told me the news."

I winced.

"It had been a pretty long-term thing, and then losing Grandpa... He thinks I've gone off the deep-end, but it wasn't that."

I felt marginally remorseful for my flippancy about his living in sin. Setting that aside, I wondered again what it *was* that had made him come here. He really didn't strike me as someone reacting emotionally after shattering losses. He also didn't strike me as someone content to live in Hammondsville. Shoot, most our *own* brightest stars got the heck out as soon as possible.

Maybe he wanted to run for governor and thought Tennessee was easier than New York. I suppose that would depend on his politics. Or maybe Senator? House of Representatives would be a better shot. That almost had to be it. Unless he was running from the law. In which case, being a DA probably wasn't a good choice. So, politics it was.

"He wants you to come home," I said, thinking of Paul and Melissa and Mary. One more thing weighing the scale against them. No one knew better than I the powerful pull of family.

"Yeah," he answered.

I had a bigger job than I had realized on my hands.

I cleared my throat. "Are you tired of shifting boxes?" I asked.

"Kind of, yeah," he said, smiling. "I know you did your level best to convince him to get rid of stuff."

I felt a pang in my heart at the mention of Henry. How many times had we bickered like an old married couple over all of his junk? "I can help you go through it if you want," I replied, throat scraping.

He hesitated a long moment, his eyes dimming a bit. And then he just said it. "I'm not ready."

I nodded. "Yeah, I understand that."

He held my eyes a moment. I heard one of the dogs barking and startled to attention, clearing my throat. "Well, I had better..." I motioned toward the door.

"Yeah, of course," he said, stepping out of my way. "Have a good day."

"Mm hmm!" I replied, tripping over the door seal, righting myself, and continuing over the threshold hurriedly.

Chapter Five

The next task in my life coaching job was to accompany Mr. Cane-Steinem as he met with a local task force on safety. He was supposed to give them recommendations on protecting the city's buildings from dangerous intruders, so that they could take proposals to the town council meeting the next night.

It was soon to be realized that I had not prepped my pupil *nearly* enough.

The meeting started benignly at a table in the middle school cafeteria, with everyone sucking up to Joseph on account of his bloodline. Then the chairman of the task force explained the committee's purposes: to secure city buildings and ensure the safety of the employees.

"The courthouse is guarded, and there are metal detectors," Mr. Warren said.

Everyone seemed to accept this as necessary due to the high tensions surrounding hearings and trials and such. There was some batting back and forth on how to properly arm the other city and county buildings, with budget always being a concern.

"Why not just put a metal detector at the doorways of all of the buildings?" Joseph said, the first time he had spoken.

"To prevent people from bringing guns into Town Hall?" the committee chairman asked, blinking.

"Yes," Joseph responded with disastrous certainty.

I sat up, trying to catch his eye.

Mrs. Anderson, who had poufy blonde hair and rather full decolletage, sat up straight. "But if they're carrying unconcealed, that's not violating the law, and if they're carrying concealed, they will have to have gotten a permit."

"Unless they are breaking the law, yes," Joseph responded. "I just don't think the clerks should have to sit there with people across from them wearing guns in their holsters. Even if there aren't any nefarious purposes, the opportunities for accidents would be numerous. What's the harm in asking someone to leave their gun in the car while they go renew their tags?"

This point of view fell over the room like a wet blanket. There was silence, until Mrs. Anderson said, "Well, I just don't think that's right!"

The committee chairman, obviously agreeing but very much wanting to avoid an awkward disagreement with Hammondsville's own pride and joy, said, "I propose that we adjourn for a brief recess and return in fifteen minutes."

Catching Joseph's eye, I none-too-gently cocked my head in the direction of the door—a command for him to follow me. Once we were outside the cafeteria doors, I said, "What the heck are you doing? Every day I expend tireless energy trying to integrate you into a harmonious relationship with this community, and you repay me by bringing up gun control?"

"Hardly!" he exclaimed in a whisper. "By asking people to leave their guns in their car when they go in government buildings?"

"Oh, yes, Mr. Cane-Steinem. You are treading a thin line here. You are going to have to walk it back when we get in there. You're not in New York City anymore, or did you forget that?"

He sighed, drawing his hand through his hair. "Well, the Dolly Parton look-alike is already completely against me anyway, so I might as well persevere."

I drew a deep breath. "You are going to *walk it back*. I'm not weighing in as to whether you're right. I'm just saying that you'll never change their minds, not in a million years, and all you are going to do is make enemies, and offend, and make them think you're one of those Yankees who pictures us all as a bunch of brutes who don't know how to hold a fork. So if you wish for me to stay in your employ, you will ask Mr. Warren for clarification on his point of view, say you didn't properly understand the ramifications, and move on."

I started to go back into the cafeteria but turned suddenly on my heel, looking at him fiercely. "And if you have something bad to say about Dolly Parton, you can just leave town right now!"

That evening, I went home and performed the not-so-cathartic activity of bathing the dogs. I scrubbed vigorously, still irritated. Some people had absolutely no appreciation. Even if I was never speaking to the man again, it occurred to me that now that the dogs had a rich daddy, we could afford to have them groomed in town.

"What do you think about that?" I asked, toweling Fritz's head dry. He appeared to be game, breathing happily into my mouth. All right, then. Add dental treats to the list.

After showering myself, I felt so much calmer that I put onion rings into the oven. Benefit to being single: you could eat as much or as little or as weird as you wanted. Every night.

I then settled in on my couch and turned on a modeling show, followed by a wedding show. The bride picked the perfect dress, and I wiped a tear at the conclusion of the couple's perfect Jewish wedding. I had a candle burning. It was a winter scent, but I was cleaning out my inventory, and what was wrong with the house smelling like Christmas cookies all year long, I ask you? It was soothing, and I needed that after one of my temper flares.

I was also curled up in a blanket since I had overdone it a bit on the air conditioning. Cozily, I judged the models on the screen, concocting ways they could improve their skill, and later judged the bride's choice of centerpieces. I planned to stay up until ten o'clock, at which point I would probably collapse in exhaustion. Not exactly how I had thought my late twenties would feel, but there you have it.

A knock at my door made me jump. Fritz's ears perked, and Frieda, in full bodyguard mode, turned her head discreetly toward the door while rising slowly. My heart hammering, I reached for the nearest weapon (the remote) and stood. I was surreptitious in my blind-peeking. Once I saw the person on the other side, I called off my henchmen and swung open the door.

"Joseph," I said in surprise, looking him over as he stood awash in light from the porch bulb. He was in a T-shirt and jeans, and his hair was a little damp as if he had just taken a shower.

He had done exactly as I had asked when we had returned to the meeting, but I still hadn't spoken to him on the way out. It occurred to me now that this action might have been a touch petty. "Hey," he said.

"Hey," I responded, suddenly attacked by shyness. I didn't know him well enough to show him my crazy yet. And yet I had.

"I wanted to tell you that I do appreciate you and all you have done to help me," he said, trying to make eye contact, but I couldn't look at him.

"Thanks," I responded quietly, still a little peeved if I were honest.

"And I don't have anything bad to say about Dolly Parton," he added.

I looked up quickly. His eyes were twinkling, and—I hate myself—I smiled. "I'm glad to hear that."

He appeared to be suppressing a smile, but he knew he was treading on thin ice. "Goodnight, Miss Whitson."

"Goodnight, Mr. Cane-Steinem." If he felt forgiven because my eyes were also dancing, that would just have to be.

"They're in, they're in!"

As soon as Mary burst through the office door with the *Hammondsville Herold*, we (Paul, Melissa, and I) knew what she meant. She spread open the huge newspaper leaves after giving us a brief glimpse of the headlines: "State Rankings on Crime, Education, Poverty, Homelessness, and More." We were only interested in the crime, of course.

"Oomph," Melissa said, seeing us ranked third (and not in the good way).

"Seriously, how can we have the most violence of any state in the South?" I demanded.

"Geez. That's a lot of murder," Paul mumbled, scowling.

"The poverty rate has gotten significantly better," Mary said optimistically.

"Mississippi—where's Mississippi?" Melissa demanded. I knew better in such instances than to think anyone was questioning my whereabouts.

"It's still Number One in poverty," I responded.

There was a collective relieved sigh.

We needed more cheering, so we looked at education and homelessness. "Well, we're not *dead* last," Mary said.

Still, it was bleak.

Melissa shook her head and muttered in unison at the same time as Paul, "Thank God for Mississippi."

"Okay, when you're formally introduced to the town council, you will need to stand," I said as Mr. Cane-Steinem and I walked briskly through the doors of Town Hall.

We were a little late—on purpose because I had convinced Joseph that we might be able to take a pass on a groping from Whalen Ritten, who was the city attorney, if we arrived once everyone was seated. He had mumbled something compassionate about Mr. Ritten perhaps needing to see a sex counselor, and I had responded, "He's just a little pinhead, okay?"

We disagreed on our approaches, but Joseph didn't argue with the suggestion that we show up late. Ha.

As the meeting was called to order, the first item of business was for the mayor to rise and, with a countenance of beaming fatherly affection, welcome our new District of Attorney to the meeting. "We are so grateful that you have joined us tonight, Mr. Cane-Steinem. Your office is a vital cornerstone of our community, and the council always maintained an excellent relationship with it while your grandfather lived. I know this will continue under your leadership." The man smiled patronizingly at me, as one might to a cute five-year-old girl. "And thank you also for joining us, Miss...?"

Why, I ought to... Oh... Oh! What was that sound? My blood boiling—the slow, gurgling rumble of something threatening to explode. "Whitson," I responded through gritted teeth.

"Ah, yes," he confirmed. He glanced around the room, saying, again in the kindergarten tone, "Miss Whitwell is Mr. Cane-Steinem's assistant."

My blood pressure was not in a good place. My temples were pounding, and I wasn't sure I wouldn't pass out. I tossed an ugly look at *Mr.* Cane-Steinem. *See? You see?!*

His eyes were glittering as his gaze rested on me for a moment. Yes, he knew perfectly well. Suppressing quivering lips, Joseph transferred his gaze back to the mayor, standing as I had bidden him when he was formally introduced, and thanking the council. The meeting proceeded from there in an agonizingly boring fashion.

On our way out, we were waylaid by one of the Big Bank Men in town, Mr. Reynolds Buford. I had participated in the bank's youth leadership program, which he always led, for a total of four years during high school, but I could see there was ab-so-lutely no recognition in his eyes. He asked if he could speak to Joseph for a moment, and we all moved a little away from the board room.

Mr. Buford said softly, "I'm sorry to catch you like this, but… I've been feeling a little nervous."

Joseph lifted his brows enquiringly.

The large, balding man drew a long breath. "The truth is, I think I'm being threatened."

My brows lowered. In *Hammondsville*?

"How so?" Joseph asked.

"There was a note left on my table in the bank's breakroom the other day. It said, 'Watch yourself.' I'm the only one who eats at that table."

"Does the public have access to that part of the bank?"

"Anybody could have gotten in. And anybody could have known I eat at that table at noon every day, just by looking in the windows from the street. That was what shook me up a little: the thought that I was being watched."

Joseph glanced at me.

I said, "You think it might be a bank matter? Like a planned robbery or something? Have you talked with your security officer?"

Not sparing me a glance, he said, "The security officer said the camera doesn't show anything conclusive. Lots of people amble up those stairways." Focusing intently on Joseph, he added, "I was *convinced* someone was watching me the other day as I left."

"The words 'watch yourself' would seem to imply that you know something or are doing something that another person considers a threat. Does anything come to mind that might explain that, Mr. Buford?" Joseph asked.

There was the slightest silence. The man answered smoothly, "Nothing at all." But I saw a flicker in his eyes. There was something he wasn't saying.

Joseph nodded, thinking. "Well, you know, I'm really out of my depth here, Mr. Buford. I don't come into play until an arrest is made or an investigation is opened. This is really a police matter. But I do encourage you to speak with the police chief if you feel you may be endangered."

Mr. Buford nodded, looking deep in thought, and I could see that, for some reason, that was not an enticing option for him. He bid Joseph (not remembering my presence) goodnight, and we departed.

The streets had darkened when we descended the stone stairs of Town Hall, and the streetlamps were just starting to flicker on. Joseph glanced at me. "Think there's anything to that?"

"I don't know. He's kind of a Nervous Nelly."

"Yeah, I caught that," he answered, seemingly pondering it.

"Probably just pissed someone off at work over the copy machine," I said darkly.

He choke-laughed, glancing around to make sure no one was listening, given his depth of amusement. We walked back toward Legal Row before I realized his Jeep was parked outside Town Hall. "You're over there," I reminded him.

"Yeah. I'm just going to be honest, he has me a little creeped out," he admitted with self-deprecating humor. "I'll walk you to your car."

I glanced up at him. Gentlemanly to put it that way so that I didn't notice that he actually wasn't concerned for himself. "Thanks," I said.

"I'm just saying I don't trust him."

Imani and I were out walking in her somewhat swanky neighborhood, seeing as how there was too great a risk we would be hit by a car or stuffed in a trunk on the secluded highway leading out to Cane House. I was trying to get fit, and since my friend was a fitness coach, I decided to take advantage of her skills. Despite the bearing of two babies, she was toned and perfect. I was skinny and winded after a half mile.

"Yeah, me neither. I don't trust anyone the Town People tend to worship. I'll need to get to know him a little better before I can issue the final judgment, I guess," I said, trying desperately to keep pace.

"Come *on*, Mississippi," she said semi-encouragingly. She checked her watch. "Mitchell will be home with take-out in forty-five minutes, so that doesn't leave us as much time as I would like." Thank goodness for Mitchell.

"I told him to pick up a salad up for you, too."

"Gee, thanks," I said bitterly.

"You'll thank me later."

"Sure, okay, right." Mitchell was one of two local doctors, not a native, but not what we would call a transplant either, since he was from Tennessee. Imani had met him during that one year I had been at college with her. He had been a senior, and I had been skeptical. When he went away to medical school at Meharry in Nashville, I had thought she would never hear from him again. I had been comprehensively wrong. Fast-forward five years, and they were married, and he moved from the city to Hammondsville because this was the only place Imani could ever call home. And here we were five years after that, about to perspire on the pavement.

"I am glad this gives you a few more months to get your life rolling, though," she said, going back to our conversation on my job. "Does he have that sense of entitlement, though?" she asked. We both knew it well from the social climbing variety in high school.

I thought this over. "I haven't really seen that. Yet."

"He asked you to stay, didn't he?"

"Yeah. But he didn't really demand it," I admitted grudgingly.

"Listen, Mississippi, I just want you to be careful," she said stopping in front of me, grabbing both of my arms.

I was startled. "Careful? He's not dangerous, Imani."

"Oh, yes, he is!" She pinned me with a stare. "He's cute. He seems to get your jokes. He has a good sense of fashion. He doesn't dip. You've always been a sucker for blue eyes. You're living in close quarters, working in close quarters..." She looked me over. "You could fall for him, you know. And then he'd leave a big hole in your heart, and *he* would move on and never look back," she said.

I laughed, snorting. "For heaven's sake, I never even thought of that! I promise you we are *extremely* professional. I'm so used to working for his grandpa that a dalliance with my employer never entered my head." Not to mention that we (the gentleman in question and I) both knew who was really the boss in this situation. And it wasn't him, in case you were wondering.

She regarded me warily. "All right. Just watch yourself. And get your legs pumping again!" she exclaimed forcefully.

God help me. I should just get a treadmill.

Chapter Six

I could smell bacon cooking when I was still a mile away. It would be the Easter usual: ham, turkey, potato soup with bacon crumbled on top, mashed potatoes, sweet potatoes, potato casserole, carrots, corn, green beans, lima beans, pinto beans, cornbread, rolls, coleslaw, pink salad, pistachio salad, and regular salad. And at the last minute, I would find three more dishes on the stove consisting of homemade macaroni and cheese, a separate, emergency dish of mashed potatoes, and a squash casserole.

Imani was going to kill me.

I made a left turn and soon heard the gravels of my mom's driveway crunching under my tires. My childhood home was a tiny, white bungalow which showed the lack of a man's touch on the outside. I looked at it for a minute, emotions acute and painful, and got out of my car, reaching for my cupcakes with the bunny tails and feet.

I side-stepped my grandma's truck and Cousin Al's dog, who, tied to a tree, lunged at me with every indication of intent to voluntary manslaughter. Possibly murder. Who cared? Either way, I was dead.

"Al!" I screamed when I had made it to the door. "For the love of heaven, what if the freaking chain breaks?!"

I heard, "Aw, he's harmless," from the living room. I breathed in through my nose, incensed. I mean, I had vicious dogs, but you kept them under *control*, for crying out loud!

My mom was at my side, taking the cupcakes and trying to find room on the dessert counter while my grandma enveloped me in a hug. "Hey, sugar lump," she said. I patted her back, happy to see her, gagging on her perfume.

Everyone still wore their Sunday finest, of course. "Honey, is that the dress you wore last year?" my mom asked.

I looked down. It was cute-ish. Not what I would have bought given unlimited resources, but the structure was good, nipping in at the waist and flowing in an A-line nearly to my knees. It was pink, and my cardigan was white. And I wore heels, something I rarely did. It wasn't Kate Middleton, but it was reminiscent. "Yes, Mama."

"Honey, Easter is about looking your best. Well, probably no one noticed at your church anyway."

I was considering retaliation, trying to think of a dig about her church, but Grandma called everybody to order. She chose her brother-in-law, my great-uncle Dan, to say grace, and locked her hand down on my third cousin's child's little head full of curls to keep him in place for once in his life.

After the prayer, we filled our plates, said child circling the table at least six times, screaming at the top of his lungs and knocking things over with airplane arms, until my grandma said to his mom, "Eugenia, if you don't bust him, I'm going to!"

Eugenia was morally (and rightfully, according to the American Psychological Association) opposed to spanking, something widely ridiculed by the elders whenever she happened to be absent from any family gathering. She swept Braden up with tears in her eyes, tossing an accusatory glance at my grandmother, and left the room.

Cousin Al proceeded to lecture his brother on child-rearing, reminding him not to let the wife rule the roost. Jack quietly stewed. "Maybe you could get your dog under control before giving other people advice!" I spat across the table. And then pandemonium broke out. In the midst of Al's flaming retort, the fire alarms started to go off, reminding my grandmother that the third meat was still in the oven. Little Braden busted free again, sweeping his Easter basket off a chair and proclaiming that he would, "HUNT EGGS NOW!" All the while, of course, Al was still trying to defend himself.

Later, when everyone had left, my mom, grandma, and I sat around the table, silent. I nibbled on a piece of a cupcake, wondering if my hearing was permanently damaged.

It had been just us three for a long time. My grandpa had died when I was little. Both of my parents were only children, and we weren't close to my dad's side of the family. We got together with my grandma's sister's family for a few holidays and funerals, but for the rest of the year, it was the three of us. My grandma was a plump gal with white hair, which was perfectly curled and kept in precision by her weekly standing appointment at the beauty salon. She lived a few miles down the road with her cat, Otto. My mother had brown hair, darker and richer than mine (it was now dyed, but that *was* her original color, she insisted). She was a plump gal, too, and beautiful, I thought.

"Honey, how's your new job going?" my mom asked.

"New job?" Grandma breathed, startled.

"Same job, new employer." So far, I had mostly been showing His Highness our court filing system, introducing him to people he needed to know, explaining cant phrases he didn't understand, and helping him familiarize himself with our current caseload. I explained this to them. "And it's temporary, Mama. Remember?" I asked, cutting her a look.

"I think it could be extended if you wanted it to. Everyone knows you're invaluable at that office," she said proudly, licking the spoon from the pistachio salad. Crap. I had wanted that spoon.

"Mama, I don't think so. And I kind of need to move on anyway. I was thinking...of going down to the beach for the summer."

I will spare you the details of what happened next. Suffice it to say, it was ugly: there were tears, recriminations, and accusations. I, of course, felt the need to defend my position, and argued in a way that made my mom feel like she had the upper hand, and it all ended with my grandma leaving, slamming the door behind her.

After Grandma left, I was able to explain to my mom that my plan was to go back to college, something that appeased her so much that she wrapped me up a plate to-go.

Monday, I was back at work. Everyone except the DA was traumatized from the holiday, so very little work got done. Tuesday, it was our day to go up to Berry for court, and I had been asked to accompany Mr. Cane-Steinem. He had enquired gravely whether it was okay if he picked me up at the cottage, or if we needed to drive the full thirty minutes up the mountain separately. There was some gleam in his eyes that made me think he wasn't quite as serious as his voice sounded.

"You may pick me up at the cottage," I had replied grandly, sweeping out of the office.

And sure enough, at seven o'clock, I saw the Jeep pulled up outside. I locked the door behind me. Today, I was dressed serviceably. Black slacks, old ballet flats, lavender cardigan. He was in a suit. It was tan, well fitting, extremely attractive, and well-complimented by his white shirt and blue gingham tie. Oh, shoot. I had stopped with the car door open, and I was staring.

He was lifting his brows in question. "Everything okay, Miss Whitson?"

"Sure, yep, yeah," I answered, climbing in and putting my purse at my feet.

"How are the dogs?" he asked. "Did you find the food?"

When I had gotten home Easter night, there had been a stash of an excellent brand of dog food on my porch, along with two new collars, one pink and one blue. That had made me smile. "They're great, and yeah, they loved it. Freida feels glamorous in her new collar. Fritz has no idea anything has changed."

He laughed softly, turning down the heat. The days were warming up exceptionally quickly now.

I told him about my Easter, which drew several delighted, surprised laughs out of him, something that was happening more the longer I spent with him. My guess was that he may have been a little depressed when he moved here. Loss of grandfather or beautiful girlfriend? Well, anyway, he'd only been in Hammondsville a short time, but there wasn't time in Hammondsville to stay in the dumps.

"What the heck?"

I looked up at his incredulous tone. We were about halfway to Berry on a really narrow road in the middle of a meadow. Filling said road in front of us was a whole brood of chickens. They clucked and pecked and wandered around aimlessly, a bunch of hens and a single rooster who seemed to be squawking orders to which nobody paid any heed. "Oh, for the love of... Jake Dillon's chickens have gotten out again. Scratch that, they were never put *up*."

My employer looked at me, eyes wide.

"They roam the countryside," I explained, reaching for the door handle.

"Should I go find the owner?" he asked.

"No, Jake's a druggie," I whispered, glancing up the hill at his shack. Geez. The kids were roaming the yard, too, even though they should've been on the way to school, and their mom was at the clothesline smoking, with the baby attached to her by a sling. "And he'll be in bed until noon anyway."

I went forward like the durable, stout-hearted girl I was, waving my hands and saying, "All right, all right, part ways, ladies. Move along!" There was a lot of clucking and a couple of frightened shrieks. I heard the other door close and saw Joseph come to stand beside me. I could feel him keeping his eye on the shack. "Oh, gosh!" I exclaimed. The rooster swaggered toward me, clucking something very disrespectful, as if to say that he was the boss, and I'd better just keep that in mind.

I heard a choked laugh beside me as I continued trying to shoo them away. "Maybe we should just get in the car and start driving. I'm sure they'll scatter."

"No, Mrs. Dillon will come down and start accusing you of running over one of them, saying she's going to sue," I hissed.

"They're in the road!" he exclaimed. "*I* should sue."

That brought a giggle on, which I soon stifled, as a certain rooster with a superiority complex lunged at me, flying through the air and squawking so loudly he sounded like a siren. There were two advantages to this, though you might see none. One, he didn't hit me, and his little flight had landed him off the road. Two, his womenfolk were truly alarmed at this outburst of rage and left the road rapidly.

"All right," I said, collecting myself. "That's not the way I would've chosen, but it's done."

We walked back to the car, Mr. Cane-Steinem's eyes dancing as though he had hugely enjoyed this excursion, but I was still rattled and annoyed.

"I'll talk to the police about paying them a visit. It's a road hazard."

"I wouldn't do that," I replied, re-buckling myself since his car was beeping at me incessantly. "Jake's a nice enough guy, but when he's under the influence, he can be a nasty cuss."

He looked back over his shoulder. "What about the woman?"

"Yeah, I'm not sure if she's using or not. And lesson of the day: Don't say 'woman.' I heard you doing that the other day." He looked at me, eyes wide, expression baffled but anticipating amusement. "It's *ladies*," I exclaimed. "Say *ladies.*"

"Am... Am I allowed to use the term 'men?'" he asked, voice quivering ever-so-slightly.

I considered this. "Maybe. It is an expression of masculinity, after all. But I would prefer you to use 'gentlemen' or 'fellas.'"

"I can't say 'fellows.' That's not going to roll off my tongue right."

"As you have so fluently demonstrated," I agreed. He had an interesting accent. He had been raised among the fashionable world in Paris. He sounded like an American, largely because of his mother, her staff, and the circle of expat friends she had. And he had attended an American (or at least English-speaking) school. I knew that because Mildred Weatherford had flat-out asked him in the office last week when she had swung by, revealing the depth of Hammondsville's interest in his mother and his past. He had seemed startled by the question, something which amused me. He had absolutely no idea of the level of intrusiveness he was in for.

But anyway, he had also spent most of his summers with his grandparents in Tennessee, and of course, the largest portion of his life in New York. He didn't really sound like anything, except cultured, but not in a snooty way. In a pleasant way. He said the word *been* like *bean*. Occasionally he would surprise me by throwing out a Southern pronunciation. There was some upper crust Northeasterner in there, too. So it was a mixed bag, always interesting to listen to, but not unnatural. His words flowed as elegantly as if there were villages of people who sounded just like him.

I cleared my throat. "I'd stick with 'ladies' and 'gentlemen.'"

"I live to please, of course," he said without a hint of irony. But his eyes could not be tamed.

"Listen, you're going to have to take this seriously! Especially today. It could be dangerous up here if you don't listen to me."

"I am taking it seriously, and I will listen," he responded. His tone was convincing, but we'd see.

Chapter Seven

The Berry courthouse seems to sit at the very top of the mountain. The court square consists of about five businesses and a post office, and that is *it*, my friend. His Royal Highness got out of the Jeep and looked around with the amazement of one who has stepped into an alternate universe. Rough-looking people were filing into the courthouse doors and arguing with court officers about retaining pocketknives.

"Come on, I'll show you the way," I said.

I shimmied past everyone, getting long stares, as if this same batch of law-breakers hadn't seen me with Mr. Cane a hundred times. At the door, one of the officers waived us to the side past the metal detectors, and I introduced him to the new DA. He was polite but responded with a refreshing lack of fawning and told us we could go on up to the courtroom.

We took the old stairs since the elevator was a one-person crank deal, and I took Joseph to the prosecution desk. He laid his files down in one stack and looked around, getting the lay of the land.

"The procedure is a bit different up here," I said. "Think you can pivot?" Corporate counsel was a far cry from a one-man-show prosecutor. This day took stamina. The kind I wasn't sure he had the experience for. My ire at the town council for their choice was stoked again.

He turned back around, looking me over. A slightly amused expression bloomed. "Yes, I think I can."

Such confidence! I flicked my brows dismissively. "Okay, then. Tell me if you need any quick refreshers on Tennessee law." Did I sound pert? Yes. I was still ticked that he could walk in without much experience and just run the whole show. People killed for his job in other, more livable parts of the state. Well, not literally killed, but still.

His lips turned up at the corners. His eyes sparked with something I couldn't quite define.

The public defender came in. They had already been introduced in court at Hammondsville, so I settled in to watch the morning's circus. *Marijuana, marijuana, marijuana.* Wife slapped husband. Husband threw bottle at wife. Meth. Violation of probation. Driving ninety on Main Street in Berry. *Sheesh.* DUI. Hunting without a license. Marijuana, marijuana, marijuana.

I kept an eye on Joseph to make sure he didn't require fluids. Overall, he handled it pretty well. Berry was always a long day, with one attorney handling all offenses for a month in a single day. I had always worried about Henry doing it after he hit, you know, eighty-five.

His grandson obviously didn't operate like a well-oiled machine this first time out of the gate. There were a few pauses, a few moments of consulting of notes. But he could've handled things a lot worse, and he had obviously come prepared. Having been a straight-A student myself, I had to give him points for that.

As we finally walked out, it was late in the afternoon. I handed him a Halls cough drop on the way down the steps, and he looked at me with true gratitude. "I have bottles of water in my bag," I said.

"A shot of insulin?" he asked hopefully.

I stopped. "You're not diabetic, are you?"

"Joking. We should probably get dinner, though. It's been a long day." He looked like he was on the verge of a headache, probably from an actual drop in blood sugar, diabetic or not, because the judge had refused to recess for lunch. I had sneaked some peanut butter crackers and an apple juice into the courtroom. Rebel to the core.

"Yeah, sure."

"Berry or Hammondsville?" he asked, glancing at me.

"Berry," I answered immediately.

His blue eyes looked across the square at the town's sole, questionable-looking diner. "Really?"

"Up here, people expect the court contingent from Hammondsville to eat together at the diner because we have to eat. In Hammondsville, people would think we are dating, or at least there would be talk, unless we go out as a whole office."

"Because we ate together?" he asked for clarification purposes. I could hear that he was straining not to sound incredulous. "I went out to lunch or dinner all the time with women—ladies—in New York. *Without* amorous intentions."

"Well, you aren't in New York anymore," I retorted. "Don't say amorous. Come on."

I led the way across the street to Bill's Diner, a place of many wonders, including vinyl booths, low-hanging light fixtures, and a salad bar that had been left out since morning. "Don't touch the salad," I whispered as we sat at our assigned table, the cushions squawking and moaning.

He picked up the menu. I took it from him. "You're going to order a baked potato and a piece of toast, okay? It's dangerous to stray into anything cooked in grease or anything not actually cooked. And order sweet tea so you know the water has been boiled."

His eyes danced. When the waitress came, he did as I bid. "I think I'll run to the restroom," he said after she shimmied off with our menus tucked under her arm.

"I wouldn't," I cautioned, looking up from checking my emails. I reached into my bag and brought out a fruity hand sanitizer.

He held out his hand, studying me with that look of amused joy. My hand trembled as I squirted the sanitizer. I gave him too much. "Sorry. Here, I'll take some," I said, reaching to scoop some out of his hand. Not a good idea, rubbing his palm. Who would have thought? Okay, so there was some attraction here. Nothing new for me. I was attracted to boys in high school all the time whom I absolutely despised. Just because you didn't warm to a person didn't mean they couldn't have physical merits.

"Thanks," he said, seemingly unaware (thank goodness). He tilted his head up to read the sign above the bar.

It said, and I quote, "*I don't care who you are, who your daddy is, or what you say—if my politics offend you, get out of my restaurant!!*"

He looked delighted. "That's a great sign!" he said. "Has to be good for business."

I met his smile reluctantly. "It's not so much his politics which offend me as the salmonella."

He choked on his tea, which the waitress had brought. He pretended to be recovering from a cough while the waitress plunked our plates down on the table. Two steaming and safe baked potatoes had officially been delivered.

We dined and then headed out for home in the Jeep. He looked tired. "You want me to drive?" I asked when we had been on the road for about five minutes. It still felt funny to be driven by someone in this job.

"No, I'm fine. Hey, why don't I know you from my summers here? I was thinking about that. My grandma would always take me to the community things and church functions."

"Well, you're a little older than me. We wouldn't have been in the same groups." He seemed to accept my answer. He had no idea that we wouldn't have run in the same circles either.

We had made it back to downtown Hammondsville by now, the church steeples illuminated against the dusky sky. He braked as a person randomly crossed in the middle of the road, yards from a crosswalk, because why would you use those? Other than that, the streets were pretty deserted, and we easily made it through the stoplights.

We headed out on the highway that would take us to Cane House. The evening was rapidly falling, making the shadows of the old tree limbs stretch eerily across the road.

He passed the big house and drove on to my cottage. I reached to unbuckle to seatbelt, and he said, "Do you want me to walk the dogs?"

Gathering my purse, I answered, "No. I do not want to have to take you to the hospital. We are not ready for that yet."

He laughed. "Okay. Thanks for all of your help today."

"Just doing my job," I answered briskly, setting the purse strap on my shoulder as firmly as a seventy-year-old woman bent on taking advantage of a sale at Alfred Dunner. Just to kill any possible attraction. Just to keep things professional. *Professional* was my middle name. Never mind that he didn't seem to be the one feeling any attraction. There was something about a man dropping a woman off at her door at night, say what you will. "Goodnight."

I closed the car door and walked briskly up my little sidewalk. The motion light came on, already attracting bugs even this early in the spring. Geez, the blooms hadn't even fallen yet. He didn't drive off until my key worked and I was in the house. Which made my heart flutter for no apparent reason.

Chapter Eight

I went to dinner with Mary and Melissa the next Monday night at the local bar and grill. We could only attend this restaurant off season for football and basketball if we wanted to be able to hear each other over the TVs and enthusiastic fans.

Mary was a few years younger than me, but we had hit it off when she had come to work as the office secretary a few years ago. She was petite, adorable, and currently dating what my mother would call A Nice Boy (looking at me pointedly as if they grew on trees and were mine for the plucking).

Melissa was in her forties, a mom of four with a cluttered van. She had gone to law school after her last child had started school. Her husband was a probation officer, and she had always been interested in the work, she said. She was shy, nervous, and extremely meticulous.

Paul never joined us, seeming to sense that it was a girls' thing while also suffering from social anxiety and longing for nothing so much as his empty, quiet house.

"Well, I think things are going as well as can be expected," Melissa mused quietly.

"I do, too," I agreed bracingly.

Mary hesitated, and we looked at her. "It's just... It can be so hard sometimes," she said, lifting her napkin and blotting her eyes. "People can be so rude on the phone."

"I told you, you've got to just start expecting that as part of the job," I said gently. We'd been over this a million times. "Like a bank teller would expect people to cash checks or a fast-food worker would expect people to order lunch."

Mary nodded. "Yes. You're right. That always helps. Do you think he's going to stay, Mississippi? I mean, because we could get someone completely different in there, and we could all lose our jobs and be turned out on the streets."

"I haven't heard him say anything about leaving," I answered, skating over his father's phone call.

Mary perked up when our queso and chips were brought. Dipping a chip, she said, "Do you know, we've been doing this for a while now, girls?" Her phone was brought forth from her purse. Opening the photo app, she tapped a file. We always took a selfie when we did an office girls' night out. She pulled up the first one, from six years ago. Melissa and Mary had just started at the office. I stood in the middle, my arms around them.

"You look *good*, Mississippi," Melissa said softly.

My cheeks warmed. I studied the picture. I sported a short haircut and wore a form-fitting black dress with a belt which accentuated my narrow waist. Gray tights and charcoal suede heels that matched the belt did give it a certain flare. I swallowed. What had happened to that girl?

Well, I mean, that sounded a little dramatic. The girl was the same. But the fashion… I mentally reviewed my current outfit. Slacks that were about ten years out of style, a shirt that was balled from too many washes, and a necklace which didn't really match.

Before I could mentally hash this conundrum out, our server brought our plates, saving me from the disturbing questions in my mind.

"Do you plan to attend church?"

We had completed a successful morning of cultural coaching. I had asked the question while we were locked in Mr. Cane-Steinem's office, knowing that he needed to get plugged into a church pretty quickly if he didn't want to face charges of being a Sunday Morning Slacker, a good-for-nothing who slept in on the Lord's Day, or a member of The Great Unchurched.

I noticed him hesitating, and I said suspiciously, "What?"

"I'm…Jewish," he said from his desk, where he looked up at me.

"Oh," I breathed. "I completely forgot."

He lifted his brows in surprise. "Is that a problem?"

"Of course not. Don't be ridiculous," I responded. I leaned against the tall, wooden bookshelves which housed a complete set of *American Jurisprudence,* thinking.

Blue eyes regarded me. "You can raise the dogs Christian," he said. "I don't mind."

I nearly choked. Stifling a laugh, I said, "This is going to be a bit...tricky."

His face changed subtly. I thought he perhaps stiffened. "Is there anti-Semitism here?"

"No, there isn't," I answered. I nibbled my lip in thought while I considered the conundrum.

"I'm a little lost, then," he explained, the confused twinkle returning to his eyes.

"Are you practicing?"

"Sort of...?"

"Answer the question. I'm trying to help you here!" I slapped the table for emphasis.

"I'm from New York. Everyone is Jewish," he answered, looking completely baffled. "People don't ask whether you're practicing or not."

"*I'm* not asking. *I* couldn't care less. But as your social instructor, I am trying to prepare you."

"For what?"

I studied him for a long moment. Fine, I would just say it. "They will want to know whether it's in your blood or in your soul."

"*What?*" His eyes were *so* wide.

"They'll be asking you if you know Jesus."

Finally, realization dawned. "They'll be worried about me."

"With all the well-intentioned arrogance of a culture which believes unabashedly that it is right," I confirmed.

He bit his lip, surveying me with smiling eyes.

I said, "They'll just be having a sort of anxiety for you if they feel like you're on the fence, so you need to tell them one way or the other pretty firmly."

Eyes softening, he responded, "Mississippi, look..." My skin tingled at his use of my first name. Stupid skin. "I was raised in both traditions, and there was never any awkwardness for me. My father was the more religious of my parents, so I do consider myself to be Jewish, but..." He sat back. "That's going to be hard for people to understand, isn't it? I always forget my experiences have been so different from everyone else's."

That was an understatement. I actually thought it was rather lovely, what he had said. My own faith meant a great deal to me, and I could see from his eyes that his did to him, too. And so I resolved not to make him pander to Hammondsville whims. Not on this one. "All right, here is the plan," I said, having gathered myself. "When someone asks you, just state it outright. They'll think you're a bit of an unknown to study, they'll tell you that they stand unreservedly with your people, and then they'll leave you alone."

His lips twitched, and he nodded. "Thanks. I'll do that."

An awkward second passed. He closed the file we had been working on. Looking up, he said, "Hey, I have a cultural question for you."

"Go for it." I was already tacking down a file's papers, getting ready to close it. *Another successful conviction*, the ruthless side of my brain touted happily. I looked up at him.

"Why does everyone not just say *goodbye* and get on with it?"

My forehead wrinkled. "What do you mean?"

"I mean, like I'll be on the phone with someone or bidding someone farewell in the courtroom, and they say, 'Goodbye.... All right, have a good evening... Okay, take care now.... All right, see you soon Cane-Steinem.' And the worst part is, between each one of these *adieus*, I find myself responding."

Mirth bubbled up inside of me. "But we don't want to be *rude*!"

"Rude? How could it possibly be rude to just say *goodbye*?"

A laugh escaped. "I can't explain it. It would be like cutting someone short, I guess. We want you to know that we still really like you as we leave. Think of it like a dance."

"It feels more like milking a cow."

"What on earth?" I exclaimed. As his comparison settled over me, I erupted into laughter, and, after his lips twitched as though he were trying to avoid it, he did too.

The door exploded open, and Mary crashed through, startling us. I hadn't realized until then that our gazes had been locked all this time. "I'm so sorry, but I've got Jepp Lewis out here saying Mr. Howell has put up a fence across his line, and I don't think I can make him wait a *second* longer!"

Even though I had attempted to duck out the window upon Mary's announcement, I hadn't been quick enough. Jepp bounded in and captured us for an hour and fifteen minutes. Sometimes you had no choice but to submit to the chaos.

My phone rang, vibrating and lighting up on my desk the next day. It was my mom, and, since we were pretty lax about taking phone calls in the office, I answered.

"Okay, let's talk Sunday dinner," she began immediately. "Did you put those beans on to soak?"

"It's Friday, Mama."

"Never too early. I've got the broccoli soaking in mayonnaise for the salad."

"I'll start defrosting the roast in the fridge," I said, doodling designs of dresses on my legal pad.

"We're having roast? You need another meat."

"For you and me and Grandma?" I protested in irritation.

"If the Cane boy is going to come."

I pulled my phone away and looked at it, wondering if I had missed something. "Why would he come?" I asked, lowering my voice.

"You cannot have Sunday dinner at your cottage, on the same property where he lives, without inviting him. It's not Southern, Mississippi. I'm surprised at you."

"Ohh-kay," I said. I knew he wouldn't come. What did New Yorkers do on Sunday afternoons? Go for a run in the park? Decompress? I could almost guarantee they didn't commit gluttony in the company of all of their relatives. "Anything else?" I asked.

"I talked to Fanny Barksdale." As an aside, she said, "She's dotty! Talking about some kind of sinus massage. It was just gross, considering she runs the bakery. Anyway, you know Peggy Wilton?"

"Yes. Bless her heart, she's been dying for twenty years," I said, getting into the spirit of things, despite myself.

"Well, she died."

I winced. "I'm so sorry to hear that," I said gravely.

"Anyway, I thought if you want to put on an extra pot of beans, it should be just in time for the funeral, and we can take it over there."

"Mama, I'm not going to the funeral home for a woman I met three times," I whispered frankly, glancing around me to make sure no one was listening.

"She was your father's third grade teacher!"

"My point exactly," I retorted through gritted teeth. "I'll do the beans for you, and I'll invite Joseph, but I'm not going to the funeral."

My mom sighed, which meant she was preparing to accept my resistance to her full bill of decrees. "All right. We'll see you at one o'clock on Sunday, then. I'll bring Grandma."

Joseph and I were the last out of the office that evening. The parking lot was deserted, and the Friday winding-down vibe was in full swing. As "the Cane boy" turned to lock up the door, I said, "Hey, my mom demands that I invite you over to the cottage for our Sunday dinner." I flushed. "I mean, not that I don't want you to come. Of course you're welcome." He looked at me, turning from the lock. I continued, "Just my mom and grandma and me, and you, too, if you want. But you totally don't have to come. She just didn't want you to feel left out. I mean, *we* didn't." Oh my gosh, kill me now.

He stared at me with his wide, perhaps amused eyes. There was something of innocence in them as well, some unadulterated enjoyment of the moment and the social customs he couldn't quite grasp. "I'm confused. Do you want me to come or not?"

"Of course!" I answered enthusiastically. "I mean, not if you don't want to. What I'm trying to say is: I can give you an out if you don't want to come."

"I can come," he said, smiling.

I flushed all over. Geez Louise. "Okay, great! One o'clock."

"Should I bring anything?"

"Just yourself!" I said chipperly, fleeing toward my car. I was going to kill my mother.

My Saturday morning started with a phone call at eight o'clock before I was even awake.

"Honey, I just happened to think: he's Jewish. What on earth are we going to do?"

"Wha...?" I asked in a whiney, morning put-out voice as I rubbed my eyes.

"You're having a *roast*, Mississippi. Think about that. This is a disaster!"

I sat up, running my hand through my hair as I tried to grasp her meaning. Jewish. Roast. Disaster. *Oh!* "It's a beef roast, Mama."

"Oh!" She sighed with relief. "Thank the good Lord for that. Is he kosher? I'm going to have to do some research if he is."

I smiled, loving my mom. "I think he is mostly, but he's not going to kick up a fuss. He wouldn't have said he would come over if he were worried about it. And I've seen him eat the heck out of a pepperoni pizza at the office. So I think we're good."

I could hear her thinking for a long moment. "I'm going to leave the bacon out of everything, just to be on the safe side."

"What were you going to have bacon in?"

"Everything," she answered honestly. "All right, bye now, honey."

I got up, decided to take no more calls from my mom, who was making me neurotic, and put my beans on to soak.

I high-tailed it from my car into the cottage after church on Sunday. The beans smelled heavenly, as did the roast, as soon as I opened the door. Tossing my purse and keys out of sight, I skittered into my kitchen and became a whirlwind of mindless activity. I put a pot on to boil for the tea, set my tiny table (which would just barely seat the four of us), and started peeling potatoes.

My cheeks were red, my hair was mussed, and my feet were tired, but everything was perfect when my mom and grandma arrived ten minutes early. It wasn't until Joseph knocked and I opened the door, seeing him in perfect trousers and a crisp shirt that I realized that I was standing there in a maxi dress I had worn in high school. With a pattern that had been "in" when I was in high school. Which obviously wasn't now. Great. Just great. Why the heck couldn't I get it together and go through my closet?

More importantly, why hadn't I invited him in? "Hey! Come on in. I hope you're hungry."

"I am," he affirmed, smiling. His eyes lifted across the room to the table, where my mom and grandma were sitting. "Hello, ladies," he said, glancing at me as if for approval.

I rolled my eyes, shutting the door.

"Why hello, young man," my mom replied, patting the chair next to her. "You just come on in and have a sit down. We already poured you a tea."

And that was that. We hadn't been eating three minutes when my mom asked Joseph if he had a girlfriend.

"No, I'm single," he answered, taking a bite of his meat. He winked. "But if you're asking, ma'am..."

"Oh!" She swatted his arm, delighted. "Listen at him!" she said in a scolding tone, as though he were a recalcitrant but cute little boy.

Great, the Crown Prince had now won my mother over as well. Was I the only one left standing? Well, there was Imani, but she hadn't met him yet. "Mom. Honestly. You can't ask personal questions."

She sighed, looking at me like she wondered where she had gone wrong. "Honey, what would we talk about then?" She turned her attention back to Joseph. "Now, your daddy—is he all alone up there? Does he have people?"

Joseph looked equally delighted with her. "He has some family and a lot of friends. He never married." He winked again. "He says that was for me, but I think being tied to *just* one woman terrifies him." My mom and grandma gasped and chuckled with delight, riveted.

"Now, do you still have your grandparents on that side?"

He nodded. "I do. They're in good health." By that measured comment, I took it that they weren't close.

The personal questions continued, but it wasn't until he was asked where his family had been during the Holocaust that I choked and nearly died.

"Well, Mississippi!" my grandma exclaimed in an accusatory tone, as if I had meant to choke. She whacked my back. A glance at my houseguest during this interlude revealed that he was struggling to maintain his gravity.

When I had recovered, he answered, "They were in New York. They were fine." His face turning more serious, he added, "There were some more distant relatives who...were not so fortunate." His voice trailed off. Oh, no. That was terrible. And bless my mama, if her inappropriate digging didn't lead us into a very good, very intimate conversation. We talked about history and its consequences, and my womenfolk acted like the rational, loving humans they were.

I smiled as I cut the pie for dessert, feeling peaceful. I heard something and looked up as Joseph entered the kitchen. He smiled. "Need help?"

"Sure," I said, motioning him toward the small plates, which he brought for me.

I felt him study me as I plated the pieces. "They're pretty great, Mississippi."

I winced, shaking my head as I put the garnishes on the pie. I looked up, finally saying, "Look, probing questions and choking and the Holocaust aside...thanks for coming today. They miss male company."

He smiled, eyes twinkling due to my caveats. But sincerity laced his expression, something I hadn't initially expected from him. He paused as he took a plate from me, and we both held it in our hands for a few seconds before he took it fully into his own. "Thanks for inviting me."

Chapter Nine

Back at work, it was business as usual. Monday and Tuesday passed uneventfully, except that Mr. Buford came into the office to reiterate that he felt threatened. When he heard that Joseph was in court, he looked defeated, saying with a wheeze caused by his two-block walk from the bank, "Well, is there someone I can speak to?"

Mary said nervously, "Well, all of the attorneys are in court today. There was a trial."

I walked forward from the copier, where I had been running some stuff for Paul. I laid the papers on his desk as I passed and said, "Mr. Buford, how can we help you?"

He sighed. "It's just that I have a...situation. Someone... That is, I believe someone may be following or threatening me."

He literally said this to me. Literally. "You may not remember, but I spoke with you after the Council meeting," I said. I tried not to grit my teeth.

He stared at me blankly.

"With Joseph Cane-Steinem," I said. If my tone was a bit clipped, probably only Mary noticed. She shifted on her balance ball chair, picking up a paper with which to fan herself.

Mr. Buford's skin tinged pink. "Ah, yes. Yes, of course. Well, as I said..." He cleared his throat, taking refuge in a coughing fit. I rolled my eyes. "The thing is, I saw a man across the street as I walked out of the bank to my car last night."

Oh, boy. He was getting to be as tedious as Jepp Lewis.

"And in the restaurant where I had dinner."

I perked up. "The same man?" That did sound like something.

His skin mottled again. "No. But why were they both looking at me?"

"Maybe they liked your tie!" Mary said in an effort to be helpful.

He didn't spare her a glance. She wasn't a Town Person either. He didn't know her daddy from the Country Club, after all. Hadn't attended her baptism or anything. How many people could a man really be expected to notice?

Pretty hot under the collar, I said, "I will relay your message to Mr. Cane-Steinem."

Which I did, and we agreed that our Nervous Nelly was probably just having a bout of paranoia. After informing the police of his concerns, we called it a day.

"Okay, a couple of things you need to know about Phil Tuck," I said as Joseph drove us out of town down country roads. They weren't charming, these roads. They were full of potholes, hair-pin curves, and (you guessed it) chickens. My travelling companion had remarked something innocent about the buttercups lining the road just before having to lock it down when somebody's suicidal dog decided to cross unexpectedly.

We were on our way to a neighboring town where Phil Tuck, an ancient attorney, kept an office. He was the appointed counsel for the drug-addicted Jake Dillon because the public defender's office had a conflict of interest. Said conflict was something about Jake having, while high, marched in and threatened to slash all of their tires (and possibly their throats) the last time they had defended him.

We thought we could reach a plea deal with Mr. Tuck, and as a courtesy due to his antiquity, Joseph had offered to go to him. And driving to Pickensville was definitely a job that called for one's cultural coach to be present.

"Is he handsy, too?" Joseph asked, a little nervously.

"No, thank heaven. But he's a hell-raiser. He has no concept of the rules of procedure or professional conduct. He is from a different era where if you can scream the loudest you win. He will not back up his statements with any law. For all of that, he has been surprisingly effective."

"Fair enough," he responded.

"I'm not finished," I said, lest he think he was going to get off easy. "I'm not certain he bathes regularly." Joseph looked at me, his eyes widening with surprised delight. I held up a finger. "And he cusses like a sailor." I drummed my fingers on the door panel. What else, what else? I looked back at him. "He is passionate about Jimmy Carter, and you don't need to say the word 'Republican' near him, or we won't get out with our lives. Got it?"

He hesitated, seeming to be unsure. "I mean, it would probably be better if you would write it all down," he said in all seriousness.

"You'll be fine," I responded with more confidence than I felt. "Just if I nudge you or step on your toe or hit you or something, you will need to follow my lead."

"Got it," he said, eyes twinkling again. We'd see what there was to twinkle about.

The scene grew slightly less rural as we emerged into the small town. We got out at the building which had been built before Mr. Tuck's president of choice had been in office. That was also the last time repairs had been done, if the firm's shingle, hanging at an angle, was any indication.

Joseph opened the door for me, and I unwillingly stepped inside to be assaulted by the smell of cigarette smoke. Joseph started coughing uncontrollably, and I whacked his back.

"Thanks," he said, eyes streaming. "I think."

"Come back!" We heard a voice utter this command not very pleasantly and started walking.

Joseph stopped, turning his head to the side and sneezing three times. "Dear God," he whispered, wiping his eyes again. What had I said? Not for the faint of heart, this excursion.

But he walked forward manfully—I have to give him that. Most people would have bailed at the sight of the shingle. "I think I smell weed," he said as I lifted my hand to open the door.

"You do."

"This puts me in an awkward position."

"Pretend you don't smell it," I instructed. "I promise you won't *see* it."

He obeyed. We settled in across from the old man, and, after establishing who both of our grandfathers were, Mr. Tuck said, "Well, she took good care of Henry, young man!"

I flushed.

"I know she did, sir," Joseph said.

I glanced at him, and he looked quite sincere. I blushed more deeply still.

"Now, what's this young fella's name you've come to see me about?"

"Jacob Ryan Dillon, sir."

"What's the charge?"

My protégé looked stunned for a second. Poor kid. So much to take in. After absorbing the shock of the lack of professionalism, he said numbly, "Possession of a controlled substance—heroin."

"Well, now, Mr. Cane, you know these young kids make mistakes! And this damned *possession* is a law that criminalizes addiction, which I don't stand for! I don't stand for it one bit!" he exclaimed, raising his voice and pounding his desk.

"Nonetheless, it is the law, and I am required to enforce it."

"Well, hell! What are you going to tell me next: that you didn't make mistakes as a kid?"

"I can't say that I snorted opioids," Joseph answered. I glanced at him, afraid he was growing annoyed, but I could see that he was amused and just doing a good job hiding it. He was also standing his ground, not an easy thing with Phil Tuck. "And this 'kid' is thirty-three years old and the father of five." And of a recalcitrant flock of chickens that had almost attacked me, lest we forget.

Mr. Tuck raised a dismissive hand. "A mere baby, at least from where I sit! Now listen here, Cane, I—"

"Cane-Steinem," I said.

"Heh?" Mr. Tuck looked at me, raising his bushy white brows.

He refused to wear hearing aids, and female tones were difficult for him. So I screamed, "It's *Cane-Steinem*!"

Joseph laid a hand on my arm briefly, content to let it pass.

"Eh, yes, right, right. But you can't tell me you really believe you should be prosecuting someone in these circumstances, young man!"

"My personal beliefs don't enter into it, sir."

"Of course they do! It's the purpose of the justice system!" the elderly gentleman exclaimed, punctuating this comment with a stomp.

Joseph said, smiling slightly, still calm, "That sounds more like the political system. From where *I'm* sitting, I have no choice but to follow the law as it is currently written."

"But where is the *justice* in that? Where is the sense of equity, the sense of *right*, which is the heart of law?"

Joseph looked at me, apparently touched. *See? I told you he was (surprisingly) effective*, my smug gaze replied.

They worked out an agreement. Joseph was equally effective, and, for all of Mr. Tuck's rabble-rousing, his younger nemesis got what he wanted. We left on the best of terms, certain he would forget our names within thirty seconds of our departure.

I got paid on Friday—*hallelujah*—and I slipped my envelope into my purse to take down to the bank on my lunch break. I went to the old drive-thru and ordered something Imani must never know about. When I finished, I pulled out the envelope just to check that the amount was right.

This time, however, there were two checks. One was my regular paycheck with the added three percent. *Thank you very much.* Brow furrowing, I switched to the other check, which was for one-hundred dollars. On the memo line was written "Child Support." My lips turned up in a smile.

I skimmed the check to see where my employer banked. Pinnacle. Not good. We needed to get all of his accounts switched either to First Hammondsville Bank or Hammondsville Community Bank, or there would be a lot of people getting offended.

Which reminded me... I picked up the phone and dialed his number back at the office.

He picked up on the second ring. "Mississippi?"

My heart did a little flip-flop at the concern in his voice. I never called him on my lunch break, generally needing mental space from the office. *Get on with it, Mississippi!* "Yes! Yeah. Um..." Why had I called again? *Geez, enough!* "Mr. Baker, the lawyer I hired for your grandfather's estate, called me yesterday to let me know that we're out of the creditor period and can start wrapping things up. He has everything ready for me to transfer the assets out of the estate into your name, and he said it would be easier if you were there."

"Oh, sure. Do we need an appointment?"

"He said we could come around three o'clock today. I forgot to tell you this morning. Does that work for you? It's just down the street on Legal Row."

"Sure."

"Okay, thanks. See you in a few."

I finished off my milkshake and set out for the bank. Checks deposited, I returned to work, which seemed a little calmer today for a pleasant change.

At three o'clock, we walked down the street toward the white Victorian that housed The Baker Firm. "Does Whalen Ritten work here?" Joseph asked warily as we kept pace down the sidewalk.

"Nope! Small mercies..."

He appeared relieved, although he didn't say so. "You're going to take an Executrix's fee, right?" he asked.

"Your grandpa did this odd thing in his Will where he actually built in a continued salary during the administration of the estate."

"That was for taking care of the house and helping out at work. I mean the usual percentage for handling the administration of the estate."

I stopped, looking at him. We needed to hash this out before we got in there. "Look, there is no percentage, unless we go less than one, that would be small enough to be fair for the time I put in. I told you, didn't I, what I have in the estate account?"

He said he didn't remember exactly, and I took out the bank statement Virgil Baker had asked me to bring in. Joseph took it, glancing at the balance, and then looked up at me. "A half percent, then."

"That's twenty-five thousand dollars, Joseph," I whispered. I felt the blood drain from my face at the thought, going white.

"Are you going to pass out?" he asked, taking my arm.

"No, I just... I don't want it. He gave me the car. It was enough." I swallowed. "He meant a great deal to me, Joseph. He asked me to do this for him, for you, a long time ago, and I agreed. As a friend."

He studied me a really long time. Something shifted in his expression that I couldn't quite discern. He slowly released my arm. He looked away for a moment. When he returned his attention to me, he said, "Pretend you are a lawyer charging hourly. What would it have come to?"

I calculated. "About two thousand," I said reluctantly.

"Can we agree to that?" he asked. "Please, Mississippi. From me, not from him. You took care of everything from day one, and I know you made it all as simple as possible for me. I don't know what I would have done otherwise while I was trying to wrap up my life in New York."

I swallowed. "Fine," I said. Then I realized I sounded like a belligerent teenager and added more gently, "Yeah, no, I think that's fair. That's fine with me."

He nodded, straightening. We walked on down to the office, and a *whoosh* of air conditioning hit us in the face as soon as we walked through the door. *Geez!* It was hot out, but... Tucking my arms, I wished I had brought a cardigan.

Hetty Gibson popped up from the secretary's desk, push-up bra and all. "Mr. Cane-Steinem!" She strolled forward. She was the married casserole dish lady, and I still couldn't figure out what her game was. Then again, she knew the contents of The Baker Firm's estate files. Was I crazy to think the distribution amount of a certain heir might be at play? I think not.

"Oh, it's just so wonderful to see you again, and looking so well! What a perfect suit. Love the tie!"

His eyes twinkled. He soaked up all of the attention he received, but I sometimes thought it was in a direct effort to annoy me. One couldn't stand within a square mile of my presence and be unaware of the inner growl butt-kissing produced within me.

"Thank you very much. And thank you for the casserole. I will bring your dish into town next week."

"I'll just drop by and get it, how about that?"

"He'll bring it into town," I said firmly, sending Hetty a glare. "Is Virgil ready for us?"

"He is!" she answered sunnily, sweeping her arm back to the next room.

We got everything settled really quickly. I wrote out the necessary checks and signed the deed for the house over into Joseph's name. We both signed the statements for the paperwork with the court. That finished, we talked with Mr. Baker for a few minutes.

He was a classy older gentleman in his sixties, soft-spoken, calming, and pleasant. "I can't tell you how glad we are to have you filling your grandfather's role, son," he said, and for once, this statement didn't irritate me because it sounded genuine. He and Mr. Cane had been friends, and if Mr. Baker said something kind, he meant it.

"Thank you," Joseph responded.

"You're going to run once your special term is up, I assume?" Mr. Baker asked encouragingly.

"Yes, I intend to."

"I don't imagine you'll be opposed," he mused. I could listen to him talk all day. His voice was very soothing. "Mississippi, how is your mother doing?" My mom was about fifteen years younger than he, so I thought he was probably just asking out of friendship rather than a special interest. Mr. Baker's wife had died a few years ago, and they had never been able to have any children. I had always worried he might be a bit lonely, but he kind of seemed like my mom in that he wasn't interested in a second marriage.

"She's great. Still working remotely in customer services for Southwest. Making knitted accessories on the side." *Harassing me to marry daily...*

"I'm glad to hear it. Tell her and your grandmother hello for me."

I promised I would, and we left soon after.

"Nice man," Joseph said as we started down the sidewalk back toward work.

"The best," I agreed, checking my watch. An hour was left until five o'clock. I looked at him. "Hey, I'm going out tonight. Would you mind just checking the water bowls in the fenced off area? Fritz tends to dump them accidentally."

He looked at me quickly. There was a really long pause. "Yeah, sure. Of course."

The air thickened and got really awkward. *What on earth?* The atmosphere remained, even once we had returned to work. Instead of staying his usual fifteen minutes late, he left two minutes early, uttering brisk *good evenings* as he strolled through the front part of the office.

Chapter Ten

I tossed my purse in the car and dialed as I headed toward Imani's subdivision, hoping my Bluetooth would pick the call up soon.

"Hello?"

"Hey, Imani. Sorry, I'm going to be a few minutes late." Mary had needed to hash out why Joseph had left early. She had been concerned that he might be mad at her, which was cute, but it did take a while to talk her down from those ledges.

"No problem at all. Mitchell was a little late, too. I'll see you in a few."

"Great, thanks."

Almost immediately, my phone started ringing. My mother.

I answered. Immediately, as though we were picking up in the middle of a conversation, she said, "I'm just saying, you're my one shot, Mississippi."

"One shot for what?"

"Grandchildren."

"Ugh. Mama. I'm twenty-eight. Do you know that in other parts of the country that's considered a perfectly acceptable age to still be single? Did you know that some people never marry at all and are perfectly happy?"

"Oh, honey, *don't*." I could almost *hear* her shudder. "I just don't see why you won't go out with the McCallister boy."

"Because he's a user."

"He takes meth?"

"No, mom, I mean he *uses* people. He used me in high school for help with math. He used Mitchell to get that job at the hospital..."

"I just think you're blowing it out of proportion, honey. What would one date hurt?"

I sighed. "Mom, he asked me out once seven years ago. I don't think it was an open invitation."

"Becky says he'd be willing enough." Of course. He was my mom's best friend's nephew. They had worked it all out.

"You tell Becky Gimble to mind her own business!"

"I'll do no such thing, young lady! You need to respect your elders. It's just a date, Mississippi. What would it hurt?" There was a long pause, during which I didn't answer. My mom's voice softened. "I don't even remember the last time you went on a date. You're stuck, honey."

Moisture filled up my eyes. That hurt. Mostly because it was so true. "I...fine. One date. I'm not promising anything else."

My mom was off to the races. By the time she finished celebrating, I was turning in at Imani's drive and had to let her go.

"I've got to go, Mama."

"Okay, bye."

"Bye-bye."

"Love you."

"Love you, too."

"Okay, bye."

"Bye." Shoot. We were doing it. I clicked to end the call rapidly.

I waived to Mitchell, who was standing at his grill.

"Hey, Mississippi," he called. "Hey, can you take these in to Imani?"

"Sure thing!" I answered, scurrying to take a plate on which was piled a bunch of grilled vegetables. "Ugh, this was a plot!" I declared.

He laughed. "There are steaks, I promise."

"Probably carefully portioned ones," I mumbled.

"That's Imani," he agreed. "Work going okay?"

"Yeah, pretty good. Just crazy busy."

I went in soon after, delivering Imani's precious vegetables and giving her a hug. Immediately, their two Corgis, William and Harry, emerged from the living room and fluttered around me. I was bending to pet them when DeShawn and Marcus came running out, sliding in their socks.

"Sippi! Sippi!" I leaned to scoop up their embraces, breathing in the fountain of youth. They were four and two and really fun. I did, however, miss when they were chubby babies, giggling and blowing bubbles. Oh, geez, maybe my mom had a point.

After I kissed both of them, I pulled them each out a cookie that I had bought at the drive-in, their favorite. "Save them for after supper, okay?" I trusted they couldn't overcome the thick tape which sealed them.

"Okay!" the exclaimed, running off.

When I stood, Imani was nailing me with a look. "You've been to the drive-in."

I tucked my hair behind my ear. "Um, yeah."

"What did you order?"

I swallowed with difficulty. "A cheeseburger?"

Imani slapped the table. "No. No." She shook her head. "Not on my watch. I'm packing your lunches. I'm coming over there on Sunday, and we'll just meal prep for the whole week. You're not at the point you can be trusted."

"Okay," I answered meekly.

Mitchell came in then, saving me, and we all sat down to eat, the two sweet babies saying the blessing in unison. Supper was healthy but good, and the kids were told they could be excused to go eat their cookies in the living room.

"I was talking to your mom today," Imani said, leaning back in her chair.

Sheesh. "Let me guess: she was enlisting your help to get me back out there on the dating scene."

"It's not a matter of *back* out. You were never in it."

Ouch.

"Imani!" Mitchell protested.

"Honey, I just think Barbara is right." She returned her attention to me. "She said she is going to set you up with Luke McCallister?"

"Yeah, I agreed to a date," I answered, eating a spoonful of some low-carb chocolate thing that was actually pretty decent. But I would never admit it.

"I'm just not sure he's right. What you need is a man like Mitchell."

"I *know*, Imani," I said with annoyance. "Is it my fault you married the last good man in Tennessee?"

Mitchell smiled smugly.

"What about the new DA? He hasn't hit on you, has he?"

"What? No. He's very professional."

"You like him," Imani said, reading my soul as per usual.

I blushed. "What? I don't know what you're talking about!" My voice squeaked. "The Crown Prince? Don't be ridiculous." Not certain I had been convincing enough, I added, "Besides, today he acted all moody and weird."

"How?" Imani took a bite of her dessert.

"Well, I told him I was going out, and asked him to check the dogs' water. He agreed but just got really quiet. I swear it was something about that which made his mood change."

"See? He doesn't want responsibility. So many men don't. All you asked him to do was a simple thing for the dogs he actually owns."

"Come on, Imani, he seems like a nice guy," Mitchell said.

Two pairs of female eyes turned toward him. "You've met him?" Imani asked.

Mitchell got really cagey. "Yeah. Like I said, he seems nice."

"How did you meet him?"

"I don't remember."

"He's your patient, isn't he?" I demanded. "He came to your office."

Mitchell shifted uncomfortably, and I knew I was right. My heart leaped. He had been sick? Why had he not told me? "What was wrong with him?"

"You know I can't answer questions about anything to do with work."

"He has syphilis, doesn't he?" Imani said, eyes narrowed. "If you don't answer me, I'm going to assume that's what it is."

"What are you...? Stop! We can't do this, ladies."

"Oh, gosh. What's wrong with him?" Southern men didn't go to the doctor unless they were at death's door, which is why, I think, all of the men in my life had sudden catastrophic events. Therefore, my mind went straight to cancer. "Cancer. He has cancer."

"Cancer?" Imani said. "Oh, my gosh, this is terrible!"

I looked at her, swallowing. "I have to talk to him—"

"Enough! He has migraines, okay?" Mitchell exclaimed.

We both looked at him again, quieting. Migraines. Okay. A perfectly legitimate reason to go to the doctor.

"And that stays strictly at this table," Mitchell said, giving a poor impression of an angry teacher. He was too nice for sternness, bless him. "The only reason I told you was that I know the pair of you. You were going to tell him that Dr. Reed says he has cancer. Or syphilis. Now please, can we change the subject?"

"Sure," Imani said. She turned to me. "Maybe he had a migraine today. You think that was why he acted strange?"

Mitchell sighed deeply.

Ignoring him, I considered this. "I don't know. It was like it changed in a second, you know?"

"Then we're back to that sense of entitlement."

"Oh, come on, step into a man's shoes for just a second," Mitchel said in frustration. "Try to see it from a different perspective."

"What are you talking about?" his wife asked.

"Mississippi told him she was going out." He raised his brows and nodded once, significantly, as if that said it all. When we stared at him blankly, he added, "And that made him jealous."

We both sat back. This was a fresh perspective, indeed. I thought it over. He had given me absolutely no indication of interest of that kind. He was very much in need of my help all day every day, and he made that very plain. He had even joked that he probably wouldn't be alive at this point if not for me. But I hadn't noticed anything of that nature, except that we might hold glances a little longer than usual sometimes. That was just because it was so rare to meet someone who understood your humor. But honestly, I was 99.9 percent sure I was *not* his type.

"I don't think so," I said. "I'm not his type."

"Yeah, me neither," Imani agreed. I tossed her a look. "What? I'm just agreeing with you!" she said, holding up her hands. "All right, are we going to watch *The Crown*, or not?"

The excellence of *The Crown* and my friends' company notwithstanding, I was a little blue when I put my car in Park that night at my cottage. Even Imani thought I was stuck. I sat with my hands on the steering wheel, staring at my dashboard, a sick feeling twisting in my gut. My mom, Mary and Melissa, and now Imani. That was four people. Oh, I could argue that Mary hadn't really said anything. But she had pulled out the picture. Melissa had reacted honestly to it. My mom and Imani obviously thought I was permanently closed for business. One person was one thing; four was...

I took out my phone and found my equivalent of Mary's picture, a slightly different one but taken the same night. I looked good. I'm not saying that in an arrogant way. I mean that I looked happy. Like I knew who I was, and like that was who I wanted to be. My eyes glowed with the confidence of youth, the kind that is aware of its inner worth before life comes smashing in and puts a big question mark on it.

Oh, I had grown a lot since then. In many ways, I was a better and stronger person. My faith was certainly deeper. It wasn't that I had gone completely backwards. But still...

My clothes looked great in the picture. It wasn't about the material things. But style was a part of who I was. A gift. Most people wouldn't think of it that way—having a knack for picking pieces, putting them together, and wearing them correctly. But I had once read something in the Bible about when they were building the tabernacle. And God had said about the people who were to design the robes and garments and things, "*Tell all the skilled workers to whom I have given wisdom in such matters that they are to make garments...*" That had clicked for me. I had been given wisdom in such matters. There was no doubt I was supposed to use that somehow.

But that hadn't been possible. Adulthood has a way of derailing all our best-laid plans. Or was that a cop out? Why did I think that just because I didn't get to make a career out of it, I had to stop being who I was? All I knew, with blinding light that moment in my car, was that the *last* thing I was supposed to be was anything but *me*. God hadn't created me for me to regift myself to the world with a watered-down version of me.

I swallowed, swiping the moisture from my left cheek. Something white caught my eye, and I looked over at the console. I sniffed, staring at the object for a second before plucking it up. It was the check for my work administering Henry's estate. I looked at the amount again, biting my lip. Henry's last gift to me. I folded the check, staring off into the night sky as an idea formed.

Chapter Eleven

Reader, I spent all day shopping in Nashville. My penchant might be for haute couture, but I could bargain shop with the best of them. I piled my Accord high with bags and bags of expensive-looking clothing, shoes, and accessories—including a knock-off bag that was a dead-ringer for Givenchy—and slammed my door shut on a job well done. My mother would be proud. Except for the fact that I had driven alone to a highly populated city, where she felt the only fate that awaited young women was that of untimely death. But this was something I had needed to do alone, and there was yet one thing left to be done.

I drove to the expensive salon where I had made an appointment that morning. In an hour, I came out with an adrenaline rush and excitement bubbling up inside of me. Sitting in my car, I opened my mirror and looked at myself. My straight brown hair was cut in a bob that didn't quite reach my chin, and thick bangs danced across my forehead. I looked like a flapper girl in the best way.

I snapped my mirror closed, wondering whether people would even recognize me. Probably not: I had even bought an eyebrow pencil, for good measure. It had been a while since I had done real makeup. But I was committed to being just who I was. And I'm just going to drop this here: the world had better watch out.

Okay, my last statement was arrogance based on a shopping high. As I walked up the sidewalk at work on Monday, I felt a bit like I was heading to one of those transformation shows in which everyone is insultingly amazed at the end. Probably everyone wouldn't even notice, though. I was going to hope for that. I would just keep my head down, like Mia Thermopolis, and get to my desk quickly.

I opened the door with a *whoosh* that set the bells tinkling.

"Mississippi! Oh-my-gosh!" I heard instantly. Mary stood, gasping as she examined me from head to toe. Melissa smiled, staring at me without a hint of embarrassment. Of *course* everyone would happen to be in the front room. Paul's brows drew together as he tried to process what exactly was different.

Joseph, who had been standing beside Paul's desk, dropped the folder he was holding. It hit the floor with a *smack* that reawakened us all. I'm not sure why, but it was his eyes that mine were locked on. For a second too long.

"That's a great outfit," Melissa said in her kindly mom-voice.

"Yes, yes, *yes*!" Mary exclaimed, bouncing around from behind her desk to come and take full stock. "And your *hair*!"

Her movement seemed to snap everyone else out of it for the second time. Joseph scooped up the folder, laid it on Paul's desk, and bent over it again as their conversation continued. Obviously aware of HR and stuff in a way that probably most Hammondsvillians weren't, he couldn't comment appropriately even with the most mundane compliment.

I smiled as Mary grabbed my hands. "Pencil skirt alert!" she said, doing a bubbly little dance.

I widened my eyes, sending her a message with them. She looked over her shoulder at the guys, who were obviously trying not to listen but listening. Horror entered her expression. "Oh, my gosh," she hissed in a whisper. She mouthed, "Sorry!" Then she skittered back to her desk.

When the three attorneys had left for court, she came to my desk, her hands on her cheeks. "Oh, my goodness, do you think I'll get fired? I was *exuberant*, Mississippi, which is completely inappropriate in the workplace, and distracting, according to our manuals. And it was pretty obvious to him, I think, that I let that one phone call go over to voicemail. And when I handed him his stack of files, he just said, 'Thanks!' Usually, he says, 'Thank you!' Does that sound ominous to you?"

Laughter boiled over. "No, you goose, it does not sound ominous. And I think Joseph knows we're friends."

"Okay. Whew. Okay." Looking me over, she said, "You really do look great. Is this for Luke?"

Shoot. I had forgotten we even had a date next week. "Um, no, actually. This is for me."

A slow smile formed on Mary's face. "I like that. Girl power!"

Mary was out of the office the next day, so I covered the phone calls. While simultaneously doing this task, I hosted a thirty-minute lesson with the boss on managing the high temperatures in Tennessee. As per usual in the South, as soon as the middle of May rolled around it felt like we were living in Hell's kitchen. I cautioned my protégé on being careful getting into his vehicle (black leather can burn the bum), touching his seatbelt and steering wheel, and leaving any chocolate in the cupholder. Eyes doing their thing, he reminded me that he had spent many a summer in Tennessee. We would see how he faired.

I also sat in on our fourteenth meeting with the Big Bank Man, Reynolds Buford, since Joseph had asked me to do so. Of course, Mr. Buford's eye contact was *all* for General Cane-Steinem, as he called him, using his fancy title. I might as well have been an insect on the shoe mold for all he acknowledged my presence.

"Maybe you will believe me now," he said, eyes wide with borderline hysteria. "Last night, I received a *voicemail*."

"A threatening message?" General Cane-Steinem asked.

"It was heavy breathing. Just like you see in horror movies!" He wiped his brow. "And then they hung up."

I thought it was more likely that a smoker had butt-dialed him and left the line open for several seconds accidentally. But don't ask me. Just the insect here.

"Mr. Buford, I've never not believed you. I have merely told you that I possess no power or authority to help you. I have reported every word you have told me to the police. I don't see what more I can do in my circumstances."

"Have me taken into a protective program!"

"That will not be possible at this time."

"You will not act to protect me?" Mr. Buford questioned in a half-manic voice.

"I will, as always, forward your information to the police and convey your sense of urgency. I cannot, however, guarantee that they will open an investigation or even think about a protective custody situation until you are willing to have an interview with them."

"Well, that," he retorted, bringing himself to his feet in indignation, "will not be possible!"

Chapter Twelve

Mary sidled up to my desk the next morning as soon as she walked through the door. She was beaming, and she extended her hand, revealing a massive rock. "Sutton proposed!" she exclaimed in a whisper, tears trembling on her lashes.

I gasped (though we all, including Paul even, had been expecting this soon). Standing, I wrapped my arms around her and said, "I'm so happy for you!"

Wiping her streaming eyes, Mary said, "It's all planned. A year from now in June. My sister will be the maid of honor, and will you be a bridesmaid?"

"Of *course*," I answered, touched.

"And I'll need you to go with me, probably to Atlanta, to pick out the dress. I trust your style as I trust my own," she said soulfully, touching her chest. "It's going to be big, Mississippi. We're talking like two-hundred people and thousands of dollars. It may kill me, but we're doing it."

I laughed. "We'll try not to let it kill you."

"We're already behind schedule, really. Do you think your best friend could train me? I want to get in shape for the wedding. I've heard she's good, but she so pretty, and I'm afraid to ask her."

This reticence amused me so much that I looked up. The rest of the office had been listening, of course, while Mary chatted enthusiastically. My eyes met Joseph's for a minute, and I saw the humor in his as well.

"I'm sure she would be glad to help you. I'll text her over lunch."

"Congratulations, Mary," Joseph said. Everyone else chimed in, and she turned a lovely shade of pink.

"Thank you!" she said joyfully. "You all have to come!" Turning back to me, she squeezed my hands. Whispering as everyone went about their business, she added, "And we have to make sure *you* bring a date who is well on his way to being your *forever* date by then!"

Since my mom had decreed that I must not set the precedent of "half-dating," as she had regrettably seen many young people do, Luke McCallister was ordered to pick me up at my house. I would have preferred to have driven myself, being an independent force to be reckoned with. But my mom had said, "No. Absolutely not. He doesn't need to get the idea that half measures will be acceptable from him. Make him work for it." Imani agreed.

Grudgingly admitting they had a point, I twitched the blinds back in place as I saw a car coming down the drive past the big house toward my cottage. I had changed out of my fancy work clothes into a pale blue sundress that fit me really well. When the doorbell rang, I picked up my new purse, threw a *be-good* look at my dogs, and swung open the door.

Okay, no one ever said Luke McCallister wasn't handsome. His hair was an indeterminate shade between brown and blonde, but it was really lush and fell nicely on his forehead. His features were pleasant, and his build was good. To be honest, he struck me as not really being my type, although I couldn't have said why.

"Hi!" I said, suddenly very nervous. It just hit me that I was extremely out of practice with the whole dating scene, and I didn't even know how to do this.

"Hey! You look great!" He said it like it was a surprise. Not an auspicious beginning.

By the time we had made it to town, I had decided I didn't like his car. I knew I was nitpicking, however. He had been perfectly nice as we made small talk. We slid into the booth at the Mexican restaurant and were given salsa immediately. Hey, the night was already looking better.

"So you're in HR at the hospital?" I asked.

"Yep, for a couple of years now," he answered, reaching for the chips and salting them. Wouldn't have been my choice, but whatever. I would not, however, be as docile if he continued to devour my chips at such an alarming pace.

I stuck my hand in the basket, staking a claim. He frowned. I laid like seven on my plate.

He aggressively pulled the basket toward him, looking at me like I was a little shocking and a bit of a naughty girl, but not in a sexy way. Okay, then. This was...hmm.

"Your mom said you haven't dated much," he said.

I choked on one of my precious few chips. "I mean, I wouldn't say *that*." It was true, but I wouldn't say it.

"I think that's great. I've heard that you're really sweet."

I lifted my brows. "I...wouldn't say that." Pretty sure *no one* would say that. Spitfire, maybe. Pistol. Hellcat, for the more spiteful, like my fifth grade Sunday school teacher.

"Nah, you're a sweet girl," he said, flashing a smile. "I can tell." Why did it sound like he was talking to a golden retriever? The server, Mateo, brought our drinks, which was the only thing that stopped me from assuming a very un-Southern, argumentative tone.

He asked about my church, which was a better direction. "I go to the Episcopal church. Not originally, but it was where my late employer attended," I said, having adopted a friendlier tone. "He needed a driver, so I started going with him. I'm not going to lie, the smell of mothballs is pretty fierce, and the crowd is almost entirely in the seventy plus category. But I don't know... It's a good fit for me somehow."

He winced. "Not really my variety. I think the best thing about sweet girls, though, is that they are usually willing to change churches. I bet you would," he said with another smile.

"No, I wouldn't," I responded flatly. "Not just like that, I mean."

"Not even if your man was a different denomination?"

I narrowed my eyes. "Why shouldn't he change?"

He sat up taller, plunked his cup down with a thud in my territory, and left his hand on it. Signals of aggression. Pretty easy to spot, like a lion pawing the ground. You knew these things when you had German shepherds, although it wouldn't be fair to compare their behavior to this. Fair to them, I mean.

The food arrived, which saved him from me again, and we tucked in.

"So you like your job?" he asked. Okay, maybe we were steering into safer territory.

"Oh... Well, you know, I like the people, which is ninety percent of happiness at work, I think. I may not be there much longer, though."

He smiled. "Well, it was a great sort of job to tide you over."

"Until what?"

"Marriage."

"Oh, I've never seriously considered marriage," I answered. You may be thinking I should be surprised that he had said this. But people said stuff like that to me all the time. Therefore, I took it in my stride.

He did the cup thing again in my bubble. "But if you did marry..."

Not really any of his business, but just to set the record straight... "I don't see why I would stop working upon marriage. That wouldn't make a lot of sense."

"My mom didn't work. Are you saying that was a bad choice?" he crossed his arms, leaning back in his seat as his eyebrows slammed together.

"Every woman is capable of making her own decision. I'm just saying it wouldn't make a lot of sense for *me*."

"Why not?"

"Because I would lose my marbles not getting out of the house!" I exclaimed. Remembering to be graceful, I added in a calmer tone, "I just don't feel like that's for me."

He laid his palms on the table. Not very sanitary, but who was I to judge? "You're saying that you would let someone else take care of your *children*?"

Okay, we were finished here. I lifted my hand. "Mateo, could we get to-go boxes?"

I had gone to school with him, and he seemed to grasp my desperation. Grinning, he said, "Sure thing, Mississippi. I'll be right back."

"*Thank you*," I said, with far too much emphasis.

"You didn't answer my question."

"About my imaginary children?" I flashed a charming smile.

Mateo came back with the boxes and—God bless him—the checks. Two separate ones, which was all the better, given the circumstances. It would be really nice if I had driven my own car right about now, *Mom*. And *Imani*. I crossed my arms as we waited for our receipts. I continued to hold the pose for pretty much the whole car ride back to the cottage, which had begun unpromisingly with Luke slamming his door loudly.

See, this was why I didn't date. I knew that was a bad attitude to have toward the whole mating ritual, but I just could *not* find a guy willing to accept me on my terms. Or who was even remotely compatible. Or normal.

We got out at the cottage, and to give him credit, he did walk me to my door. "Thanks, Mississippi. I had a good time," he said.

He must have dug deep for that one. Not sure I could have said it. "Thanks, Luke." I was mustering my *it's-a-shame-we'll-never-see-each-other-again* smile.

Before it could form, he said, "So, you want to go out again next week?"

Holy crap. I mean... *What the heck?* "Um, okay, wow..." I tried to channel...something. I must have had *some* ancestor with a mild temperament. I doubted it in this moment somehow. I tucked my bobbed hair behind my ears. I said delicately, "This just goes to show how differently people can perceive the same events, I think. Which is useful to note for my job." Like when that man had driven a spike through his tongue, nailed himself to a table, and tried to blow up the Tasty Freeze. He had probably thought that was a reasonable idea at the time.

Like Luke thought this was a good idea. I, meanwhile, felt a bit as though I needed therapy after exiting a controlling relationship that had lasted an hour and forty-five minutes. "I just think maybe we're...on different paths. But thanks anyway. And be safe driving back into town."

Irritation flashed in his eyes, but he managed a decent response and left soon thereafter.

Thank heaven.

My files looked pristine in the drawer, as did my running catalogue (which sat on the edge of my desk) of things I had taught Hammondsville's new DA. I, like the maiden aunt at heart that I was, enjoyed keeping a neat desk. Now, besides the catalogue, the only file which sat on my workspace was a newly opened case file for a crime committed against the bank.

General Cane-Steinem had asked Mary to set up an appointment with the bank officers to discuss the case and had requested that I accompany him. Until then, with nothing left to do, I was sketching the silhouette I imagined for Mary's wedding dress to show her later.

Joseph came out of his office in a few minutes. He had looked a bit exasperated when he had walked through the door. That wasn't like him. Usually, he was good at catching, deflecting, or circumventing anything thrown at him like a particularly good dodgeball player, all the while with a twinkle in his blue eyes. His eyes, I meant. Not sure at all what color they were.

I hoped nothing was wrong with his family back in New York. Or maybe he had a migraine. But whatever the cause, his temper was a touch thin.

Glancing at his watch as though he had allotted just enough time to get down to the bank, he said, "I think the rain is going to hold off, so we can walk on now if that works for you."

"Yep, no problem!" I answered, trying not to focus on his blue Ralph Lauren suit. That was, the pants. He had taken the coat off, presumably since the day had reached a balmy eighty-seven degrees. The blue tie and crisp white shirt were... very nice.

Okay! I stood, gathering the file, and, waving it, said, "I've been reading it if you'd like a refresher."

"Yeah, that would be great," he answered, straightening his tie as he opened the door for us. "It was twelve-thousand dollars, right?"

"Yep. A smooth debit card fraud move by a daughter against the parents. Anyway, the problem is that the bank is on the hook for it, so they feel like they have to press charges."

"Got it." He glanced at me. He looked as though he might say something, but he didn't.

We walked for a time. When the bank was reached, I said, "I think the president also said—" I broke off, seeing Reynolds Buford coming down the steps. Of all the bad luck... I had timed the appointment with the bank president for noon when Mr. Buford had told us he *always* ate lunch. But there he was in the flesh, coming down the bank's marble steps.

Out of nowhere, I heard something that sounded like a loud blast, thundering with a *boom*. I, after my heart seized, registered the sound as a gun. We froze where we were, confused and astonished, as did everyone else out and about on the sidewalks. Then, clutching his chest, Mr. Buford suddenly slumped to the ground.

There was a moment's stunned silence as comprehension eluded us. "*Shit.*" Joseph said the word slowly and fiercely. He grasped the situation about two seconds before I did.

Coming to myself, I ran. "Mr. Buford!" I screamed.

Joseph got down beside him while I did a quick scan of the perimeter just in case the gunman imagined he hadn't finished Mr. Buford off and decided to try for Round Two. But there was literally no sign of a shooter anywhere. Not that I was trained to know where to look. But the only people I saw were

Fanny Barksdale screaming her head off at the door of her bakery, Mildred Weatherford speaking into her cell phone as she ordered an ambulance with the cool head of a mother of four, and William St. John, Imani's preacher over at the African Methodist Episcopal, who appeared to have been on his way back to his car after leaving the bank when the shot was fired.

I looked back. Joseph was on his knees beside Mr. Buford, from whom blood was pouring like a fountain. He was pressing his hands on the wound in an effort to staunch the flow, and let me tell you, my Sex-Ed classes had been a little too thorough to permit my doing that. Blood was soon all over Joseph's shirt. It soaked his arms and leather watch.

I got down, saying again, "Mr. Buford?" But he was clearly unconscious. He was completely pasty, and maybe dead. But no, he wouldn't be bleeding like that if he were. I stripped off my blazer. "Here, Joseph, use this," I commanded tightly. He took it from me and folded it up to make a pad, which worked a little better.

"What the *hell*?" Joseph whispered under his breath while we waited for the ambulance. "Did you see anything?"

"Nothing," I answered, elevating Mr. Buford's head.

Mr. St. John jogged over. "I just got off the phone with the police. They're on their way, too," he said.

Joseph nodded. The pastor closed his eyes, moving his lips in silent prayer. It wasn't long until we heard a terrible roar of sirens, and two ambulances and four police cars blocked the road. The police chief, seeing Joseph, exclaimed sharply, "Are you hurt, too?"

"No. No."

Joseph and I receded while the paramedics did their work.

"We need to secure the scene," a policeman told us while the others fanned out to comb the area. He looked at Joseph, Mr. St. John, and me, and said, "Meet us back at the police station in an hour. Were there any other witnesses?"

"Fanny and Mildred," Mr. St. John answered for all of us.

The policeman nodded. "I'll go tell them, too."

I drove us toward Cane House so Joseph could shower and change. He sat in my passenger seat on the garbage bag which Mary, after seeing him and yelping, had retrieved from the back cabinet at the office. I glanced over at him as he looked out the window. "You did really well," I said.

"I'm not sure I was supposed to do that. It reminded me of a gang incident I had seen once in Paris, and..." He shrugged. "That was what the guy had done to save him. We'll see."

He fell silent once more. I glanced at him again. "It's not your fault, you know."

He didn't respond.

"You told him what he needed to do, and he refused."

Joseph looked at me. "I didn't believe him," he said, mouth twisted wryly. "I didn't take him seriously. If I had, I would have marched down to the police station with him and demanded he tell them his concerns."

I bit my lip. "I don't think he would have gone," I replied in complete truth.

Nothing more was said. I had some blood on my skirt, so I opted for a shower, too. I tried not to think of all the blood-borne pathogens of which I had learned in such gruesome detail—*thank you for the pictures, Nurse Candace.*

Joseph walked down to the cottage when he was finished. He glanced over me, almost as though to check that I was all right. He didn't say anything, though, just smiled kindly, and we headed back into town. We were there forever. Of course, part of the reason for that was that Joseph would have to play a role in the investigation.

Fanny and Mildred had seen nothing, but William St. John said that he believed the shot had been fired from a window in the empty shirt factory across from the bank. The police confirmed that the angle of the bullet would sustain that theory. Joseph had again carefully detailed all of the threats Mr. Buford had received.

But there was not a single lead, not a single suspect, and not so much as a theory. I had a feeling only Reynolds Buford knew, but he was in critical condition in Vanderbilt Hospital in Nashville.

I sat in my pajamas on my couch that night, staring into the distance. Fritz was curled up beside me, sensing my distress, and Freida was covering the back door on the off chance said distress was caused by a threat to my person.

I jumped when there was a knock at the door, but I was pretty sure I knew what it was. I had almost felt him coming.

Therefore, I collared Freida and opened the door. "Joseph," I said. His name usually felt strange on my tongue, but not tonight, somehow.

He was still in his second work outfit: a white shirt with a loosened blue tie and the trousers of his tan suit. "Hey," he said, meeting my eyes for a long second.

"Do you want to come in?"

He shook his head, staying on the porch. "I came to see how you were doing," he said, looking up the step at me.

"I'm fine," I answered, well aware of how minimal the disorder in my life was compared to the Buford family's right now.

He nodded. He drew a hand through his hair, and I saw, in that betraying action, deep fatigue. "Mr. Buford's brother called me. He wanted to thank us and tell me he'll keep us updated. His condition is too unstable tonight to know."

I swallowed, inclining my head. "I'm afraid if it had been up to me, he would have completely bled out," I admitted, voice cracking. "I froze up, or...something."

He looked at me with compassion in his eyes. "Like I said, I'm still not sure I did the right thing. Neither of us was trained for that sort of thing, you know."

I nodded.

"Now we just have to help the police, and then prosecute whoever did it," he added. "*That* is our job."

I studied his face. "There has to be a reason Reynolds refused to go to the police, Joseph," I said.

He held my eyes. "Do you suspect corruption with the police?" he asked bluntly.

I bit my lip. "People can surprise you, I know. But I wouldn't have thought so. They always seem to take their job so seriously."

"Then it is most likely one thing," he responded. "Reynolds Buford was already on the wrong side of the law. And he was afraid an investigation into why someone wanted to kill him would turn up some damning things about him."

Friday had never met with such acclaim as it received from our District Attorney's office that week. Not that we had an easy day precisely. But no one cried, which was a plus, and we ordered in lunch (a welcome relief from Imani's perfectly healthy meal-prepping) and locked the doors.

When Saturday dawned, I slept in and resolved to do some gardening and outdoor work. I had all of the supplies but just hadn't gotten to it yet this year. I thought it might help me relax and unwind from a really horrible week.

I packed soil over a new plant in my flower bed. Sweat was running down my neck and in other, less presentable places. But it felt good to be here, not worrying about anything. I had swept my porch clean, knocked down the spiderwebs from the white boards of the cottage, and rearranged the pillows on the porch swing. I had a rocking chair near the door that I had found in Henry's shed a couple of years back. It had been flaking, but I had saved it, painting it a snazzy teal blue. I had cleaned it this morning and watered my ferns. The sun kissing my skin was pleasurable, although I would have to be careful; there was only so much I could take.

I heard the door of the big house shut and turned from my hydrangeas. The house's owner looked over and saw me, lifting a hand. He called, "Hey!"

I lifted my hand, shading my eyes as I replied, "Hey," sincerely trusting that he would not come any nearer. Let's be honest here: I did not want him to see me like this.

"I'm going into town for some groceries. Do the dogs need anything?" I could see his smile, so I figured he must be coping pretty well with everything.

I tilted my head, thinking. "Actually, they could use a bag of food," Mentally apportioning what we had, I realized we could only get to Tuesday.

"Got it. See you later."

He left, and I got back to the soil, calculating how long I had to make myself presentable before he returned. I hadn't spent an entire two weeks looking stellar only to have anybody's image destroyed. I wrapped things up in about thirty minutes and went in for a quick shower. I put on fresh clothes and decided to tidy up the kitchen. My hair hung in wet, loose clumps that cooled me down as I washed my dishes from last night.

I heard his car about fifteen minutes after that, and shortly answered the knock on my door.

Joseph held the same expensive, healthy variety of dog food he had bought the time before. Fritz and Freida had no idea how fancy they had become, but they did love the food. "Thanks," I said. "You can just put it down in the laundry room, if you don't mind." No need in lugging it when there was a perfectly healthy male around for once.

Once he had set it down, his eyes seemed to roam my face before he looked away. "I had better get out before Freida catches my scent." He smiled, eyes crinkling.

"That is not unwise," I admitted.

"Where are they? Do they need anything?"

"They're playing in the yard. I don't really think they need anything, except I wish I could spend more time with them and give them more exercise. They're still young and have *so* much energy."

He considered for a second. "We could take them to the state park on Memorial Day next week. I mean, obviously they would have to be leashed, and obviously you would have to be the one to hold them." He smiled again. "But I would be there for moral support."

My heart did this weird sort of quickening thing. Almost like it wished he had asked as a date instead of a co-parenting thing. Weird. "Um, yeah, that would be great, actually," I said, cognizant that I had flushed to the roots of my hair and hoping he could *not* detect it.

We agreed to make plans later, and he left after we wrapped up the conversation.

Jepp Lewis came into the office the Monday after the shooting. If you are inexperienced in working with the public, you might think it was unusual for repeat visitors to bombard the office with run-of-the-mill annoyances after a crisis. But, of course, your inexperience would excuse that belief.

As soon as he saw the slightest crack in Joseph's door, Jepp barreled through, all friendliness and good humor. "Well, howya doin'? Never mind; saw you on the front page of the newspaper this morning with blood splattered all over you. Terrible thing. He's a piece of shit, but still a bad thing. Mississippi, how are you?" he enquired, formally inclining his head.

"Jepp, I'm fine, but we don't have long," I answered from my chair. "We're fielding calls from the press. What's going on? Mr. Howell again?"

He settled into the chair across from Mr. Cane-Steinem's desk. "It's not about the encroachment. Well, I suppose it is, but of another variety. You see, the cows got out."

"Your cows or his cows?" Joseph asked.

"*His.* They got out and trampled all of my wife's tulips. It was like a massacre. Merla's going to have a come apart, I tell you, if this happens again." He paused only for the breadth of a moment. "You know Tommy Bonner? Keeps a zebra."

Eyes wide with a mixture of awe and delight, our district attorney shook his head in wonder.

"He told me that the neighbor's dog was getting out, harassing his horses and the zebra, and he got a prosecution. I just thought: can't we prosecute Dan Howell's cows in the same way?"

"Did he fix the fence?" I asked irascibly.

"Well, yes."

"Then what's the problem?" I demanded, exasperated.

"Well, I'm just wondering if we can nail him on this."

There were, technically, criminal laws on roving animals. I was reluctant to tell him this, however.

"If it was accidental and the problem has been fixed, I would be hesitant to prosecute," Joseph said, God bless him.

Unheeding, Jepp continued, "I'm just thinking that we could use it to show he's encroaching *all* over the place. We'll just use one law to get him for something else, so to speak." He then waxed eloquent on this theme. Disgusted, I slipped out halfway through the soliloquy, leaving the door cracked, and sat down at my desk. I thought I might get back to work on our press release, but I couldn't quit hearing the man's voice, dadgum him.

When Mr. Lewis came to the end of himself, I heard Joseph say calmly, "Here's the thing, Jepp. It's illegal."

"Aw, shoot," Jepp countered in disgust. I could picture his face of exasperated confusion.

There was some back-and-forth, which Joseph won with firmness. There was a brief hush. Then I heard Jepp slap the desk, undaunted. "Well. There's more than one way to skin a cat," he said in excitement, apparently forming an idea.

Silence reigned from the other side of the desk. Then I heard Joseph ask a bit faintly, "Is there?" Shoot. That was a phrase I had left out of his lexicon.

"Sure is! All right, Cane-Steinem, I'll be seeing you around. I've got a new idea. Stay away from bloodbaths if you can!"

Jepp strode out through the foyer, an unabashed, undaunted grin on his face. The door had barely closed when Joseph emerged from his office, eyes brimful with humor, and sought out my gaze. I met his eyes, and, unable to contain the bubble within me any longer, I erupted into laughter at the same time he did. This startled the whole office to the extent that everyone stared at us, but I could scarcely catch a breath, let alone explain. "He...He didn't mean it—about the cat," I promised, wiping my streaming eyes.

Gasping for air, he replied, "I figured that out. It's—the zebra!"

"I know!" And we were set off again, struggling to breathe around the convulsive laughter—the kind that would make us feel sore tomorrow, but it felt so good.

Chapter Thirteen

The county-wide Memorial Day ceremony was always held at my church on the Saturday before the holiday. There was some haggling at a town council meeting I had been unfortunate enough to attend. The subject was whether it was respectful to host what might be construed as a celebration while Reynolds Buford lay unconscious in critical condition. Phil Tuck (he of the inauspicious pot and cigarette combination) had demanded to know whether it was respectful to forget that four-thousand Tennesseans had died in World War Two. And so the show had gone on.

Phil Tuck, while from Pickensville, had been the president of the two counties' Democratic Party, which hosted the event, for about a hundred years. The Republican Party also attended, and both parties set up outside the meeting place with booths and pamphlets. This was strictly in violation of the minister's terms of hosting at the church, but they did it every year. The Republican Party's entourage also brought with them a roving mural, which flanked one entire side of the parking lot.

Joseph blinked. "That's the biggest depiction of Ronald Reagan I've ever seen."

"It won't be for long," I assured him, reaching for my purse.

"Oh, gosh. Mr. Tuck and Mr. Gerald are arguing at the door," Mary said, biting her nails.

"I wish I'd stayed home," Melissa responded gloomily. As did we all. Paul had done so, preferring an afternoon spent with his classical music and cats to a politically charged memorial to the fallen at a place of worship. I, however, had seen the bigger picture. Joseph was going to be an elected official, and it was important for him to attend such events. And when I had reminded Mary and Melissa that their jobs depended on Joseph keeping his, they had high-tailed it to the car. Nothing like a bit of motivation.

We walked toward the ancient double doors. In my final words of advice to my protégé before entering, I said, "I want you to preserve neutrality. Things are too charged for you to be taking political sides."

"Why are things charged?" Simba asked.

Poor, innocent kid. "They always are," I explained. "There doesn't need to be a reason for it." Having nothing else to add on that score, I continued, "You will need to speak both with Mr. Tuck and Mr. Gerald, who are the opposing party presidents. Compliment Mr. Tuck on the event and Mr. Gerald on the music. Since he attends church here and is our music leader, Phil always deigns to let Frank Gerald choose the arrangements." I considered other need-to-know tidbits. "Frank Gerald is originally from New York. You might talk about that. Okay, now go in. Sit near the middle."

Eyes laughing, Joseph crossed into the vestibule. I was tickled that he was amused, I thought, rolling my eyes and wondering how far he could survive if he were on his own.

"Does anyone else smell mothballs?" Melissa asked darkly as we crossed the threshold. Mary wrinkled her nose, nodding in misery.

Joseph, however, was just fine. He glad-handed his way to success, schmoozing with the talent of a born politician. Babies adored him, old ladies were all aflutter, and people flocked to him worshipfully, fawning over him like he was all of the Beatles and this was 1964. Barf. I rolled my eyes, leaving him to his own devices, since he was so obviously competent.

He joined us ten minutes later, slipping in beside me and closing the door on the old pew. He was smiling—grinning, really—as he looked at me. I gave him the same look I gave Fritz when he drank his own bathwater. He appeared quite pleased to have annoyed me and entirely unabashed.

The national anthem began playing, and we all stood, covering our hearts. Then came the veterans' march, and they entered and took their seats. Mr. Tuck took the podium following this. After a speech complete with a plug for his party and an awkward few curse words dropped in, Phil read the roster of the fallen troops from the two counties from all of the wars (provided by the local historical society). Then the high school choir performed, followed by various musicians from all over town.

Mr. Tuck had been sitting serenely, apparently pleased with his choice magnanimously to allow his nemesis to choose the arrangements.

Until "Battle Hymn of the Republic" began playing.

I saw Phil breathe in through his nostrils deeply. His eyes shot around the church insanely.

"Oh, no," I whispered.

Joseph looked at me quickly. "What is it?" he whispered.

"It's about to get ugly," I replied, not removing my eyes from the scene.

He returned his attention to the front pew just as Phil Tuck shot to his feet and yelled, "Frank Gerald, you damned Yankee!" The organ came to a screeching halt.

Mr. Gerald, standing in the corner near the flag, maintained a stoical demeaner, sniffing dismissively. But the gauntlet had been thrown. "You are cruisin' for a bruisin', Mister!" Phil screamed, walking with alarming rapidity across the church. "Playing the same damn song Sherman played when he marched through here and tore up everything in sight! A *Yankee battle hymn*!"

Taking a long-suffering breath, Mr. Gerald turned and simply walked out the door. We heard Phil say, "That's the last time I'll let you choose any damned song for this sacred service!"

Apparently, this sally was too much. Frank Gerald turned around and yelled across the space, "Your son is a Republican! He has been for years!"

Mr. Tuck drew in a gasping breath, choked, and looked around wildly. This occurred just before he exited the church and slammed the door, presumably off to give chase.

There was a moment of silence. Taking a weary breath, Melissa said, shaking her head and crossing herself, "Thank God for Mississippi." Then everyone began to stir.

"What's happening now?" Joseph asked, eyes wide.

"That's the end," I said. "Everybody's going home."

"Going home?" He scanned the crowd with something like delight. No one was shaken. Everyone had simply taken the violent language as a cue that the service was over. Looking back at me, he asked, "Where is Mr. Gerald by now, do you think?"

"Probably in the next county."

Joseph bit his lip as his blue eyes danced. "But what happens to Ronald Reagan?"

Ronald Reagan was salvaged (although the pride of community could not be), and we headed up to the state park on Memorial Day. Joseph had removed the soft top windows from the Jeep, and, although the SUV was new, he didn't seem to mind Fritz and Freida's invasion of it.

Seeing the vehicle that had been provided for him was the last piece to tip Fritz over the edge from reserve to friendliness toward his new owner. He loved to ride in cars, and as soon as he had bounded into the Jeep, he licked Joseph's ear with a hearty slurp.

Obviously, this exuberance annoyed Frieda, who eyed her fellow canine as though he were a traitor. She had to be muzzled for the ride, which annoyed her further, but I couldn't risk her attempting to attack a certain occupant of the vehicle, who shall remain nameless.

"Do you think she's warming up to me?" Joseph asked as we got started down the highway.

"The important thing to remember is that once German shepherds accept you, they won't go back."

"So that's a no," he said.

I adjusted my ballcap. "Oh, look! A family of deer!"

By the time we had sufficiently admired the deer in a passing field, he was ready to change the subject, which was fortunate. It took about thirty minutes to reach the state park, and we parked in the shade of tall trees that were more than a hundred years old. I opened the back door, and our children came barreling out. I had made Joseph stand a few feet away in anticipation of unmuzzling Freida, but Fritz dashed toward him.

My heart jumping in my throat, I yelled, "Fritz!" He was usually a fun-loving guy, but helpless against the call of his inner beast, he could occasionally get over-protective and riled.

I was making a move to dash toward them when I realized Fritz only intended to hug Joseph, which he *was* doing, apparently deaf to my directives. I paused, meeting Joseph's eyes as Fritz danced happily around him. It appeared we were having a break-through here.

"You know," I said carefully, "I think he might allow you to hold his leash."

Moving cautiously, Joseph picked it up off the ground. Fritz looked at him enthusiastically, panting, and seemed to say, *I'm game, man! Let's do this!*

Joseph met my eyes again. "Wow."

"He wanted to ride in your Jeep. Who would have thought?" I turned, rubbing Frieda's head. "You ready to go, baby girl? Let's go!"

Frieda, however, was snubbing me. Given her mood, I kept her on a short leash. "I think the dog-friendly path starts here," I said, pointing.

We began. Thanks to Imani's training, I wasn't in too much trouble until we had gone a mile and started climbing a steep incline. My need to pull to the side of the path and take a break seemed to amuse the Crown Prince, who did not appear to be winded at all.

"We could go ahead and have lunch," he suggested.

"No. We need—to make it—to the falls."

"Sure. If you think you *can* make it..." he quipped, eyes twinkling.

Frieda growled at her father, calling him to order and prompting us to continue our walk. When we fell behind, I gave her a stern talking-to, which she, from all appearances, ignored completely. We heard the waterfall about five minutes before we came upon it. It tumbled out of a cliff onto massive rocks with a loud splatter. The birds around it seemed to sing louder, as if to be overheard.

"Have you ever been?" I asked, hands on my hips as I caught my breath.

He nodded. "Once. My grandparents brought me. It is beautiful."

"It really is," I agreed.

We proceeded to a cliff with a tree nearby, where we tied the dogs and gave them water. I spread out our blanket while Joseph brought out the chicken sandwiches I had made. There was, of course, also potato salad, baked beans, and coleslaw, as well as sweet tea in mason jars. I was only my mother's daughter, and there was no getting around that.

"This looks great," Joseph asked as we got started.

I hoped the chicken was prepared the right way. It came right off a farm in Hammondsville, and they were renowned for their responsible practices. I shrugged. "It wasn't too much trouble."

He studied me for a minute. "Well, it's delicious. Thanks. I'll cook next time."

Interesting choice of words. "Cool," I said. Gosh, I hated myself sometimes. Was I attracted to him? My mind skittered over this query. "Well, the day has certainly been effective for the dogs. Or one of them, at least." That's right. This was all about the dogs. *Then why are you wearing your sleek leggings, expensive T-shirt, and running shoes that make your butt and legs look good, young lady?* I did not dignify this question with a response.

"Do they like the guy you're dating?" he asked, chewing on his chicken. He was staring at me with all the intentness of a cat zoned in on a bug.

"I'm...not dating."

His brows lifted slightly. "Oh!" he said slowly, looking surprised and a bit apologetic. "I...saw a guy pick you up. Maybe he was your cousin. I happened to be outside."

I slapped my forehead. "Luke! Bless him, no. He didn't get to meet the dogs. And he won't."

He continued to look at me. "He won't?"

I winced. "He tried to put me in a 'sweet' box before we had been eating for five minutes."

Mary hadn't understood what I meant when I had told her why things hadn't worked out. Comprehension dawned immediately on Joseph's face, however, and he grimaced. "Gross."

My heart lifted. Validation.

"I just thought that it would be embarrassing if they took easily to some other guy," he said.

Were we playing it a wee bit cool? I was neurotic, so it was hard to tell. He certainly seemed quite intent on his baked beans, so maybe he hadn't been fishing. Well, anyway, what was good for the goose was good for the gander. Since he now knew something as personal as the fact that my dating life was negligible, I said, "Can I ask you something?"

"Sure," he answered, apparently unconcerned.

"Why do you work? And why Hammondsville?"

He met my eyes. He hesitated for a long moment before saying, "My grandpa wanted me to follow in his footsteps. I don't know if you knew that."

I shook my head.

He finally added, "If I had envisioned coming here, it was probably caring for my grandpa, not with him gone." He stared into the distance, seeming to regret that. He continued, "When my mom and I lived in France, we didn't have any family there." Then he lifted a shoulder, growing more serious. "I don't know. When I would come here, there was family. Stability."

I swallowed.

His eyes slowly began to twinkle again. "You're unconvinced."

My face heated. "I am not!"

"You've been wary of me from the beginning," he countered mildly.

I sighed. "It's just... People in the South are skeptical when someone moves in from another place. It's one of the reasons I knew you needed me to guide you. It takes commitment to live here. There's a lot of poverty, and inconvenience, it's humid, and...in some advancements we're twenty years behind the times. It's not an easy life. I just wasn't sure you fully understood what you were signing up for. So yes, there's a certain skepticism that someone will be willing to take the bad with the good. You have to earn trust by living here years and years." I paused. "And Paul and Melissa and Mary depend on you. They like you. I wouldn't want them to be hurt."

There was a beat of silence. He regarded me. "I understand. And I don't intend to hurt Paul and Melissa and Mary," he added softly.

His eyes held mine, and I felt myself flush. I smoothed my little ponytail, breaking eye contact. "Well, I won't be there ultimately, anyway. I'm just looking out for my friends."

He didn't answer, but I felt his eyes still on me. We let a slightly awkward silence grow. Finally, he said, "Look, could I say with absolute certainty where I'll be ten years from now? No. Of course not. But I'm not playing, Mississippi. No, I don't have to work, and yes, this life is very different from anything

I've ever known. But I take the job seriously. I take my place in the community seriously."

I had to admit, I heard his sincerity. And his honesty. Something shifted in me, something that decided to let him in, just a little bit. I nodded, giving him a smile of agreement, which he returned. "I'm sorry I may not always have been hospitable," I said.

"You've been very hospitable. I've met your grandmother, you've saved me from being bitten multiple times, and your family knows where mine was during World War Two. I'd say that's pretty close."

I choked on my sweet tea.

His grin was electric. He looked mischievous when he did that, his blue eyes full of light and life, and I could definitely see why Hetty Gibson was hot to trot. He waited only a beat before he said, "Now, my turn. Can I ask *you* a personal question?"

"Sure!" I said, mimicking his nonchalant response.

He smiled. "I want to know about this mysterious one year at The University of the South."

My smile fell slowly. "There's nothing mysterious about that. My dad had a stroke."

He gave me a sympathetic look, pressing his lips together.

"My mom needed help. They couldn't pay for the care he needed, so I moved back in. He was incapacitated for two years before he passed. By then, my scholarships had dried up, and it just didn't seem feasible anymore. I got the job with your grandpa, and the rest is history." I said it in a conversational way. But twenty was far too young for a girl to lose her dad, and there was no sugar-coating that. There wasn't any way to put a nice bow on the way my mom and I had struggled during those years either.

"I'm sorry," he said simply, but genuinely.

I lifted a shoulder. "I am where I am for a reason." But I missed my dad like crazy. And I knew that the man across from me knew that as our eyes held. Of course he did.

"And you want to go back?" he asked. "Is that why you want to go to a beach town to make money?"

I nodded. "Maybe mostly online or something. But yes."

He looked out at the waterfall for a long several seconds. When he looked back at me, he said, "If you want to move, that's fine. But I think you know you've been invaluable. I'm not sure what I would have done, or what I *will* do without your guidance. I don't feel like I fully have my feet under me yet. How much of a raise would I have to give you to make it worth it to stay until Christmas?"

"Six percent," I answered, without hesitation.

He watched me, grinning with amusement. "That was quick."

"Hey, when you grow up like I did, you learn to be scrappy."

He smiled. "I like that." He leaned off his hand, extending it to me. "We have a deal?"

I nodded, taking his hand and giving it a single shake. "We have a deal."

It was in late-afternoon duskiness and tiredness that we headed back toward Hammondsville. The dogs, having had the time of their life, were worn out and quiet in the back. I rested my head against the door, a slight smile on my lips, the happy tiredness brought on by a day in nature flowing through me. Joseph had turned on some music, and we were riding in companionable silence.

Then my phone rang, shattering the peace, and I answered. It was Imani. "Mississippi?" she said. I could tell from this one word that she was upset. I sat up.

"Imani, what is it?"

She swallowed thickly, and I could hear her crying softly. "Mitchell's dad had a heart attack." She paused, and I bit my lip. "I'm sorry, I know it's just bringing it all up with your dad."

"No, no. Go ahead."

"It was so sudden, just like the stroke. He'd had no symptoms. He's in the hospital. They took him to Chattanooga for a specialist. I think he's going into surgery now. Mississippi, my mama and daddy are on their anniversary trip in the Keys. They're on their way home. Do you care to come and spend the night with the kids until they can get here?"

"Of course. Don't worry about that. It'll be just a little while. We've been up at the falls with the dogs."

There was a pause. "You and Joseph?"

"Yeah."

A heavy silence, which I knew I wouldn't escape later. "Mississippi, you might want to bring him with you if he can come," she said, in what sounded like a huge concession on her part. Almost as if she was accepting his presence in my life. But he didn't have one outside of work, so that was confusing.

"Two boys and two dogs... It's a lot. Even for me when I have to do it alone, and I'm familiar with the routines."

I took a breath. "Yeah, we'll...work something out. Don't worry, I'll be there soon."

I hung up and then explained to Joseph.

"Do I need to take you home to get clothes?" he asked.

I shook my head. "I'll wear something of Imani's."

"What can I do? How can I help?" he asked, looking at me like he really cared.

"I..." I did love those babies and those Corgis, but they were like live wires, all four of them, and I was feeling a little overwhelmed. What if I wasn't watching and one of them got hurt? "Do you care to help me? Just until I can get them down for the night?"

"Would the Reeds want me to?"

"Imani suggested it."

He smiled encouragingly. "It's settled, then."

I directed him to their subdivision, and we turned in. Mitchell was loading bags into their SUV with tears streaming down his face, and my heart ached for him. I hustled Fritz and Frieda into the fenced-in backyard, and Joseph and I went in together.

We saw the Reeds off, having introduced the boys to Joseph and explained what was happening. By then, the Corgis had picked up on the nervous energy in the house and were zooming all over the place uttering excitable yips.

"What are their names?" Joseph asked, surveying this maelstrom with wonderment. Nonetheless, it appeared he was game to withstand it.

"DeShawn and Marcus. I told you," I said.

"No, the dogs," he called above their barking.

"Oh! William and Harry."

"That...should be easy to remember," he responded.

I held up my hand. "We are Anglophiles. We do not need your judgment."

He shook his head, smiling. I made a dash for William, and he caught Harry up in his arms. "You know," he said, "they basically look like German shepherds with short legs."

This made me giggle, which was completely inappropriate given the circumstances. Luckily, the kids were too young to know that. Once we had contained the Corgis, I scooped up Marcus, who, being only two, showed signs of growing upset. I kissed him and swayed with him. He gave a couple of cries, and I soothed him.

I looked over and Joseph was watching us. "Why don't you guys go read a book?" he suggested gently. "I'll start supper."

I nodded, reaching for DeShawn's hand. We went back to Marcus's room, which was a beautiful child's room with a bookshelf full of options. I let DeShawn pick, and we settled on the soft rug in the floor, Marcus in my lap and DeShawn tucked under my arm. It was hard to turn the pages in such a pose, but I imagined Imani's arms must feel so full. My eyes filled, and my throat burned.

By the time we had read three books, I could smell the heavenly scent of onions and peppers cooking. "Do you think Joseph is making spaghetti for us, or tacos?" I asked.

"Or maybe couscous topped with veggies," Imani's eldest child suggested. She was creating healthy monsters. We would have to have a conversation about this. I sincerely trusted we would not be dining on DeShawn's selection and continued with the story.

When we emerged about thirty minutes later into the kitchen, it was to find our district attorney with a look of true pleasure in his eyes. "She has *everything*," he said. "I'm going to have to ask her where she gets her groceries."

"I think she orders them," I said bleakly.

But it turned out that he had made us a delicious Ashkenazi soup. "This is yum," Marcus said in all seriousness, as we all four sat at Imani's elegant bar.

"My grandmother taught me how to make it," Joseph said in a kind tone. He didn't offer any more information. But let's just say the woman must be a fabulous cook.

It took us all of fifteen minutes to scarf it down. I reached for our bowls, but Joseph stopped me.

"Go ahead. It's getting close to bedtime, isn't it? I'll take care of it and feed the dogs, too."

Nodding in agreement, I took the boy's hands and led them back toward the bathroom, where I intended to dunk them both in the tub in an efficient two-for-one. I called over my shoulder, "Be careful around Frieda!"

"I will," he called back.

Thirty minutes later, both boys were tucked in their beds, asleep after an emotionally exhausting day. Leaving their nightlights on and their doors cracked, I tiptoed down the hall into the library, where Joseph was looking at a picture on the wall. This particular one was of several Black women sharecropping in the 1930s.

"Imani collects early twentieth century African American photography," I said, going to look at the same one for a moment.

I walked down a ways and indicated one of a lady in a homemade dress, thin and barefoot, not smiling. "This is Imani's great-grandmother," I said softly.

He moved to look at the picture. "I see her in Imani," he said after a minute.

I nodded. The bone structure. Beautiful.

"The local historical society was able to track it down for her."

"Was this on my family's plantation?" he asked, looking at me seriously.

"Where you live now? No."

"No, I mean the one that burned."

"Probably," I answered, tilting my head. "There were only so many farms that size in Drake County." And the historical society had thought it likely. And Imani had a family story that said it was.

He shook his head. "Life is strange."

"It is, indeed," I agreed solemnly.

He looked some more, and I could feel the heaviness in him. I slipped out to give him the silence and went into the living room, where I picked up one of Imani's magazines. *Eating Well.* Sigh.

Tossing it aside, I instead picked up the book one of the Reeds had been reading and settled in. *Persuasion.* Couldn't think of anything better, unless it was by a Brontë. I heard Joseph's voice as he took a phone call. He spoke softly for the boys' sake, so I couldn't make anything of it. Returning to my reading, I soon found myself engrossed and didn't look up until I heard footsteps in the hall.

I leaned up, looking at Joseph as he entered the room. He was a little pale, I thought, though the light was dim. He studied me for a moment as if hesitating, and I got the feeling he was about to deliver bad news.

"What is it?" I asked, heart thudding.

He swallowed, holding my eyes. "Reynolds Buford is dead."

Chapter Fourteen

Some of the most beautiful historic homes in the South are funeral homes. Undertakers are among the few able to afford the repair and upkeep. Which, I guess, is a win for the town, even if a dark one.

As Joseph drove us into the parking lot beside the perfectly manicured lawn, my spirits were low. Reynolds Buford's death had wiped me out. He had a brother. A niece. A sister-in-law. And even though he hadn't remembered my presence in the youth leadership program, he had cared enough for teens that he had headed it.

It had taken me a while to wrap my head around the news after hearing it. Imani's father-in-law was on the mend and was going to be okay after a period of recovery. I had handed the kids over to her parents the next morning and gone into work a little late.

And here we were two days later. But I couldn't shake the feeling haunting me. Murder... There was something different about it. Something I had never experienced.

I had enough presence of mind about me to prep Joseph for Southern funerals. He was appropriately attired in a dark blue suit, while I wore a black dress. I had told him that he needed to stand on the porch and talk to the people sitting in the rocking chairs for about ten minutes, mostly about the deceased, how bad it was, and how much he hated it for the family.

I had also told him that he needed to prepare to stand in the queue for as long as it took to get up to the casket. And just look at the body, for heaven's sake, even though you don't want to, and maybe drop a remark about how peaceful the dead person looked. "Just like he's sleeping," he intoned, obviously remembering a thing or two from his grandfather's funeral, when we finally made it up to the casket after two hours.

Mr. Buford's sister-in-law looked as though this resonated, saying, "That's exactly what I told Jeff."

Sometimes my protégé performed his role all too well. I refrained from rolling my eyes, however.

Jeff Buford looked earnestly at us. "Mr. Cane-Steinem, Miss Whitson...our family can't thank you enough for what you did for Reynolds that day."

He looked at us both equally, and I was touched.

"The doctors said he would have died on the scene if not for what you did," Jeff added softly.

Joseph looked a bit wry. "He might have preferred that," he said softly.

The man shook his head. "No, Reynolds wanted to live. He would have wanted us to have done everything we could. And we did."

A solemn moment passed.

"Are they any closer?" he asked, searching Joseph's eyes with the hunger of a grieving man wanting answers.

He shook his head, looking like he wished he could say differently. "The police are working tirelessly."

After the man nodded with acceptance, we moved on, stopping to talk to various people, and I slipped off to the kitchen to see if I could help the ladies. The room was pretty much covered with food, wall to wall, and let me tell you, nothing smelled better than funeral food. If the kitchen just happened to be right beside another room with a sign on the door which read *Warning: Deadly Chemicals in Use*, it was best not to think of that. I helped the church ladies slice up some sandwiches, gave the crocks a stir, and moseyed back into the parlor, taking note of the house's historic touches as I went.

I was talking to a couple of girls I knew from high school when Joseph came up to me.

"Mississippi..." he whispered.

I looked over my shoulder, raising my eyebrows. "A funeral home employee keeps asking me for my keys. What do I...?" He appeared utterly confounded.

I suppressed laughter, although I probably couldn't keep it from my eyes. "For the motorcade," I explained. "Don't you remember that Southerners *must* make a stately exit? Give the man your keys. It's fine."

"I forgot this part," he mumbled, heading off to do as I said.

Soon, we were discreetly ushered into the chapel. Here we endured the most depressing music known to man for the next thirty minutes. This was followed by a sermon on hellfire and damnation, both for the person who had taken Mr. Buford's life and for ourselves if we did not have our lives in order before we dropped dead, which could happen at any moment.

As uplifting as this was, the best was yet to come: a ten-minute display by Reynold's ex-wife, who threw herself on the closed coffin and screamed for God to take her too. As this seemed to tick his sister-in-law off, and it appeared we were moving toward a catfight, it was a blessing when the funeral director cut short this exuberant display of grief and motioned the pallbearers forward.

We mourners then proceeded to our vehicles. Joseph took a deep breath and released it when we closed our doors, pinching the bridge of his nose.

I smirked. "It's a lot, isn't it?"

"So much," he said. He looked up. Despite everything, the joy was heavily present in the hidden glimmers of his eyes. I bit my lip, trying not to smile in return. Nothing could take away the heaviness of attending the funeral of a murdered man. But there was absurdity in simply everything in life, if one knew where to look for it. And he did.

"I'm sure it was a lot for you to take in at your grandpa's funeral."

He started the car as the police began leading the motorcade. "I felt in equal parts supported and exhausted."

"The definition of being a Southerner," I confirmed.

He smiled, following the vehicle in front of us to the cemetery. "I didn't know about the ex-wife, though. Think there's anything there?"

"Tilda? Oh, no, that was over ages ago. That's why Patsy looked like she was about to jump her," I answered. Oncoming traffic properly pulled their cars over as they met our funeral possession on the road.

The cemetery rose before us with the tent constructed over the gravesite visible in the distance. Already those first in the procession were climbing the hill toward the site. We had made an agreement to hang back at the burial, so we stood on the grass at the back of the circle.

Virgil Baker, the lawyer who had handled Henry's estate, joined us, and he was a relief. No crazy antics, just soft tones and sensible conversation.

"Do you remember how long Reynolds and Tilda have been divorced?" I asked, *sotto voce.*

"Oh, fifteen years at least," he answered. Mr. Baker looked elegant in his gray suit, his hands clasped behind his back, his silver hair perfectly brushed. "I had forgotten how...difficult that divorce was until today." He paused for a moment while the pallbearers carried the casket to the site. "I represented him. One of the worst divorces I've ever seen." His eyes scanned the distance while the preacher began the second sermon.

But Joseph's eyes met mine significantly.

"It's all over town that you're dating Joseph Cane-Steinem."

This was the first sentence my mother uttered as our phone call began. I held my phone out from my face, looking at it. "Have you called the right person?" I questioned in a certain *tone*.

"It's true, Mississippi, people are talking! You don't *attend a funeral* with a man and *ride in his vehicle* in the procession without giving people a certain idea!"

I rubbed my forehead. "I must have missed that lesson in dating etiquette."

"And of course, it's not *known* that you're dating, so that means it's being kept secret, which can only mean one thing. Do you know what that one thing is, Mississippi Marie Whitson?"

I groaned inwardly. "Yes, I do."

"It means you are having sex," she plowed ahead. "You may not care what people say—"

"I do care."

"They may believe in free love up at that Episcopal church where you go—"

"They don't."

"—but, I'm going to ask you one time and one time only, young lady: are you having sex with that boy?"

"Mom. Stop. No."

She drew a deep breath. "Well, I didn't think so. And I'll tell you this: I'm going to tan Pearl Fitts's hide one of these days for her gossiping. Yes, and Lena Caldwell, too," she added cryptically. She paused for several seconds. More hesitantly, she asked, "Well, are you dating him, honey?"

"No, Mama. We went to the funeral together. That's it. Gosh. Kill me."

"I'm just saying, I don't have a problem with him being Jewish."

"Thank you. Entirely unnecessary information."

"Just saying that he would give me pretty grandchildren. Your eyes are rather nondescript, but *his*, with that blue..."

"Mom. I'm going to hang up."

"No, but Mississippi," she said, entirely ignoring me, "I'll deal with this rumor, but there *is* something I've been meaning to speak with you about."

Oh, no. Round two. "Oh?" I asked, less than enthusiastically.

There was a pause. "Honey, you know I think you're the smartest, most beautiful, worthiest girl around, right?"

"Naturally." Nondescript eyes aside.

I could almost hear my mom ruminating. "Well, all of this talk just got me thinking. Honey, you *don't* have a crush on him, do you? Grandma and I talked about it, and she said she wasn't sure you didn't."

"Mom, we work together. We take care of the dogs. That's it. He's not even my type." How many times did I have to say this?

I heard her almost sigh in relief. "Good. Because for all of the pretty babies he could make... The Canes and the Whitsons...they're cut from different cloths. Not to put too fine a point on it, they've always been rich, and we've always been... you know, just good country folk. You know there's not a lot of intermarrying between the haves and the have nots around here. I know we live in a modern world, but you still don't see it a lot. I'm just saying this to give you a word of caution: I don't think he would ever seriously entertain marrying you, honey. I think all the time about Ted Williams. You know, he liked me in high school. He liked me a lot. We even dated a while. But at the end of the day, I wasn't good enough."

"You were good enough for Daddy," I said, throat burning. I was unsure why I was defensive.

"That's what I'm saying, honey. The Whitsons and the Smiths...we were from the same kind of families. And it worked wonderfully. But anyway, all of that's just to say that I'm happy you feel the way you do. I'm not saying nothing *could* come of it, just that I'd be surprised if something did."

With my mother's brutal, yet true, statements in my mind, when Joseph Cane-Steinem knocked on my door on Saturday, I opened the door with a smile and sexless friendliness.

"Hey, just in time for lunch," I said.

He lifted his brows. "I only came to bring this. I found it in the Jeep," he said, handing me a clump of things that had fallen out of my purse, apparently. Okay, maybe my mom did have a point. Even better, among the items was a sanitary pad. Could he not have spared me and thrown it away?

"That is so kind," I said grimly.

There was a smile perhaps playing about his lips, but he didn't address it. He merely said, "And maybe I could walk Fritz? I don't want him to forget we're friends."

"Sure," I said, going to get the pooch, who, upon being told of his impending excursion, became so excitable it was all I could do to contain him.

"You boys be careful, now," I said, not entirely sure we weren't rushing matters.

By the time they made it back, I had two plates of cucumber sandwiches and kettle-cooked chips on the ottoman in front of the sofa. Sweet teas completed the meal. "Thanks," Joseph said. "Although I did promise to cook next time."

"Sandwiches aren't cooking," I answered, flapping my hand. "Plus, you made the soup and helped with small boys and Corgis, so we're even."

We sat down and ate, chatting all the time with never a loss for conversation. When he had finished, he caught sight of my *Vogue* magazines beneath the dinner tray. He looked up at me, appearing anticipatory. "You're into fashion."

"Can't you tell?" I asked, lifting my brows in mock-hauteur.

He laughed. "Of course. I mean—really into it?"

I flushed slightly. I felt a bit like an imposter compared to how "into fashion" his mom had been. "I used to want to be a designer," I admitted.

"Really?" he said, looking at me in wonder. I could see the pleasure in his expression. "Do you have drawings?"

I winced inwardly. He knew the fashion industry. No one from that world had ever critiqued me, and I was a bit afraid of it. But I nodded, slipping off the couch and back to my room for my sketch pad. I handed it to him, and he opened it. Of course, my more recent drawings were first.

His fingers turned the pages carefully. He looked at me after a few moments. "Alexander McQueen meets Ralph Lauren." He flipped another page, looking surprised anew. "Meets Coco Chanel."

I flushed from joy.

"But that's how you dress, of course, so I should have known," he said, still flipping through. About thirty seconds after he said it, a slight redness tinged his cheekbones. I got it: he was my employer. He had been swept up in fashion talk, but we normally didn't discuss one another's appearance or clothes.

He flipped on through, shaking his head in appreciation once, studying everything else with flattering attention to detail.

"You know...your mom was a big inspiration for me," I said hesitantly, afraid he would think that was trite. He'd probably heard it a thousand times.

But he looked at me, meeting my eyes. "Was she?"

I nodded. "I mean, she was from Hammondsville, right? She was so talented, and she had such an eye for fashion. She was and is an inspiration for a lot of little girls around here."

He swallowed, holding my eyes as I thought there was perhaps a bit of moisture in his. To say that he looked touched would have been an understatement.

I smiled. "I have this favorite magazine ad of hers. She was on the beach, wearing some pretty shoes and an edgy dress, and beside her was a horse. You could only see her from the waist down, and her feet were crossed in the same direction as the horse's feet."

He smiled in a reminiscing way as he cast back over his mind. "Gucci!" he said finally.

"That's the one!"

He continued to hold my eyes. "You know, I have all of the vintage *Vogues* she was in," he said.

I touched my heart, gasping. "Here?" I whispered.

He nodded, standing. "Come, I'll show you."

Without a thought, we crossed the yard to the big house, where he took me back to his bedroom. There were still stacks of boxes unpacked, but he went right to one and opened it. We sat on the floor, and I poured over them. He gave me anecdotes as I asked, and he even found in an old album a picture of him on the French beach with his mom for the Gucci shoot.

"She was thirty-five then," he said, looking at the picture where she was leaning down, her arms around his neck as she smiled with her eyes squeezed shut in laughter. She wasn't a model in that moment, just a mom. "She had completely aged out of modeling, but she was one of the first to speak out against cutting women off at twenty-one—or around that age."

"She never lost her edge," I said, looking at a photo of her in one of her later shoots. She was stunning, her jaw razor sharp, her skin flawless, her hair naturally light blonde, like his. She was just so *timeless.*

"So *thin,*" I said with envy. I was skinny, but she took it to a whole new level.

There was a moment's hesitation. "It...had its price," he said, and left it at that.

I looked at him, biting my lip.

Going back, I opened the last magazine. A paper slipped out. It was a letter, which began, *Dear Mr. Cane-Steinem* and ended with a signature, followed by a comma and *Editor of Vogue Magazine.*

Of course, I read it. They were wanting to do a special edition to mark the twentieth anniversary of Lillette Cane's death next year, and they wanted an interview. I looked up at Joseph in awe. "Have you responded to them?"

He shook his head.

"Why on earth not? Joseph, this is a big deal!"

He sat up and away a little, seemingly receding into himself. "My...mom was very famous," he answered, lifting a shoulder as if trying to explain. "She was a sex symbol, an icon. She left a legacy. All of that can be difficult to compartmentalize. I've been in legal battles over her images since I was twenty years old. I usually don't talk about it, or her, or any of it."

I studied him. "But you..." I paused. "I mean, the world remembers her, obviously. It's not your duty to memorialize her." How to be gentle but forceful, here? It was clear that he would regret not doing this if the opportunity passed. I began again, "But the fact remains that you knew her better than anyone else on earth. It might be nice to set the record straight. To remember her. Without any complicated feelings or legal battles. Just her. And you. That's all you would have to talk about."

He held my eyes, reaching for the letter. I gave it to him, and he tucked it back in its place. "I'll think about it," he said. "But I doubt it."

Something told me he planned to cling stubbornly to his original plan. He stood then and, reaching down a hand, helped me up. I had impressions of the carpet on my legs; we had been down awhile.

I looked around the room. It was absolutely crammed with his things, and I didn't know how he even found his clothes. I mean, granted, Henry's crap was splayed throughout the rest of the house, and there wasn't really room for anything else, but still... "Joseph, this is depressing," I said.

"I know," he admitted.

I looked at him. I knew it was hard to go through a deceased loved one's things, and I knew it was a bad job even without the emotional element. But we had to get him comfortable. I thought of Mary, Melissa, and Paul. Let no man say I was not willing to go the last mile to ensure their happiness at work. And really, who could be expected to want to stay in Cane House? It was beautiful, but *this* would have any rational human high-tailing it back to sleek apartments, Sunday brunches at his dad's equally expensive apartment, the girlfriend from the same world, the high-flying friends, Yom Kippur and Hanukkah with the Steinems, weekends in Vermont, summers at The Hamptons, dinners at five-star restaurants, evenings at art galleries... Seriously, how could *this* compete with *that*?

Hands on my hips, I said, "We start at dawn."

Chapter Fifteen

We started in the kitchen.

"Okay, you're going to go through and mark the crap you want to keep, and I will begin discarding the crap you want to get rid of," I announced, passing Joseph a roll of sticker dots from my mom's most recent yard sale. Luckily, my cousin knew a guy, and he had brought one of those massive dumpsters over.

"Honestly, in the kitchen..." He winced. "Just the table. And this," he said, going to open one of the cabinets, where his grandma had tacked a little framed paper of the Prayer of Saint Francis of Assisi. I took it down, laying it carefully aside.

"Got it. Now, go work on your bedroom. And bring me your pots and pans when you get to them."

He obeyed. I opened the cabinets, seeing Henry's old stuff. Geez, what had Joseph even been cooking on? I knew he was busy, but I was beginning to wonder if there was something to his dad's theory about the breakup and the loss of Henry putting him into a tailspin. He didn't show it at work, but I was thinking his devastation at Henry's loss must have been pretty thorough for him not to have touched any more than he had. And I totally got that.

The cleaning lady had kept the surfaces clean, but there was some inherited stickiness in the under-cabinets. Shuddering, I was thankful for my gloves as I ripped out all of the old shelf liner and tossed it. I cleaned, laid down a sleeker liner, and began stacking Joseph's kitchen equipment.

He ambled in, looking amazed in the way men do at the productiveness of women, and said, "I've got all of the boxes sorted. Need any help?"

I handed him the roll of stickers. "Get started in the living room."

He smiled at the command but took the roll and headed off. Two more hours passed, and, given that he was rich, I had made an extensive list of things necessary to bring the kitchen up to the twenty-first century. I took my pen and pad throughout the house, looking around, and by the time I was finished with the list, I located Joseph in the living room and said, "You're taking next week off."

He looked up from his perusal of the crap in the built-ins. "I can't take next week off."

"Yes, you can. You don't have any major court appearances, the police have gotten no further on the Buford case, and Paul and Melissa can cover your other stuff. I'm working here also next week but as part of my regular salary. I consider this just as important as anything I could help you with at the office," I said, chin in the air. "This house is going to need more work than I ever realized."

He leaned back, sighing. "I know it is."

"Well, then?" I prompted.

"Fine," he said, lifting his hands in concession. "I'll call Paul and Melissa tonight."

"That's the spirit," I approved, looking around for things he had tagged in here. A globe, a wing chair, his grandpa's magnifying glass, and a picture of Henry, his wife, and Joseph's mother when she had been about four. "What about the books?"

"I have hundreds of my own," he answered.

"Okay, I'll call the library and see if they want us to donate any of them." I bent over, picking up an intricately woven split oak basket. "You're keeping this."

He grinned, handing me a sticker. "All right, then."

I scanned around, locating a gold figurine of a goose that had been Mrs. Cane's. I had always loved it. Since it was on the top shelf of one of the built-ins, I said, "Can you reach that?"

Joseph looked up and then reached to get it.

"Are you sure you don't want to keep that?" I asked.

He turned it over in his hands before extending it to me. "Why don't you keep it?"

I held it to my chest. "Are you sure?"

He nodded, lifting his eyes from the figurine to my face. I took a breath. "All right, back to work. Get to tagging—throughout the whole rest of the house, mind you!"

"Yes, ma'am," he answered meekly, but in the way of a naughty adolescent boy who is actually undaunted. Recalcitrant, that man. I would bet he had been a trying child.

I set to work dumping out old papers from the banker's boxes that were randomly sitting by the fireplace. *Henry, you were almost a hoarder.* When Joseph finished with his tagging, he joined me, and before long we were both coughing from the dust we had stirred up.

As I was digging through a box, I jumped back, eyeing a spider.

"What is it?" Joseph asked, pausing in his own box perusal.

"I think that is a black widow, and you are going to have to come kill it, or I will blow this place up."

He duly did so, and I had never thought anyone so gallant. "A lot of bugs here," he commented.

The understatement of the year. It was like a Biblical plague of every swarm of insect imaginable every summer, and why our ancestors had thought this was an appropriate place to settle was beyond me. We didn't stop for lunch, and by the time we had noticed our growling hunger, said insects had started their nightly, deafening chorus outside.

Joseph made us something French. And Reader, let me tell you, I could have sold the farm and moved in with him once I tasted that dish. Keeping my mother's admonitions in mind, however, I restricted our conversation to his plans for the house.

"I would really like a master bath. The one that's there is just kind of in the hallway, and...dated."

"What, you don't like pink tile and fifty years' worth of grime?" I asked, incredulous.

"It's the clawfoot tub that kills me. What am I supposed to do with a clawfoot tub?"

I pointed my fork at him. "That tub could be fabulous. Build a nice, walk-in shower and leave it alone." His eyes laughed at me, but he agreed. We discussed contractors and had a plan by the end of the meal.

Then we moved into the living room with our peach cobbler (my contribution) and ice cream. Sitting on the couch in the warmth of the lamplight, with the bookshelves cleared out and most of the junk gone, I realized for the first time that this was a really beautiful room. "This house could be a stunner, you know."

He nodded. "My mom used to talk about how it looked when she was younger. Sometimes I wonder, though... Is it too much house for just me? Five bedrooms, five-thousand square feet... Should I just sell it and get a nice, manageable house somewhere closer to town?"

I searched his face. He had said it in a conversational way, but this was his family home we were talking about. The family that was all gone except for him. "Don't you want a family?"

He lifted a shoulder. "Of course. But it's just my dad and me."

"I mean a family of your own." I watched him.

He paused in his cobbler-eating, continuing to look down into the bowl, as if to study the food. "I did."

Two words, not *spoken* sadly, but filled with broken dreams and heartache, nonetheless. I swallowed. "What happened?" I asked softly. I had sacrificed my pride, my cleanliness, and my upper respiratory system today; he could tell me something personal.

He looked off into the past, lifting his head. It was compelling when he turned serious like that. "I don't know. It was good, you know. Until it wasn't."

I bit my lip. "Was the break-up cordial?" I pictured him being the 'consciously uncoupling' type. Super mature, having drinks with her family soon after...

"It was surprisingly dramatic," he responded candidly, looking a bit wry. "I mean, I wouldn't say Taylor Swift level, but pretty close."

I choked on a laugh, drawn by his ability to be self-deprecating. "I like Taylor. Don't be judgmental."

"I'm not judging now that I've been in the exact same boat," he responded, eyes twinkling.

I laughed. But then I said, "I'm sorry. There's no easy way to lose someone."

He held my eyes a long moment. "No." There was a pause. "But she'll be fine. I'll be fine, too," he said finally. And he sounded like he really meant it.

I set out for the big house early the next morning, trying not to obsess over whether Joseph had held my eyes a moment longer than usual there on the end. He hadn't, and I was crazy.

The dining room was pretty atrocious. Let's just say if the IRS ever wanted to conduct an audit of the past forty years, we would absolutely be covered.

"The shred truck is coming tomorrow," Joseph said, wiping his brow with his sleeve as he cringed over an old magazine with coffee stains on it. I hoped it was coffee.

"We may need two trucks," I responded. I opened one of the corner china cabinets. Stacked on its shelves was dainty china with a delicate floral pattern, the kind no one had used for at least fifty years. "Keep or sell?" I asked.

Joseph looked my way, his eyes running over the dishes. "It was their wedding china. So...keep."

"Will do. Not sure what else you put in a china cabinet anyway."

We paused for lunch, and then we started back on the dining room. A rainstorm set in, so it was all indoor work for the rest of the afternoon. Joseph put on some music, which seemed to help us work more efficiently. Having moved out most of the furniture, we tag-teamed rolling up the massive rug, which had been under the table collecting crumbs and dust for about thirty years. It became really heavy at some point, and I couldn't push it any farther, which made us laugh. I swept while Joseph dragged the rug out to the mudroom, its final fate being the dumpster when the rain slacked.

"Oh, hey!" I said, pausing as I saw Henry's old record player. Next to it, of course, were boxes and boxes of records.

Joseph walked over, smiling nostalgically. He paused the Bluetooth on his phone, picking up a record. "I wonder if it still works?" He placed the record, pushed a few buttons, and then we heard the comforting staticky sound before "Dance with Me" started playing.

"Your grandpa did love Orleans," I said.

He smiled, looking up at me. Suddenly, the words, the cadence of the song struck me. So gentle and intimate, sweet and yearning. It flowed throughout the room, sounding ten times better than the modern speaker (not really, but there was something about the crackling). My mouth was dry suddenly. What was wrong with me?

I jumped up, tucking my hair behind my ear. "They had to have some country albums," I said, flipping through another box.

There was a beat of silence. Then he said, "I was never much of a country music fan."

I paused, going stock still as I looked at him, everything else fading. "What?"

He lifted a shoulder. "It's just not really my thing."

I blinked. "You come to Tennessee, and then say something like that?"

He grinned. "We don't have to tell people," he pleaded, eyes twinkling.

"It's going to come out," I said firmly. "You mean...*no* country music? I'm not talking about this newfangled stuff. What about from the '80's and 90's?"

"Did you say *newfangled*?" His eyes widened.

"You are straying from the point," I asserted. I turned back to the box. "You just haven't given it a fair chance, is all." I pulled out a Dolly Parton album.

He smiled when he saw it. "What's your favorite Dolly song?"

I looked at him like he was an alien. "'Two Doors Down.' Of course." What was his problem? I played the record, and after a while, he looked favorably impressed.

"She really does have a beautiful voice," he said.

"Such presumption. Who are *you* to compliment Dolly Parton?"

He bit his lip on a smile. "My eternal apologies." He stood, looking through the box with me. "I've never even heard of half of these."

I sighed deeply. He was such a lost cause without me.

"*The Judds*. Heck yes," I said, laying this one aside for later.

His eyes twinkled. "You keep looking. I'm going to go check on the dogs." We had them corralled in the fence behind the house. Fritz had dumped his bowl three times. When he did it twice, it was because he was a bit of a buffoon. Three times meant he was angry that no one was playing with him. "I might take Fritz for a walk," Joseph said.

"Okay. Just...be careful." He agreed to it. "And kill that spider on your way out," I directed, motioning toward a monster hanging upside down from the archway. I had kept my eye on him all morning.

Joseph was so efficient at killing spiders, something a girl couldn't help but admire. He wadded up the napkin and threw it into a pile of trash.

"Next one is yours," he said on his way out.

"I don't think so!" I called seriously.

Going back to my sweeping, I changed the record. I'm telling you, Wynonna really knew what she was doing. At some point, the sweet strains of "Love is Alive" began to float throughout the dining room.

I caught sight of Fritz playing outside. Leaning against the window, I watched as Joseph threw a stick for him, high and long like I couldn't do because I didn't have the strength. When Fritz brought it back, Joseph got down, scratching his neck, talking baby talk to him while Fritz panted happily in his face. Having already learned Fritz's ways, Joseph was armed with a second stick. Fritz would never give up his first stick until another was thrown. He didn't get the concept of "fetch" at all. And I kind of loved that Joseph was okay with that.

Fritz returned triumphantly with the second stick, unconsciously whacking Joseph with it. I smiled. He would learn to be quicker.

Once we had moved the furniture back in, we went into the library. I got inspiration as we began to peel back the room's bones. I could picture painting the bookshelves behind the antique desk a dark olive green, keeping the figurine of the hound dog, and the guns hanging over the door. We could move the original mallard paintings from that bedroom onto freshly painted cream walls in here. Very Ernest Hemingway Southern Masculine. Was that a design style? More to the point, was it Joseph's?

I looked him over. He might be more Minimalist Modern Industrial (another term I quickly created in my head). This occurred to me because that was the way his fabulous New York apartment had been designed.

"Who got the apartment?" I asked, continuing last night's conversation today.

Joseph looked confused/amused.

"Come on now. You can't honestly think your grandfather didn't ask me to stalk you on Facebook for him," I said.

His eyes twinkled with that joy I was used to seeing by now. "I didn't know that." He paused a moment. "She offered to buy me out."

"Was that her style or your style?"

He thought for a moment. "A little of both. But more hers, I would say." He looked at me questioningly, not without amusement.

"I ask because I figure I'll be coordinating with the contractor after you go back to work. Men are generally hopeless with this sort of thing. But your mom was a designer, so that intimidates me. I don't want to take it in the wrong direction."

"Ah." A smile played about his lips. "What were you thinking?"

I sketched with words my general idea for the library, and he nodded definitively. "We're definitely on the same page."

"Good." I turned back to the desk drawers, which were, of course, crammed.

"But nothing cutesy or antique in the kitchen or bathrooms."

"Got it." I foresaw a battle ahead over the clawfoot tub. One which I would win, Reader, I assure you.

I thought he had gone back to work when he said, "Just nothing too feminine."

"It's like you don't know me at all." I tossed him a look.

His eyes twinkled as they met mine. "Sorry."

We worked for three more hours, barely making a dent. Just take it from me, people: recycle your papers. Everything you get in the mail, you do not have to keep. Set some sort of time limit, and then shred that crap. Then maybe when you're dead, your grandson and employee will not be driven perilously close to losing their minds.

Needing a mental break, and also to get the blood to stop rushing to my head, I stood up. I took a breath, scanning over the room to see Joseph. He bent over to lift a stack of books. He really was a very attractive man. What can I say? Sometimes a look grows on you? Don't judge me.

He jerked back suddenly, looking down at the floor.

Coming to myself, I asked ominously, "What is it?" A bug, obviously, but what were we talking here?

Not breaking his focused attention, he said seriously, "I don't know what the hell that is, but it has a stinger."

I yelped, jumping up. "No, no, no," I said, darting for the double doors, where I considered it very gracious that I stopped. "You have to kill it."

He reached behind him, not removing his eyes from his prey. Or predator. It was all a matter of perspective. "Give me your shoe."

"I'll keep my shoes, thank you very much."

He looked up at me briefly. "If I lose it, you'll have a head start. I'll need both of mine to save myself."

I weighed this. Not by any means pleased, I reached down slowly and removed my sneaker. "You have to let me get ten feet away before you go for it."

"Agreed."

I took him the weapon slowly, and he delayed the agreed upon time. I waited at the door with fear and trembling, but he apparently wasn't taking any chances and got it on the first whack. It was all over very quickly.

"We need an exterminator," he said darkly, drawing his fingers through his hair.

"Indeed," I responded, taking back my shoe with a cringe. It was not exactly in the same condition in which it had been given.

He winced, taking it back. "I'll be right back." He went into the kitchen and returned with a clean shoe.

"Thank you," I said with false dignity, which made him smile.

"Indeed. You are most welcome."

Chapter Sixteen

The rest of the week was spent in completely exhausting physical activity. By the end, however, we had Cane House clean, sanitary, and uncluttered. Since the contractor couldn't get started for a couple of weeks, I went back to work at the office the following Monday. And let me tell you, they were lucky I did.

I sat at my desk, a little antsy because the police chief had come in with the bank president, and they had been closeted with Joseph for about fifteen minutes. I knew this was something about Reynolds Buford, but I couldn't have said what. But I really needed to be back there.

To my surprise, the door opened, and Joseph met my eyes. "Mississippi, do you care to come back?"

I studied him. "Sure," I answered, getting up and going to him.

The police chief and Mr. Morton greeted me solemnly as I sat down.

"As you all know, Miss Whitson is my personal assistant, and, being that she knows the town better than I do, I keep her up to speed on important investigations." Joseph looked at me across the desk. "An audit of Mr. Buford's email account shows that someone impersonated his niece through an email on the day he was shot. The impersonator asked Mr. Buford to meet them at the Tasty Freeze for ice cream. It appears that an email account may have been set up for that purpose alone. The address was identical to Britta Buford's, except the false address had an underscore at the end."

I swallowed. "That was why he was coming out of the bank that day." To meet his niece for ice cream on his lunch hour. Geez.

"There's more," the police chief said. "General Cane-Steinem tells me that you are under a confidentiality agreement with the State, so I feel that I can tell you. Mr. Morton has discovered that Mr. Buford was using the bank to launder money for close to two years." I glanced at the bank president, who looked sick at the thought.

"He failed to file numerous Suspicious Activity Reports, despite taking in large amounts of cash. We're required by law to file them for cash deposited that is over a certain amount or any activity that might indicate laundering. He overrode the tellers multiple times," Mr. Morton said, shaking his head. "We had no idea."

"It seems he must have decided to stop about three months ago," the police chief continued, meeting my eyes. "Which would be just about the time he started being threatened. They were afraid he was about to squeal."

I bit my lip. "So...drugs."

Joseph nodded. "Drugs."

Having sat on the revelations for a night, I went into Joseph's office the next morning. He looked up at me from his desk.

"Look, it would have to have been someone who knew Britta Buford's email address," I said. I had the daily office mail in my hand, and I retained the envelopes as I met Joseph's eyes.

He nodded. "They called her in for an interview yesterday evening." He turned to his computer and opened an email. "She only uses the address personally for family and friends, as well as when she wants to double-enter a contest online." We both smiled briefly. My eyes were already scanning the list Britta had compiled. "See anything?" he asked after a time.

Not really. Her mom, dad, uncle, her boyfriend, a handful of friends, a few extended family members. I said really softly, "I'm guessing she never gave it to her ex-aunt Tilda?" I was a little ashamed to suspect the ex-wife, just because she was the ex-wife. Only, Virgil Baker's obvious suppressed suspicion kept returning to me. He had handled the divorce, and he had said it was one of the messiest he'd ever witnessed... And I trusted his instincts, so I couldn't rule it out as a possibility.

"They haven't spoken since the divorce, and Britta created the account about ten years ago, which was after the divorce. They asked her that."

"Well, nothing stands out to me," I said, straightening. I crossed my arms and nibbled my lip as I thought. "She's absolutely sure these are the only people who have ever had it?"

"No, she said..." He scanned the email to get the exact wording. "She was pretty sure, but over that long a time, there was a possibility that she had missed someone." He looked up at me. "And she was completely wrecked to learn that her uncle had been going to meet her, so it's possible she could have forgotten someone given the state of her emotions."

"Hmm." There was something niggling at the back of my brain, but I hadn't had enough sleep to bring it to the forefront. "Well, I'll think about it. Here's your mail."

He took it, our fingers brushing. Ignoring the hair standing at the back of my neck, I said, "I've already shredded all of the junk mail. Here's a few court documents. Some stuff from the State. A letter from the county executive and his husband inviting you to their swanky Independence Day celebration."

He was flipping through, but he looked up as I spoke. "Should I go?"

"Yes. All of the big wigs will be there. You'll likely be running unopposed, but you still need to attend. And they're not butt-kissers like the mayor, who, by the way won't be there because the county executive and mayor hate each other, on principle."

He smiled. "Where do they live?"

"I don't remember," I answered, taking the letter from him, and accidentally coming away with the other piece of mail he hadn't read yet. "Elmhill... Oh, that's Social Climbing Avenue," I said caustically. Something dinged in my head again. Something about Britta Buford's email list, but again, it wouldn't come to me. I looked at Joseph, and he was smiling at my sarcasm. "Just drive until you see what appears to be the Loire Valley, but in subdivision format."

His eyes twinkled. "Turrets, vineyards, and all?"

"Just you wait. And last, a personal note," I added, handing him the notecard he had accidentally given back to me.

It was a note from Hetty Gibson, inviting him to try *all* of her casseroles any time he wanted. He choked and coughed into his elbow. But he met my eyes, and apparently they were dancing with as much laughter as his, because he had to fake coughing again.

It hit me at 2:00 a.m.

Social Climbing Avenue. That was why the lead had tried to trigger in my brain when I had said the fake street name. That was where Reynolds Buford's brother lived (and hence where Britta Buford had grown up). It was also where Tony Tonneau had lived with his mom, dad, and the brother who looked so much different from him. (This wasn't important, but Jackson Tonneau wasn't nearly as hot as his brother.)

I remembered the location of the Tonneau house because a girl doesn't forget getting lost on the way to a bathroom at a party during high school. I had heard that Tony had moved back in with his mom and dad after his recent and unexpected brush with the law. Probably they were hoping to get him back on track.

Anyway, all of that was irrelevant. Britta and Tony had dated. I remembered that because while Tony was my age, Britta was two years younger, and everyone had pretty much thought she was the luckiest girl to have died and gone to heaven. Of course, she *was* a cheerleader, a thing akin to dating a goddess at Hammondsville High. I smiled, remembering her waiving her pom-poms.

They had dated pretty seriously—even after he had gone away to college—for four or five years, I think. I remember everyone being surprised when they had broken up. Still, it had been a long time ago now. Was it possible that Britta had forgotten he knew her email address? Because *I* was almost certain he would have known it.

I told all of this to Joseph the next morning when he came to walk Fritz while I walked Frieda. It was a routine we had developed while cleaning out Cane House. Joseph was afraid of losing ground with Fritz, and I couldn't say his concern was entirely unwarranted. My big fluffball was fairly protective of me. He had sent the UPS man running about a week ago, which had required a written apology.

Joseph was already in his work clothes, but he did at least wear waders to protect his khakis from the dewy morning grass. I did the same.

I cringed. "First suspecting the ex-wife, and now a person with a drug charge. Could I be more prejudiced?"

"Since you called the people up at Berry 'Mountain People?' No," he answered. He stopped, looking at me. "You thought of him because he was her boyfriend. That was a good catch. I think we need to tell the police to ask her if it's a possibility. Look, Mississippi..." His eyes scanned the panoramic view of the meadow before us, blanketed in fog, gentle sunshine, and dew like a Tennessee morning should be. "If I'm being honest, something never felt right about John Anthony Tonneau's plea of nolo contendere. There was no evidence of drugs in his system." I met his eyes. I hadn't known that. "There never has been, on any of his probation reports. If there hadn't been such a big Ziploc of drugs in his console, I would have dropped the charges. But there *was*, and there was no getting around that. I thought he might be protecting a friend, but now... I'm not so sure."

I swallowed. Something felt slightly ominous about this information. The skin on my arms tingled. I knew just enough to know there was a lot I *didn't* know about this type of situation. Sure, I'd seen countless drug addicts convicted of possession, even selling. I knew all of the signs of addiction, all of its implications, its devastations, what it did to the poor souls it had in its grip, to their families, to the people the drugs made them hurt. To the legal system, like us, who tried to sort it all, day in and day out. I knew the fatigue, how it etched on your soul a sort of hopelessness, a weariness like no other. I was intimately acquainted with drugs.

But if Joseph suspected there was a supply hub in Hammondsville or its vicinity... Here, I was entirely out of my league. I couldn't even begin to understand the implications of a large-scale drug business. The money laundering, the linked crime, the violence, the national concern...

I don't know, putting two and two together, something clicked. And I think, as we both stood there in the gentle morning light, it dawned on us both. There was Reynolds Buford to launder (now dead). Poor addicts across the state and possibly the South to buy. And a ring driving the operation somewhere at the center. And Tony Tonneau might be the first door into that center.

The police were interested. So interested that by noon that day, calls had been made to the TBI, who declined to open an investigation without more concrete proof. I thought we *had* some pretty concrete stuff. Britta Buford had been contacted. She had verified that Tony Tonneau had emailed her on numerous occasions, even bringing in her laptop and showing the police some pretty embarrassing and juvenile emails from several years ago between the two.

I had been there, attending the meeting, standing quietly with my arms crossed and looking stellar in my pencil skirt and coordinating top, if I may say so. I felt like I was on set of one of those crime dramas.

Britta dabbed her red eyes with the tissue she was holding. Time had rounded her face and form, although I could still see the skinny high school girl who had loved Tony Tonneau.

"Tony..." She bit her lip, shaking her head. "Look, things didn't end well between us, but he's not violent."

Joseph met my eyes over the computer screen. I knew what he was thinking: who to know that better than a long-time girlfriend? And she had sounded sincere. So I hoped very much that we had the wrong end of the stick.

I had a joint training session with Mary and Imani that night. The session did not go well. Well, for Mary it went fine. *She* was taking the healthy lifestyle seriously, Imani had said with a pointed look at me. *I* collapsed on my sofa afterwards with aching muscles, wounded pride, and the determination never to exercise again. It wasn't until Saturday that I could again sit down on my toilet, and by then, I was scheduled for a salon day with my mom and grandma.

"Just perfect," my mom said, right before she opened the salon door. "Hetty Gibson's in there in rollers in Lena Caldwell's chair. Two of the biggest gossips in town."

"Well, go in. Maybe we'll learn something," Grandma said grumpily, but with a tinge of optimism.

They got started on my mother first, since her color would have to set. Then they took Grandma to another chair and put me right by Hetty Gibson as she sat reading *Garden and Gun*. Darn it. I had wanted that magazine. I still wasn't over her trying to hit on Joseph in Mr. Baker's office that day. Married with kids! Casserole dish, indeed.

"Hi, Mississippi," she said, sickly sweet as Paige Prentiss pumped my chair up.

"Hetty," I responded cautiously by way of greeting.

"This is a cute cut," Paige said, flicking my hair, playing with my bangs. "You had it done in Nashville?"

"Yep, it just needs a trim, I think."

"I can definitely do that," she answered with a wink. I had always liked her.

"Your mama let us know that it wasn't true, what was all over town," Lena Caldwell said as she started to unroll Hetty's hair. "That you were having sex with the Cane boy."

"Thank you for being so specific, Lena," I responded.

"But wouldn't you just like to!" Hetty of the casserole dish said, with all of the innocent relish of one speaking of diving into a chocolate cake. I bristled.

"Well, he's a looker, I'll grant you that," Lena said, not best pleased with this talk.

I did not deign to respond.

Lena finished up with Hetty, and Paige continued with me. As soon as the bells tinkled on the door after Hetty had paid and left, Lena said like one in possession of Big News, "That girl is asking for trouble, if you ask me!"

Paige and I looked at her. "She says she and Jason are on the rocks, so it doesn't matter what she does."

I couldn't care less. I saw Hetty pop into the coffee shop next door, bouncing her new hairdo, and I sincerely hoped that was the last time we ran into each other for a while. I twitched up the discarded *Garden and Gun*, trying to tune the Town Gossip out, while Paige and Lena continued talking.

Something that was said about five minutes later made my ears perk, however. "And here she is telling me the Cane boy inherited five million from his Grandpa. She said she was going to drop in on him at the office this week, *just to say hi.*"

I slammed down the magazine. "She *said* that?" I demanded.

Both women looked a little startled. "Well, yes, she did," Lena responded cautiously.

I came to my feet, glancing out the window just in time to see Hetty exiting the shop. "Excuse me, Paige, I have some business to attend to."

I charged toward the door like a crazed scientist, clips pinned here and there, causing my hair to stand at every angle possible, salon cape flapping.

"Mississippi!" I heard my mama call in confusion.

But I was on a mission. I pushed open the door none-too-gently and yelled, "Hetty! Hetty Gibson! You stop right there."

She did so.

I advanced toward her, pointing my finger. "You and me are going to tie up. What in the world do you think you're doing, giving out information about Virgil Baker's clients? Do you not know you could get him in big trouble? Five million indeed! Listen here, you are going to take your sites off of Joseph Cane-Steinem right now."

She looked a little daunted, but she quipped saucily, "Trying to eliminate the competition, Mississippi?"

I looked down my nose at her. "It is *not* right for you to be out telling his business, let alone endangering Mr. Baker's career. Do you not think I can fight dirty? I'm Scotch Irish, thank you very much. All I would have to do is tell Mr. Baker that you can't keep that mouth shut, and you would be out of a job. Go home and work it out with Jason, or don't, but for heaven's sake, don't try to get with people for their money!" With this screamed on the air, I turned back around and strode into the beauty salon.

"I'm just saying, I don't know how we're supposed to hold our heads up in public if you're going to bless people out in the parking lot," my mom said, dipping her chip into salsa at Los Lobos. "I like to have died."

"That was unfortunate," I agreed, with dignity. "But it had to be done."

"Well, she is a shameless woman, and you set her to rights for her sin," Grandma said.

"No, that wasn't—"

"That *is* true," my mother said, taking a brighter view of the matter.

I sighed. It was useless to argue.

"Are we doing anything for the Fourth?" my mom asked. "I need to start planning now if so."

Grandma sighed. "Bev and Dan said something about having it at their place. But I swear, those screaming kids make me want to run for the hills."

Being around Cousins Jack (of the screaming children) and Al (of the vicious dog) was not something I could contemplate with serenity after the stressful past few months. "Why don't we go somewhere?" I suggested.

"We can't go somewhere; you're saving money for college," my mom pointed out.

"I have an emergency stash," my grandmother offered. "Anything to keep us away from those kids."

"We're not digging into your emergency stash. We'll accept Aunt Bev's offer. There. That's that. Tell her I'll bring the baked beans."

Chapter Seventeen

With my hair cut and Independence Day sorted, I went into the office for what I hoped would be the last week before the contractor got started at Cane House. I needed out of here in the worst sort of way. I would much rather be choosing wall colors and trim designs. And maybe by the time the house was finished, I would have had a nice mental break. Then I could return to the office until Christmas, by which time I would have a very nice nest egg socked away. And then...

I turned my thoughts away from that thought quickly enough.

I readied my files for court with Joseph, Paul, and Melissa. We all walked over to the courthouse together. There, an overly zealous deputy made me walk through the metal detector because I didn't have a licensure card, even though I was surrounded by three people who did, and who were not, presumably, attempting to smuggle a terrorist into the building.

Annoyed, and casting a nasty look at Joseph as his eyes danced with laughter, I laid my personal items in the tray and walked through. *If my last name had been Cane or Buford or Riley, this would not have happened, I can guarantee you that,* my mind was growling. That was why I handed *General* Cane-Steinem his folders none too gently as we sat down in the courtroom.

While a hearing ran a bit long, Melissa showed Paul pictures of her cat on her phone. I was pretty sure that Jake Dillon (he of the chickens and drug problem), who was sitting on the first bench, was following along. What can I say? Everyone loves cats.

It was during this time that Joseph nudged me. "Look at this," he whispered.

He put his court docket between us. He started going down the list of cases, most of which were Schedule I drug offenses. He started drawing a line and listing what they were out next to them. *Heroin. Heroin. Heroin.* Again and again.

"Sheesh," I whispered.

"You told me the problem was growing, but it seems like a significant uptick even just in the time I've been here." I decided to forgive him for his earlier privilege, because he was being a nerd. And again, as a straight-A student, I appreciated that.

"I mean, where are people even getting that much?" I whispered.

He gave me a significant look. My shoulders slumped as I exhaled. A supply hub. This again. Joseph and I were definitely on the same wavelength about there being something big out there. But were we just being paranoid? After all, many of the most brilliant conspiracy theories weren't even true. Just because some pieces of a puzzle seemed to fit together didn't mean we were on the right track.

Apparently this must have shown in my eyes, because Joseph felt the need to reiterate some things. "Something had to be significant enough for Reynolds Buford to be laundering that much money," he whispered. "And for him to be dead now."

Sheesh. I mean, *geez*. Yes. He was right. There was more than likely something big at the bottom of this, unless it was just a series of huge coincidences. We weren't equipped to handle this sort of thing. The State was going to have to get with the program.

"State of Tennessee verses Jacob Ryan Dillon!" the clerk bellowed.

Joseph stood, as did Phil Tuck. The man reeked of cigarette smoke, but luckily, I couldn't smell marijuana on him today. At least...not from here. An officer took Jake Dillon forward to the stand, and the lawyers informed the judge of the plea deal they had reached. The judge began going over the man's rights with him and asking the requisite questions about his understanding.

"Mississippi..." I saw the hand before I heard the voice. It was slithering on my knee.

"Mr. Ritten," I said, sounding about as pleased as if it were me making the plea deal instead.

"It's been so *long*," Whalen Ritten said in *that* voice, drumming his fingers on my kneecap. Right there in the open courtroom. I slid away as much as my chair would bodily allow. "You look *good*. I like your new style."

"Old style, really. How's the wife and kids?" I asked pointedly, keeping my voice moderated.

Not embarrassed at all, he replied, "Great, just great. We have a vacation coming up in a couple of weeks. Here, I'll show you some pictures of the kids. Growing like weeds." Genuine affection shaped his features as he extended his phone. I would never understand the man if I lived to be a hundred.

"They're really pretty, Whalen," I said, dutifully surveying his kids.

"Most of the credit goes to Layla," he said, looking fondly at his wife's face in the picture.

He had called the office the day after Reynolds was shot, offering his support in any way possible, and the thing about it was: he had *really* meant it. But that did *not* mean I had to let his hand slither up my skirt, as it appeared to be doing. I slapped him. Right there in front of God and everybody. I'm not saying I meant to do it, but I stand by it.

The slap echoed across the courtroom, and everything seemed to come to a halt. The judge, Joseph, Jake Dillon, the clerk—everybody (except Phil Tuck, who was partially deaf or high)—looked our way. There was an awkward moment. The public, of course, had no idea of what had happened. Some of the attorneys seemed barely able to contain themselves. The judge looked stupefied, and, while I am sure he was fully supportive, he seemed unsure how to proceed.

Unheeding, Mr. Tuck broke the ice by slamming his fist against the podium. "I'm telling you, this man has *rights*, Judge!"

The room snapped out of it. Whalen Ritten slinked off (possibly because Joseph was looking at him thunderously) and court proceeded. When it was finally adjourned and we were all walking out together, the tension was sliceable. Joseph's jaw was clenched, and it was clear to everyone that he was angry. This was unprecedented, so we were quiet. "What did he *do*?" he demanded suddenly in the hall, stopping and looking at me.

"Just the usual. Hand on the knee, hand up the skirt."

His eyes flashed. "I'll be back to the office later."

I hurried down the hall after him in my heels, Paul and Melissa watching. I caught his arm. "Joseph. Don't. It's just Whalen."

His pretty eyes seemed to shoot fire. "I will *not* allow you... an employee to be harassed. Go on back to the office, all of you. I'll follow shortly."

I watched, speechless, as he set off. I looked at Paul and Melissa. They were of a nervous nature generally, but there was something else amidst the feeling in the air as we set off. They kept glancing at me. Opening the door of the courthouse to the baking heat of the sun, I felt compelled to say, "He would do it for any of his employees!"

Somehow, that didn't ring quite true when I said it, but I was vindicated a few hours later. Upon Mr. Cane-Steinem's return, everyone immediately waylaid him with, "What did you do?"

"It won't happen again," he answered, adjusting his tie as he walked back to his office. He shut the door.

"I'm assuming he didn't kill him," Mary whispered. "We're assuming that, right?"

I searched his ancestry for Scotch Irish blood and found none. "We are," I confirmed.

Later, just as we were all getting some real work done on our files, Dan Howell strolled in. He of the encroaching sewage. He of the roaming cattle. Jepp Lewis's neighbor and archnemesis. By the end of his visit, I was in pure harmony with Jepp on wishing the little turd could go to jail. (Not literally, but I did see how the man could get under one's skin.)

I had heard that Mrs. Howell had recently filed for divorce after a forty-year marriage, saying ominously all over town that she "wasn't having any part of it anymore." What "it" was, no one was quite sure.

"Can I help you, sir?" Melissa asked, since Mary was taking a call.

He ignored her completely. Joseph had just strolled out of his office to get something he had printed, so he glanced up at the man. "You needed to speak with an attorney?" he asked.

"That's right," Mr. Howell said. "Doe-mestic."

"That would be Ms. Robertson," Joseph answered, indicating Melissa. Apparently thinking he was finished, Joseph began reading through what he had printed.

Mr. Howell strolled up to Melissa's desk. "My son's been in a little scuffle with his wife. This might be a job for one of the fellas." He looked Melissa over dubiously. "You're a *lawyer*, you say?"

"Yes," Melissa responded, deadpanning as usual.

"A female lawyer?"

"Yes."

The man appeared to be much struck. "A *full* lawyer?" he demanded, incredulous.

His mood apparently bubbling over, Joseph looked up, scowling thunderously. "What the hell is a full lawyer? As opposed to a half lawyer? Get out of my office! And don't come back until you are prepared to speak respectfully to Ms. Robertson."

Dan, frightened, had been backing out the door slowly, and at that last command, he tripped over the threshold and fled. I wanted to clap. I was looking at Joseph, eyes shining with more approval than ever, and Mary appeared to be about to crumble on the spot. Joseph went back into his office and slammed the door.

"I think it's safe to say we've all been under quite a bit of stress," I said that night at the office girls' night out at the bar and grill.

"If I were porcelain, I would be in a thousand pieces on this floor," Mary said, trembling.

Melissa took a more sanguine view, dipping her chip into our spinach and artichoke dip. "I just have to say, the fact that he's feeling protective of the employees, standing up for us... I don't know, it just seems like a good sign to me."

I reached across the table, covering the other woman's hand. "It's a very good sign, Melissa," I said. A sign I had trained him well, thank you very much. "I think he's going to stay."

"Why *anyone* would stay is beyond me," Mary said into her napkin, blotting her eyes. "Between the murder and the groping and the misogyny, he must think we're a bunch of *hooligans*."

"Well, *I* didn't murder anybody," Melissa said.

A fair point. There was nothing more to be said, so we talked wedding plans.

"Honey, I need you to pick Otto up at the vet."

I gave a sigh. My retired, bored grandmother seemed always to be able to find a job for me to do for her.

"Why can't you pick him up, Grandma?" I asked, gathering my files to lock up for the day. I pulled my trash can out from beneath my desk and placed it on top since the cleaning service was coming tonight.

"Because I have my life group." Her life group was a quilting bee that met regularly to gossip. "You know this, Mississippi."

"Why couldn't you have taken Otto to the vet at a different time?"

"Because rabies shots are ten percent off this week. You don't get a deal like that every day."

I pinched the bridge of my nose. "Fine. I'll do it." Twenty minutes later, I was driving back toward my cottage, a large male tabby in a carrier in my backseat. He was a bit of a ladies' man, so I was going to have to be careful not to let him out.

I picked him up, staggering a little. "Otto, you are a very big boy."

He yowled at me, so I took it we were on good terms. Fritz and Frieda were a tad annoyed at having to stay corralled outside. But I had no choice. Frieda hated cats, and Fritz always good-naturedly wished to tree them. Somehow cats didn't find this predilection so genial.

"All right, young man, don't pee on anything," I directed, letting him out to roam in the cottage.

Going to my bag, I took out my phone. Eight missed calls. *Oooph*. I had put my phone on silent earlier when a group text thread from my church had threatened to send me over the edge with its numerous dings. "I don't *care* if we have duplicate egg salads at the Sunday dinner, Cindy," I grumbled, scrolling through what I had missed.

I slid my thumb across my mom's name and was soon hearing her ringtone.

"Where have you been?"

"Running errands for my grandmother."

I heard tapping. I could picture her at her little computer desk, solving someone's travel problems from afar. "Miss, I have found a man who will go on a date with you."

I groaned. "Do you *hear* yourself?"

Apparently not. "It's Mateo Rodriguez from your class. Wasn't he always such a cutie! I saw his mama shopping at the Tienda Mexicana—"

"You shop at the Tienda Mexicana?"

"I get my salsa there."

"I had no idea."

"I have for years," she answered simply. "Queso, too."

"Huh," I said in surprise. Just when you thought you knew a person and all of their almost-too-ritualistic habits...

"Anyway, she was always so spiffy in her heels, and I'm just telling you: I couldn't do it all day at the restaurant if it was me. Maybe it would be different if I owned the place, but I'm doubting it. Anyway, it's all set up."

I really needed an aspirin. And the cat was clawing my curtains. I walked into the living room, swatting him away. "Mom, you can't keep doing this!"

"What? Setting you up with nice, attractive boys? Well, sue me for living. You *promised* me you would put yourself out there, Mississippi!"

I gave a long sigh. "You are going to send me over the edge, and when you do—"

She broke in, not hearing. "I forgot to tell you about this set-up yesterday... I was using my gift certificate for the manicure and got completely distracted. Anyway, he may be calling today."

"Mom!" I shrieked. Then I noticed my grandmother's feline inching toward the vases on my fireplace mantle. Otto had some sort of obsession with breakable china, and a bad history with the same.

"Mississippi, if you would just open your heart, I think you would find, after all, that you *could* share your life with a man—"

"Mom, I have to go," I hissed. "I've got a cat situation. Bye." I ended the call. "Otto Frank!" I screamed, remembering that, for reasons unknown, if you said his name really loudly, he would cease and desist with all shattering of porcelain.

He halted and tossed me a wary look.

"You heard me," I said, holding firm.

My phone buzzed.

I looked down. It was a number I didn't recognize. I swallowed. "Hello?"

"Hi, Mississippi, this is Mateo Rodriguez. I hope it's okay that I called."

He sounded a little embarrassed, and most of my irritation at my mother faded. He *was* a nice guy. And he *was* cute. "Hey, no, that's fine. My mom had...said something about it." Why wasn't I blushing? I would usually be blushing. We both knew he was calling to ask me out, after all.

"Yeah, she called me, too."

I bit my lip, wincing, horrified.

"She said she doesn't mind that I'm Mexican."

I gasped, choking on my own saliva.

"You okay?"

"Fine," I croaked. I was going to kill my mother.

"Look, Mississippi: I know this is a little odd, but your mom saw my mom in the grocery store, and—"

"Trust me, it's a lot less odd than you would think," I said grimly.

"Oh! Well, that's good. Would you like to have dinner some time?"

I paused. My brain seemed to be having trouble formulating an answer. "I would," I said. "When were you thinking?"

"Next Friday?"

"Yeah, that works for me!" I answered. "Where would you like to go?"

"Somewhere that's not my parents' restaurant?" he suggested.

I smiled. It never really mattered to me where I went on a date. I had a theory that anything was fun, or at least bearable, when you were with the right person. Even the diner up in Berry, for instance, could work in the right circumstances. "I get that. I know a great pizza place in Pickensville. Sorry, I know that's not fancy. Did you have something else in mind?"

"No, that sounds great. I'll pick you up at six o'clock?" he asked.

"Sounds great!" I affirmed.

My phone rang while I was loading dishes in the dishwasher. I had deposited Otto at my grandmother's house, where he had proceeded to cling to her as though I had been abusive. Grandma had looked at me suspiciously, so I was not surprised she was calling.

"Hey, Grandma," I said. Had I really had fish sticks three nights in a row? I scrubbed the crumbs from my plates, choosing not to think about the implications of that.

"Your mama tells me that you have a date!"

"Yeah, she keeps setting me up with people," I said, letting my irritation show.

"She's here with me. You're on speaker phone."

I rolled my eyes. I refused, however, to be ashamed. "Mom, did you say that you don't mind that Mateo is Mexican?" I demanded, putting a plate down on the counter with undue force.

"I'm telling you, Mississippi Whitson," my mother responded, "I worry for your generation. You're so worried about *giving offense* that you can't see the meaning of what I *actually* said. I said I *don't* mind that he's Mexican, which a lot of people around here, to their shame, couldn't say. At least now if you date him, he doesn't have to wonder where I stand!"

I sighed. "Could you at least say Hispanic?"

"I thought we were saying Latino now?"

I heard my grandma in the background ask, "What's Hispanic?"

I rubbed my temples.

"Mom, Grandma: I am going to hang up now," I said firmly.

"Fine. Just don't end this one after the first date, Mississippi," my mother tossed at me.

I gripped the phone, catching a second wind. "May I remind you that Luke McCallister tried to get me to change my religion within the first hour of our first date?"

"Are we back to that?" my mother asked in a long-suffering voice. As if she herself hadn't, in fact, brought us back to that. "Just give him a shot, Miss."

"I will!" I exclaimed, wanting to hang up *so bad*, but you didn't come back from hanging up on your mother and grandmother around here. So I waited out the rituals of closing down the conversation and only then signed off.

Chapter Eighteen

Where shall I begin about the Fourth of July? It all started with a sparkler incident. And yes, my grandmother had been right: it involved the children, little devils that they were. An ambulance call averted, we all dined on grilled hamburgers. They were sub-par to what my dad's would have been. I bit my lip, thinking how much he would have liked to have been here. It was his favorite holiday.

While we *baked* in chairs on the lawn and swatted off mosquitos, I sat wondering why in the world I always felt compelled to go to these family events. Admittedly, I loved my family and usually couldn't imagine myself anywhere else. Tonight, though, I could imagine myself on the lawn of the county executive's swanky property, looking over the river, surrounded by foliage that had been sprayed for mosquitos, watching as magnificent fireworks boomed across the river. Joseph was likely dining on catered delicacies, not tough hamburgers. I wondered suddenly if he minded going to these functions solo.

I had kind of thought he would ask me (as a sort of extension of my job) to go with him. But he hadn't.

The night went on, long and boring, loud and often annoying. Quilting and hunting: the night's riveting conversations. Braden and Sam got into it over some sort of newfangled toy that looked nothing like what we had played with back in *my* day.

Tomorrow was my birthday, and that had just about made my mood foul. Biological clock... And why was that what I always thought of on my birthday, when I wasn't even sure I wanted to have children? Maybe women were hard-wired to think about these things?

I was trudging back to my chair with my dessert when the fight spilled over. The boys were fighting with the toy above their heads next to the oversized kiddie pool, Eugenia looking on lovingly. I got the no spanking part, but...nothing?

Suddenly, one of them knocked me in the head, while the other fell against me, and we all three (or four if you count my slice of strawberry pretzel salad) tumbled into the pool. Gasping for air, I splashed up amidst the screams of all of the ladies. Eugenia was demanding to be told whether her babies were okay (her cousin-in-law be damned). *I* should be the one screaming, but the cold water had been a literal bucket over the head for my bad mood. Braden and Sam were looking at me like they were afraid for once that they had gone too far. "Oh, you little *stinkers*," I exclaimed, grabbing them and tickling them. They gave delighted giggles. My cousin Jack had run over, looking horrified. "Mississippi, I'm sorry!"

He extended his hand, and, despite the genuine expression of concern, I took it and yanked him in with me. They were his kids, after all. He splashed in with a huge *thunk*. "Mississippi!" he exclaimed, although not with surprise. We had played together as children, after all. And I had pretty much dominated the pack.

He came for me, dunking me under water. I yelped, shimmying away, but the kids joined in, and the game was on. And I defied them to have more fun even on Social Climbing Avenue.

My bad mood had returned by the morning.

Twenty-nine... What to say about twenty-nine? I felt like my youth was slipping away. Simultaneously, I felt like if I could just get to thirty my life would stop being so crazy and I would have figured things out. I wondered if I had squandered my youth living as though I were older than I was. I wondered how long it would be before I had to start worrying about wrinkles. Would I have to start dyeing my hair within five years? Was forty still my upper age limit to have a baby?

Bleak. It was bleak.

My phone trilled, and, seeing my mom's name, I sighed. "Hey, Mama," I said.

"It's my baby's big day," she trilled.

"Yep."

"This time twenty-nine-years ago, I was wishing I had never thought of you. But that would change in about two hours," she said lovingly.

I smiled, despite myself.

She asked, continuing with the yearly reminisces, "And you know what you were named after?" I know the possibilities that are presenting themselves to you for my name's origin: the Southern state, the mighty river, the great tribe of Native Americans—

"Your father's favorite pie. Mississippi Mud."

I had always just told everyone the Whitsons were originally from Mississippi. "Yep, you've told me," I said with forced cheerfulness.

"Well honey, enjoy your day, and we'll celebrate at Grandma's tomorrow," she said.

"Thanks, Mama. Love you."

"Love you. Bye."

"Bye-bye."

"Bye."

I jumped at a knock on my door. It was Saturday, but luckily, I had dressed. It would be Joseph, here for Fritz. I laid down my phone, grabbed the dogs' leashes, and took the pups to the door with me.

"Hey!" I said, handing Joseph the blue leash. Freida growled at him like she had never seen him, and I shimmied her away.

"Hey," he responded, once it was safe to do so. We set out walking down the long, shady drive, both of us keeping a wary eye on Freida as she tossed passive aggressive looks at Fritz and Joseph.

The latter glanced at me. "Today is your birthday," he said.

I looked up, surprised.

"It pops up in the employee system," he explained.

"Ah. Yes." I tucked my hair behind my ear, not meeting his eyes. "Twenty-nine. A tough one."

"I'm five years ahead of you. You'll be fine."

"Easy for you to say. You're a man," I said with a smirk. "Meanwhile, my biological clock is ticking, according to my mother." We stopped by the tree that the dogs loved to sniff.

"Oh, come on," he said. "No one's even thought of marriage at twenty-nine in New York City."

"Well, that's not the case here," I responded. "My mom has currently fixed me up with a childhood friend. I'm her one shot, she says."

There was a beat of silence. "Who?" I looked up from my survey of the grass. Was I imagining the intensity in his eyes? Likely.

"Mateo Rodriguez."

Another drawn out moment passed. Birds sang, crickets chirped. "He's a nice guy," he said at length. Somehow, I was reminded of the same clipped tone and un-Joseph-like caveman instincts I thought I had seen on the picnic. When he had asked me about the guy I was dating... But every girl likes to imagine a man jealous when she goes on a date with another guy, and my gut had led me astray before. I will repeat that Joseph Cane-Steinem had never made the slightest romantic overture to me.

"Yeah, he is," I answered. "The best one she's picked yet, really."

I thought he continued to study me for a second, but I wasn't sure I hadn't imagined it. I tucked my hair shyly and turned the conversation.

"It was nice," he said in response to my question about the Independence Day party. He seemed reluctant to say more, abstracted even. I wondered if he *had* been lonely, staring across the river at those magnificent colors bursting across the sky. I don't know what it was about fireworks which always made *me* feel lonely. He was probably missing his ex-girlfriend.

I told him about the pool incident (he knew about Eugenia and Braden), and his eyes lit again with that recurring joy. I was glad. It felt wrong when it wasn't there. "I can picture it," he said, before confirming that nothing so unrefined had happened on Elmhill Lane.

"Oh, my gosh, he looks like Max Minghella."

"You think everyone attractive looks like Max Minghella," I responded to Mary, taking my phone back and logging out of Facebook before she could accidentally like anything on Mateo's page.

"While that is usually true," Mary said in a philosophical spirit, "I will remind you that Sutton is a ginger."

Duly corrected, I closed my menu and waited for the server. We (meaning Mary, her mother, sister, grandmother, and I) had successfully chosen her wedding dress and were now feasting at a fancy restaurant to celebrate. I was extremely glad that we had taken Thursday (the only day she could get an appointment at the bridal salon) off to make the trip.

"Mary says your boss is a real cutie," her grandmother said, winking at me.

Mary flushed crimson. "I did not. I did not say that." She fanned herself. "I mean, hypothetically speaking. I mean, not like in an interested way. He's too old for me. Like ten years or something, so that would be... I just mean, in a detached way, like, he has a nice butt."

This caused all of us to explode with laughter, and Mary protested loudly until drinks were brought, and we settled down.

"I don't really see him marrying anyone in Hammondsville, though, do you, Mississippi?" Mary asked, sucking on her strawberry lemonade.

I didn't. Not if I were honest. "Maybe he'll bring a city girl down South," I said lightly.

"Or leave," she returned darkly. "I mean, he can't be celibate. He doesn't look like the type to be celibate, does he? Or maybe he's hooking up with Hetty Gibson, after all?"

"I don't... I don't think he's hooking up with Hetty, no," I said, voice quivering. But something soured in my stomach. My tea tasted a little weird. Maybe that was it. Was there someone? I hadn't really thought of this. Hmm. Well, anyway, what did I care?

"Who's going to the Cornhusk Festival?" Mary's mom asked, ready to move on from hookups and decent butts.

I told her I was working a booth. The festival was the sort of thing we had always gone to when I was a child because we, frankly, didn't have the money to vacation. It was a cross between a craft fair and a real fair, and I conjured scents of funnel cakes and barbecue nachos even now.

"Well, I'm so excited. It'll be our first time on the Ferris wheel as an engaged couple!" Mary exclaimed excitedly. I envied her innocence. And felt annoyed by her enthusiasm.

But hey! Maybe I would hit it off with Mateo and be posting silly pictures to social media on carnival rides by next year.

Mateo knocked on my door at six o'clock Friday night.

"Wow, you look great," I said. First faux pas. Wasn't the man supposed to say that? But he did look great.

I expected his eyes to twinkle, but he looked a little surprised. "Oh... Thanks." He handed me a little posy of flowers. "From my mom's garden," he said a bit apologetically. I took the flowers and placed them in one of the vases Otto had tried to destroy. "Sorry, she's...excited. She thinks we would make beautiful babies." I looked into his face. You could never tell if he was joking when he said things like that.

"Mateo," I said, slipping my arm through his as I shepherded him out the door, "it would seem that some things are universal."

He heaved a relieved sigh. "What *is* the obsession with grandkids?"

"You tell me. So your mom thinks I'm pretty?" I asked.

He held my door, and I didn't mind. He was already giving off less aggressive vibes than Luke, so things were looking up.

"She thinks you look like Audrey Hepburn," he answered.

"I always liked your mom!" I said warmly. "And that was so sweet of her to send the flowers. They're beautiful. You'll tell her I said so?"

"If we are on speaking terms. You can't imagine what working with your parents is like, Mississippi."

I laughed, encouraging him to tell me as we drove out to Pickensville. At the pizza place, we agreed upon a pizza and settled back. Conversation was always easy. We talked about how we had blown past our ten-year class reunion. About how in middle school we had been afraid to acknowledge each other at first because we had come from the same elementary school, and that wouldn't have been cool. About a few people from our original kindergarten class, wondering where they were now.

It was all perfectly pleasant, enjoyable even. But I couldn't shake the feeling that I maybe thought of him like a brother. I remembered this feeling with Patrick Cummings. He had gone on from our illustrious background at West Drake Elementary to become the basketball star of our high school grade. So many girls had asked me if I didn't just think he was *so hot*. I was always baffled by these questions. I mean, it was *Patrick*. I had seen him stick crayons up his nose. You would have to have a love that transcended time and space to overcome something like that. And then it was like a lightbulb hit me.

"Do you know who you would be really good with, Mateo?" I asked with enthusiasm. "Paige Prentiss!" Why had I never thought of this before?

He lifted his brows. "I guess I'll assume the date isn't going well?"

I had the grace to flush. "No, I mean, I like you so much. It's just... We grew up together. You were a part of my childhood."

"Which Hollywood holds should indicate we are soulmates," he said.

"Hollywood knows literally nothing about it. I mean, I keep thinking about when you snapped my bra—"

He flushed deeply. "I never snapped your bra!"

"Yes, you did. You got sent to the principal for it! Word always got out when the girls started wear them, and then the boys would—"

"Are you still holding it against me?" he asked. "I mean, you think I'm some sort of creep who still snaps women's bras?"

I choked on a laugh. "No, of course I don't." I stifled more laughter. "No, really, Mateo, can you tell me you don't think the same thing about me? Like a first cousin, at least?"

He sighed, sitting back. "I *was* thinking about when you shoved me off the climbing bars, and told me I needed to get more courage, and to watch you."

"See! It clouds everything, doesn't it? You're wondering if I'm still like that, aren't you? Well, I am, Mateo. I mean, if you had just met me on the street today for the first time, you would think: flawless woman who looks like Audrey Hepburn—"

"I mean, I wouldn't say—" I socked his arm, and he did laugh. Then he sighed. "Okay, but you're going to have to go to my parents' house with me and explain this," he said. "I mean, I'm twenty-nine. In my culture..."

"Oh, boohoo, you know what *this* culture is like! Don't tell me you have it any worse than I do."

"My mom told me a month ago that she would still love me if I had realized I was gay," he protested.

"Well, my mom asked me if I felt called to the single life, like Paul," I tossed back. I defied anyone's mother to be more panicked on the subject of age and singlehood. But I *will* say that Mrs. Rodriguez was sounding more like my mother by the minute.

We laughed together, taking our first few bites of pizza. We talked with perfect ease, much more freely than we had been. And I did go over to his parents' house with him, where they seemed to be hosting a movie night for about a hundred people. Spanish was the language spoken, and I struggled with my rudimentary high school training.

But the point was conveyed, and, while it led to some shouting in various corners, everyone thereafter calmed down, and I was invited to join the movie. Which I did, as well as being persuaded to eat another delicious supper. Imani was absolutely going to kill me. I swallowed. As was my mother.

I avoided my mother the next few days. As it turned out, there were events enough to keep me occupied legitimately without actively having to dodge parental questioning.

My phone rang on Sunday morning. Joseph. Odd. I answered.

"Sorry to call you on Sunday," he said, his voice a little reticent.

"Oh, no problem at all," I answered, curious as I slid my foot down into an exquisite high heel. "What's up?"

I was wanting to talk to you about something." My heart quickened—I wasn't sure whether with anticipation or dread. "I received a call from the police chief last night." My heart rate returned to normal.

I hopped as I almost lost my balance with the shoe. I believe I managed to maintain a professional tone, however—no small achievement when one's heels try to topple one. "Oh?"

"They've had Tony Tonneau in for questioning. They think they have enough to make an arrest and want my blessing. They don't need it, of course, but..." He sighed deeply. "I think they were thinking the same thing that I am: if there were nothing to it, it would be a tough break for a guy already embarrassed by a conviction."

I sighed, too. "Yeah."

There was a pensive silence. "I was looking through his old file and saw that Virgil Baker was lined up by his defense attorney as a character witness, in case it got to trial."

"Really? Odd for an attorney to take the stand."

"Well, he wasn't his attorney. Whalen Ritten was. Anyway, I hadn't realized Virgil had known him, and I thought: he's someone I would trust to tell me if I'm on the wrong track here. I know you were planning to continue on the house tomorrow, but would you care to go with me to his office for a meeting in the morning?"

"Can you get an appointment?"

"Hetty Gibson was apparently recently let go—"

"Thank the good Lord for that!"

I could picture him smiling. "—but I know his new secretary. I texted her, and she said we could come in at seven o'clock before they open. He was happy to accommodate."

I agreed to it, wondering who the heck the new secretary was.

It was Becky Gimble. I was so relieved I could have died. She was my mother's best friend, and I guess Joseph knew her because she was on the city development committee. I was pretty sure he had donated a big sum to the town revitalization project. So there you go.

She brought my birthday present around from behind her desk, saying, "Betcha didn't know I worked here, did you, sweetie? Hetty got thrown out on her ass for some breaches of confidentiality. So here I am! Out of retirement until Virgil can find someone."

"Thank you!" I said, smiling at the floofy pink bag with feathers.

Virgil came to his door and, with all the grace of a Southern gentleman, invited us back. We took the same chairs in front of his desk that we had when we had closed out Henry's estate. Mr. Baker knew why we were here. He said he was eager to help. "Fire away. I'm not sure I can be of much use, but I'll tell you what I know."

"You know the Tonneau family, and John Anthony Tonneau in particular?" Joseph asked.

Mr. Baker nodded. "Yes, I do. I'm old friends with the boy's parents. Good people."

"What do you know about his recent drug charge?" I asked.

He sighed in thought, looking off into the distance. "I couldn't say. I'm not sure if he was dabbling and got caught and scared straight, or..." He looked back at us. "If I'm being honest, I feel like he may have been protecting a friend. Someone who left the heroin in his car or something. That sounds more like the kid I know."

I looked at Joseph. It was what he had suspected as well.

Mr. Tuck smiled at me. "Sorry, Mississippi. I keep saying *kid*. I know he was in your graduating class."

I smiled in returned. "Oh, I don't mind that one bit."

Looking at us in amusement, Joseph said, "Would you be willing to vouch for him, Mr. Baker?" This returned us to more serious matters.

"Honestly...yes." He looked up at us. "Any day of the week. I know that may sound strange after recent events, but... I know Tony Tonneau. He might have made a mistake here or there. But as to anything deeper? No, I'd swear against it on my life. He just doesn't have it in him."

We left the Baker Firm kind of deflated. If Virgil Baker said he trusted someone, well... He was just the sort of person whose word you took as solid. Like Pastor St. John. And Dolly Parton.

Joseph was feeling the same way, obviously. He called the police and told them our point of view. The chief called him back and assured him they wouldn't make the arrest, in that case.

As we walked along the sidewalk (which I hoped would soon be part of the town revitalization project), I pointed out that the city's flower beds could really use some work, by way of a hint. Joseph looked at me with a smile which told me he knew exactly what I was doing. "Duly noted," he responded dryly.

"So have we hit a block wall?" I asked.

"I kind of think we have," he answered. "This blows my whole theory out of the water."

"Or at least the 'in' we had to the ring," I added, side-stepping some weeds and nearly stumbling on a big hole in the concrete.

Joseph caught my arm, and said without missing a beat, "Yeah I know: the sidewalks need work, too."

I smiled innocently up at him while he still held my arm. He shook his head, eyes twinkling as he released me. He sighed. "I'm thinking we're going to need to order pizza for lunch."

"That is definitely a must in situations such as these," I replied.

We rounded the corner on the side of the office that didn't adjoin a building. I was debating pepperoni or cheese when Joseph came to a halt, reaching for my arm. He was standing stock still, looking at something in front of us. And he said in a tone I hadn't heard since the moment

Reynolds Buford was shot, "*Shit*," although a bit softer this time, almost a whisper.

I followed his gaze. Across the whole bricked side of the building was scrolled *JUDE*, and the writing was cloaked on either side by a swastika.

Chapter Nineteen

The TBI jumped on the situation, labelling it a hate crime, and soon we had people from Nashville in suits crawling the place. Joseph was on the phone with his dad, who was doing what dads did: yelling across the thousand-mile divide and threatening "to come down there." By the time he had him calmed down, the police had everything taped off at the office and told us it was time to go down to the station for interviews.

Mary, Paul, Melissa, and I were interviewed first. The most any of us could come up with was that Paul remembered something about two percent Jewish showing up on is Ancestry.com report. So we were fairly certain that the vandalism was centered squarely on Joseph. He was really quiet, almost pensive, but he did look up with a twinkle when Paul mused randomly about his DNA spit test. I smiled at him, trying to look reassuring.

He was taken off to be interviewed as soon as the TBI arrived. My head was spinning. I was angry and scared and feeling helpless. The office had been taped off, so we were shut down for the day.

By noon, there were protestors organized on the green beside the office with signs reading, "Racism will not be tolerated," "Get your anti-Semitic ass out of town," and "We are not Nazis." A little rough around the edges, but the spirit was in the right place. I gave them a thumbs-up as I got into my car.

I ran a trembling hand through my hair. I had never seen anything like this, and it was really shaking me up. Luckily, before I could have a total collapse, my phone rang. It was my mother.

"If that don't beat all. I just don't know what's gotten into this town. The whole place is going to riot and ruin, and I tell you what I think it is, Mississippi: it's that pagan statue downtown."

"Really, Mom?"

"No. But it's a symbol. We've gotten away from God. And what do we get for it? Murder. Drugs. Fornication. Anti-Semitism. Yes, and your generation afraid to mention the Holocaust! Well, let me tell you, Mississippi, this is what happens when you don't tell people what hate can do!"

I pressed my temples. "I..."

"Is he okay? Poor boy. Invite him over here for some mashed potatoes."

"Mama, I don't think he wants mashed potatoes."

"Don't be ridiculous. All anyone wants when they're sick or having a miserable day is mashed potatoes."

"I... Mama, I've got to go, okay?"

"Okay, sweetie. I love you."

I swallowed. "I love you, too."

Crickets set in for their nightly chorus about the same time the lightning bugs lit up the yard between Joseph's house and mine. Putting a cardigan over my sundress (more for comfort than for warmth), I started up the path. Two policemen were posted for protection on the property.

"Mississippi," one of them said in greeting as I passed by.

"George," I returned, inclining my head. I continued up the path and knocked on the door.

In a few moments, Joseph opened it, looking almost as disheveled as he had on his first day in Hammondsville. I swallowed, looking up into his face. "When I said there wasn't anti-Semitism in Hammondsville... It's because I thought there wasn't anti-Semitism in Hammondsville."

"Come in, Mississippi," he said gently.

He opened the door wider, and I slipped in. We stood in the kitchen, and he looked down at me for a minute. I wanted to ask him if he was okay, if his dad had calmed down, what the investigative officers had said, but I stayed quiet.

"Have you heard of any extremist activity around here?" he asked.

I sighed, shaking my head. "I haven't, but..." I lifted my shoulder.

"Has Imani?"

"I'll call her," I said, taking out my phone.

He covered my hand, stilling me. I looked up, swallowing. "It can wait," he said softly.

I lowered my head, fighting tears.

A long silence passed. His hand stayed. I fought the almost inexplicable pull to move closer to him. The air felt thick, and I could hear him breathing.

At last, he lowered his hand. He took a step away, running his fingers through his hair. "I think I may be crazy, and you're going to think I'm a complete conspiracy theorist, but... At some point, it crossed my mind that that this could have been done to distract from the investigation. Like they thought we were getting too close to cracking this, and..." He lifted his shoulders. "I don't know."

"Have you ever been targeted for being Jewish?" I asked softly, holding his eyes.

"No. But my dad has. Too many times to be naïve."

I drew a deep breath. "I hope he was okay."

He nodded. "Just upset. He can be kind of protective. I never knew that until my mom died."

"He's a dad." It didn't matter that he had been young and the situation was unique. "Mine would have killed for me, and I'm not even kidding."

He nodded, a corner of his mouth lifting. "I was thinking the other day: he was thirty-four when he came to get me in Paris after Mom and Aman were killed. My age, and he had a fifteen-year-old kid. We've had our ups and downs, and I didn't even know him *that* well, but I never doubted I could count on him to protect me." He lifted a shoulder. "I guess that's why I called him today—some sort of calling back to childhood. I don't know."

I had a feeling his dad had been a constant during his childhood, but not a very present one. It could never be an easy situation when parents were split up, divided by a continent and an age gap. And Joseph was still that kid sometimes. He was thirty-four and just realizing he could enjoy having a dad, and all of the benefits that came with that. I smiled. "See, if it were me, I would *have* to call because my mom would *kill me* if I didn't tell her. Slaughter me and lay me out for burial."

He cracked a smile. "She would."

Speaking of... I reached for the container in my tote bag. "Joseph... This may sound strange, but: would you like some mashed potatoes?"

He lifted his brows, looking amazed. I'm pretty sure my face had flushed, but the lighting was dim, so it was fine. And then he stunned me. "I *would*, actually. That is exactly what I was wanting for supper."

I've always had a bit of a photographic memory. Images come to me just between sleeping and waking, playing like an old-fashioned movie reel in my mind. A courthouse. Cat pictures. An interested defendant looking over my shoulder. Jake Dillon. Joseph's hand holding a pen, drawing a line. *Heroin. Heroin. Heroin.*

I sat up with a jolt, drawing in a breath as I tried to orient myself. My polka dot sheets were mussed, as if I had tossed and turned all night. Frieda was staring at me from across the room. I drew a hand threw my matted hair, turning my face away from the window. The curtains were drawn, but the light was nevertheless intense, and birds were already singing.

My brow furrowed. I had been onto something there, but I had lost it.

"All right, kids," I said, getting up. Frieda nudged me toward the food, so I took care of that first before any necessities for myself, of course. I lived to serve.

Rolling my eyes, I dragged myself toward my bathroom. It was as I was stumbling back toward my bedroom that I noticed the clock: 10:00 a.m.

I gasped. Strange as it felt to carry on business as usual, I was supposed to meet the contractor at 10:30 at Cane House. I looked out the window. The Jeep was gone.

I texted Mary to ask if they had let them back in the office. She said that they had. I guessed that was a good sign, although I did wonder now if the authorities would ever catch whoever had vandalized the building.

I barely made it inside Cane House before Mr. Hicken, the contractor, pulled up. My morning was spent going over everything that needed to be done with him, and he drew all of my suggestions out on an impressive blueprint he had made of the house. His crew arrived shortly after and started demolition. I winced, feeling sorry for Joseph, who would be living in a disaster zone for a while.

Deciding to make myself useful, I went back to one of the spare bedrooms and began removing the 1980s rose wallpaper. It was not fun, to say the least. I took a break about an hour in and called Imani.

"Hey, is everybody all right?" she asked in her soothing tone.

I smiled. "Yeah." My smile slipped. "Have you ever heard of extremist race behavior around here?" I asked.

I remembered a boy in my class bragging that he had found some robes in his dad's bedroom trunk. That was the only mention of that kind of activity I had ever heard, but I'm not sure I *would* hear about such things.

Imani paused. "Let me ask a few people. I'll call my hairdresser. She might know."

"Thanks," I said, genuinely grateful.

I continued the excruciatingly tedious task of peeling paper, inch by inch. When Imani called back, she said there had been an incident in the housing projects when we were kids in school. But she hadn't heard of anything more recently.

"Thanks, Imani."

"You're welcome. And don't forget that you're volunteering at the Black History Museum's booth at the Cornhusk Festival. September seventh."

"Yep. I've got it on my calendar. Hard to believe September is just around the corner."

"Sounds good. Take care, Mississippi. I mean it. Bye."

I slipped my phone back in my pocket and continued peeling. It was weird in light of everything that this became my overwhelming obsession: getting this ugly wallpaper off the wall. I must have worked another hour when my phone ringing caused me to jump.

It was Joseph. I answered. "Hey!" Did I sound too chipper? How did one talk after a hate crime?

"Hey, is everything okay?"

I lifted my brows. "Yeah!" I said (maybe too enthusiastically?).

He paused. "If someone *is* targeting me, I don't like the idea of you being out there alone while I'm in town."

Something warm spread through my chest. "I'm not alone. Mr. Hicken and his entire crew are here."

"I know, but..." He sighed, lowering his voice, "I can't move without tripping over a protection officer, and there's no one out there."

"Joseph, it's not me they're targeting."

"Are you sure? Because I'm not," he said forcefully. *At some point, it crossed my mind that that this could have been done to distract from the investigation. Like they thought we were getting too close to cracking this...* I could see his face so clearly as he had said that to me last night.

Chickens. Cat pictures. Jake Dillon.

I gasped. My heart thumped.

"Mississippi... I'm sorry. I didn't mean to sc—"

"Jake Dillon," I blurted.

A pause. "What about him?"

"He was sitting behind us, Joseph. While you highlighted all of the heroin cases, and we shared significant looks as to the possibility of a drug ring in Hammondsville. I thought he was looking at Melissa's cat pictures, but..."

There was some more silence. Joseph said, "Look, I don't know. I only know that if someone had dropped a bomb in the middle of Main Street, it couldn't more thoroughly have derailed the investigation into Reynolds Buford's death. If you think..."

"I don't think. I know. In that way that a woman does, Joseph. The man is addicted to heroin. He's in their clutches, these people he depends on to supply him. And you were getting too close. Someone has to get a warrant and search his place."

"We can't get a warrant on a hunch."

I sighed, deflated. He was right, of course. I was ninety-nine percent sure Jake had reported to his suppliers that Joseph suspected the presence of a supply hub, and someone had taken this action to silence Joseph and distract from the investigation. Or maybe Jake had been sent to do the dirty work himself. He *was* a night owl, only coming out once the sun had set. And he could be *nasty* when he was in the clutches of drugs.

"It doesn't matter *why* someone has done this; it is a vile thing driven by hate and playing on fear," I said wrathfully.

"Agreed." There was a pause. "I'll tip the investigators off. They're going to say we don't have enough to go on, but at least maybe they'll start looking in the right direction." I waited, certain he wasn't finished. "But we're playing with fire here. We've already seen a fraction of what these people are capable of. I don't want you to involve yourself, Mississippi. You could get hurt, and I couldn't..." His voice trailed off, not finishing the thought.

I drew a breath, hesitating. "I won't say a word to anybody. You know that."

He released a relieved sigh. "Yes. I know." I heard him swallow. "Lock up if they leave early."

"I will."

Chapter Twenty

Going up to Cane House every morning, I conscientiously watched over the renovations. I chose countertops, flooring, bathroom tile, beadboard, and cabinetry. I also nudged the workers back on track when they veered off in an erroneous direction, or in a direction (obviously wrong) only a man would take.

I met Imani for frozen yogurt (she did not allow ice cream) on Thursday evening. She asked me how the date went, and I gave her an apologetic look.

"Your mother is going to kill you," she said, getting a spoonful of her sugar-free fruity cup.

"I haven't told her yet," I replied.

"Putting off the inevitable. So...you were pretty upset about Joseph."

I narrowed my eyes, trying to read her. "Yes..." I responded warily.

Imani studied me for a moment.

"What?"

She looked surreptitious for a moment. "I mean, that's natural, of course. It was a terrible thing."

I huffed. "What *is* it, Imani?"

"I just know you have a thing for blue eyes and that you've always liked Jewish weddings. Every wedding show we watch. 'Look at the chairs!'" she mimicked. "'The chuppah! I love the glass crushing!'" she continued.

"What has that got to do with the price of tea?" I asked, blushing.

She glanced up at me before looking with great interest back into her cup. "I'm just not convinced he's here to stay. Dating is already so hard, but that would be really tough. Best to just friend-zone him—I mean in your mind."

"Right. I mean, yeah. That's where we are."

"Okay. Just so you're careful," she said, reaching for my bowl to throw away.

"I wasn't finished!"

"You've had enough."

"Well, another one bites the dust in the long line of men who never got past the first date with Mississippi Whitson."

My mother had found out about Mateo.

I was sitting on the floor in my kitchen, brushing the dogs, who seemed to think I was a groomer, or at least in some sort of servient position to them.

I looked at Frieda for commiseration as to my mother. She commiserated, as always. "On to the next one!" I retorted.

"Don't take that tone with me, young lady. The devil loves a smart mouth." This sounded like an ominous prelude to a tongue-thrashing, but I was surprised. My mother drew a deep breath and said no more about it. I mean, like...nothing.

I stood up, blinking, wondering if she was okay.

"Is Joseph doing okay, honey?" she asked. Interesting subject change.

I was quiet for a second. "Um, yeah. I mean, he seems to be."

There was a beat of silence. "Well. Okay, honey. I love you."

I blinked as she hung up the phone, apparently in a benign and even sensitive mood. I wasn't sure if the Earth had stopped or pigs were flying, or what.

I *had* always thought Jewish weddings were exceptional. I'm not going to lie about that. I liked the traditions, the emotions, the symbolism... However, something like that would never cloud my vision as to my romantic prospects, I argued in my head. Imani was just overly protective. And there was nothing there. So I put thoughts of any such things (or people) out of my head.

The contractors finished the renovations at the house on the first day of September, and I decided to take my vacation week then. Joseph was off at an attorneys' conference anyway, so the timing was perfect. My mom refused to let me go on an *actual* vacation, since she seemed to think I would blow all of the money I had saved for college. She and I did get away for a couple of nights to the state park, where they had some questionable cabins but a really nice pool and endless natural beauties.

When I got back home, I drove a couple of counties over to a bigger town where they had a decent grocery store, from which I stocked my fridge and freezer. Then I reorganized cabinets, knocked down all of my cobwebs, sorted my *Vogue* magazines by publication date, and vacuumed dog fur. By the end of the week, I was absolutely stir-crazy. Luke McCallister didn't know how lucky he was to have taken a pass on me as a housewife. I was on the verge of losing my marbles—and approximately five days had passed.

By Friday when Mr. Baker's new secretary called me and told me they had a tax document for Henry's estate if I could drop by and get it, I had never been so grateful. Probably overdoing it on the hair and makeup for a trip into town, I nonetheless relished the chance to dress and resume human contact.

Air conditioning whooshed over me when I opened the creaking door on the house where the law office operated. The vaguely pleasant/unpleasant smell of an old building wafted to my senses. The newly hired secretary (I didn't know her) said she would get Mr. Baker. He came out of his office smiling, the old wood floors squeaking beneath him.

"Mississippi. How are you? Just have Joseph give this to his CPA when he files taxes," he said, handing me a paper.

"He shouldn't owe anything, but I can't give tax advice, so there you go."

"Thank you," I said. "Is everything closed out with the court? I got the Order to Close in the mail."

"Yes, this should be the very last thing," he said. "Is Joseph coping well? I couldn't believe that anti-Semitic stuff. Very jarring."

"Yeah, it was, but he has a remarkable resilience." *No need to sound like a fangirl, Mississippi.*

"Any word on who may have done it?"

I knew I could trust him, but I was cognizant of my duties of confidentiality. So I didn't tell him any of the nuances of our suspicions. Instead, I said, "There aren't any strong leads yet."

He patted my shoulder. "Well, hang in there, kid. You were the valedictorian of your class, I believe. That takes no small intellect. Whoever did this didn't count on that." He smiled encouragingly.

I laughed self-deprecatingly. "Thanks. It's really up to the police at this point." I tucked the paper into my folder. "I'll give this to Joseph. Thanks again, Mr. Baker."

Chapter Twenty-One

I had never been so happy to be back at work. Since there had been no further threats, Joseph's protection officers had left, and things had returned to comforting normalcy.

That being said, a mountain of assorted jobs awaited me. A lot of new and thrilling cases had come in during my absence. "Attempted strangulation," I said, filing to the side of Joseph's desk. "Charming."

He looked up at me, eyes laughing. After a moment, he said, "I've missed your commentary."

"That is because it is pithy and cuts to the marrow, like any good Southern commentary," I answered, cramming one last sheet into a massive file.

Apparently unheeding, he asked, "Hey, what is this?"

He had been going through his mail and now extended a letter to me. If it was another note from Hetty Gibson, we were going to have a personal chat, she and I.

I took the paper. It was from the Cornhusk Festival Committee. I looked up. "The Public Defender has chosen a list of songs, and now it is our turn to choose from them."

"To what end?" he asked.

"It's a competition. Every year, they pick a list of songs, then we choose from among them, and someone from each office competes in the sing-off. Most rival offices participate. The mayor and county executive, for example. It gets nasty. The best part of the whole festival."

Joseph looked stupefied. "Did my grandfather take part in this...tradition?"

"No, of course not. Well, he chose the song, but he didn't sing it."

"Who from this office did?"

I put my hands on my hips. "Who do you think? And let me tell you, that comes to an end this year. I am here only on borrowed time, as a curtesy to you—"

"I don't sing."

"Yes, you do." I had heard him at the Memorial Day celebration. You don't grow up wrapped in sophistication without learning how to sing.

"Not in public," he said, holding firm.

I was afraid he was choosing to make this one of his inconvenient stubborn moments. I declared, "I can only make myself sound like June Carter Cash so many times, Joseph." Did he know how hard that was? Acting like you had something caught in your throat? I handed him the paper back forcefully.

"I've never heard of some of these songs," he said, leaning over the paper. "'Your Cheatin' Heart?'" His voice handled dropping the "G" about as well as the Queen's would have.

"Patsy Cline, and I won't hear a word against her."

His eyes twinkled. "'That Summer.' I *have* heard of that one. Too close to my origin story." He crossed it off.

I choked. "No, it is not!" I reprimanded.

He regarded me steadily, suppressed amusement in his eyes. "Oh, no? My dad was one of my mom's summer interns."

My eyes must have widened, although I tried to school my expression. "Oh!"

He moved on. "They seem to like this Garth Brooks. 'Callin' Baton Rouge.' Maybe that one?"

My eyes nearly popped out of my head. He had said *Baton Rouge* with perfect French diction. "Oh-my-gosh. You cannot say it that way. You will be run out of town. Repeat after me: *Battun Rooshj*." Clearly, I had left him to his own devices too long.

"Baton Rouge," he said, much better this time. His eyes were laughing, so it was hard to tell if he was messing with me or not. I regarded him suspiciously.

He lifted his brows, appearing the picture of innocence. "So, is it a good song?"

"It is."

"That one, then. But you'll have to sing it."

"I can't. It's a man calling his love, Samantha-dear."

He rubbed his temples. "I don't have time for this."

They had really chosen difficult songs (and one—his origin story—that I suspected was chosen as a gag). There was one song left. "'There's No Gettin' Over Me,'" Joseph read. He smirked. "Well, *that's* true."

I rolled my eyes. "Clearly a song big enough for your ego." I took the paper from him. "Ronnie Milsap. He was blind, like your grandpa. It would be a good way to honor him." I looked up at him virtuously. Two could play that game.

He narrowed his eyes. "It is immoral to play on emotions to accomplish a goal."

"Only if the goal is nefarious," I countered, holding firm.

"I'm a tenor," he protested.

"Ha!" I said, slapping the desk. "I knew you had sung before! How do you know you're a tenor, huh?" I rested on my heels, satisfied. "You'll be just fine."

"Mississippi—"

"It's not part of my job description," I said, walking toward the door. "I did it for your grandpa because he was blind, and because Melissa has social anxiety, Paul has IBS, and Mary has panic attacks. *You* are perfectly healthy and sane."

I opened the door to find that Paul, Mary, and Melissa, sitting at their desks, had been listening and were staring at me. I blushed. "Well, do y'all want to sing on stage?" I demanded irascibly.

"No!" they said fiercely, almost in unison.

"Then don't judge me for speaking the truth!" I said, tucking my papers that I intended to file at the courthouse under my arm and sweeping out the door. I knew I should probably spend some time in the clerk's office. My moral high ground was fragile on this one, and I had just ticked off everyone I worked with.

Famous historian Jon Meacham once said of his alma mater, the University of the South, that it was a cross between *Downton Abbey* and *Deliverance*. The university is about thirty miles from Hammondsville. And at the Annual Cornhusk Festival, Hammondsville was heavy on the *Deliverance* aspect. I could never see a mullet, smell a cigarette, and watch two women go at each other over a redneck lover without instantly forming images of Ferris wheels, ride lights against the night sky, and a general unpleasant high caused by second-hand marijuana and a circus of people. But there were funnel cakes.

I worked the Black History Museum's booth at the festival early Saturday morning. The other two ladies working it were Dot and Esther, who revived a twenty-nine-year-old feud over who had stolen whose strawberry pound cake recipe and argued the entire time. Only older people were out and about that early, though, so otherwise things were pretty tame. I then went home, changed out of my T-shirt with the museum's logo, took a shower (because I was sticky with sweat from the heat), and went back downtown, where I met Joseph.

I was wearing a T-Shirt that read in flowing script: *Dolly and Loretta and Patsy,* which is how, Joseph said, he had located me. I gave him a look and then took him to have lunch at my church's booth. Afterwards, I partook of the redeeming funnel cake.

We walked around to most of the booths. "You should buy your grandmother a corn husk doll," I instructed as we neared a booth where Native American artisans were crafting and selling them.

He winced. "She's a minimalist."

"Ooh, fancy grandma," I said approvingly. "Okay, I can keep it, but everyone has to buy a corn husk doll."

He regarded me with amused, narrowed eyes. "Something tells me this was your angle all along." I declined to comment. But I did tuck the artisan's piece into my bag carefully after he handed it to me. His eyes twinkled.

That finished, we admired the local woodworkers' booths, petted the llamas, and saw, for the first time, Tommy Bonner's zebra. Next, we took a stroll through the art building. This included the school children's competition, more advanced paintings, and a quilting exhibition. My grandma's group had an entry, and rumor was that it was the frontrunner.

Of course, everywhere we went, we saw someone we knew. Joseph was fawned over and hardly needed any social steering at this point, so I was able to relax.

The September day was sweltering, but by the time the sun began to go down, a taste of autumn touched my senses for the first time this year. I removed my cardigan from my oversized purse and slipped it on. It was sun-warm and felt wonderful against my skin.

We went to the Lion's Club booth for supper, where we both dined on fabulously unhealthy nachos and cokes. We chatted the whole time, laughing a lot, and the time passed really quickly. The whole day seemed to have passed quickly.

"Why Cornhusk?" Joseph asked. "Or is it just the crafts?"

"Corn is what we grow here," I said. "It's what we've always grown. Haven't you seen it?"

"Is that what that tall plant is?"

My mouth fell open. He really was hopeless! Where would he be without me?

He smiled. "I'm joking."

I huffed. "Whatever. We also, yes, have always had a significant craft industry involving corn husks. You saw the Native American booth. And during the Great Depression, everyone started learning how to make toys for their children out of the husks because there wasn't enough money for anything else." There was also a significant corn-moonshine connection in these parts to this day, but Joseph was looking impressed, and I didn't think there was any need to dampen that.

Speaking of moonshine... Our county's top dealer rounded the corner just then. I grabbed Joseph's arm. "Jepp Lewis," I hissed just before dragging him out of the benches and to the left. Looking around desperately, I spotted the Ferris wheel. If we were a hundred feet in the air, Jepp couldn't try to press charges against Mr. Howell's cows. We leapt in.

I realized I was sitting on the same side as Joseph and quickly switched seats. "Where...? Oh, I see him now," Joseph said, eyes wide with delight, sitting back. His face changed. "There's Mateo Rodriguez." He looked across at me.

I smiled, glancing over the side. "Is it?"

"I'll tell him what happened," Joseph said.

I looked at him, about to respond when the carnival employee gruffly commanded me to buckle my seatbelt. For some reason (and through no fault of my own), mine wasn't working, so he shoved me back onto the other side with Joseph and, apparently having entirely lost hope in our intelligence, buckled us himself. "Of all the nerve..." Annoyed, I vented for the next five minutes.

"I don't think he did shove you," Joseph said.

"He shoved me!" I exclaimed.

"I'm just saying there's a difference in a forceful prod and a shove," he responded. His eyes were doing that thing, as though he were goading me. Well, it was working.

The Ferris wheel took us up into the darkened night sky, the multi-colored lights of the fair rides evoking fall and happy memories with my loved ones. My mood mellowed.

"Hey..." Joseph nudged me, inclining his head toward the ground.

I peered over the side of the cart. Below us, over behind the grandstands where the beauty pageant was going on, Tony Tonneau stood talking with Jake Dillon. It was a fairly secluded place, but the Ferris wheel could see everything. Jake took a piece of paper out of his pocket and handed it to Tony, who pocketed it without looking at it. Then they parted ways.

I turned my head back to Joseph. He mouthed a silent *shh*, glancing up at the cart above us. I nodded. We had barely gotten the cart door open and moved away from the crowd when I said, "They are from completely separate socio-economic backgrounds, Joseph. There is absolutely no reason those two men would be talking unless drugs were involved."

"Are you sure you're not generalizing again?"

"Of course I'm generalizing! And I will apologize for it later, but there are strict social lines around here, Joseph. They are completely unspoken, and nobody really thinks about them, but few cross them either. I mean, it's like the spheres don't even know the others exist. And you may say that Hollywood indicates differently, but there is very little chance the high school jock would be best buddies with someone from the fringes, with a history of drug addiction that goes beyond partying to poverty."

"I haven't said anything about Hollywood," Joseph protested, looking baffled.

"Oh, right—that was Mateo. Sorry."

Joseph's jaw tightened. There was a brief pause. "Look, Mississippi, I do think we're onto something here. But we don't have enough to go on, you know. Jake Dillon could have been handing him a number for a good barber."

I gave a long sigh. "Yeah, I know. You're right."

Before I could add anything, I saw the county executive and his husband and knew my next duty. "Here is Mr. Bellenfant. Tell Mr. Nelson you like his beagle: Bailey."

"I've met Bailey, thank you very much," Joseph replied. As they approached, he knelt, greeting Bailey first, which delighted his fathers.

"How are Fritz and Freida?" Mr. Bellenfant said, looking between us.

"Very well," Joseph replied. He explained that he was still trying to ingratiate himself with Freida, which amused them. It *was* amusing.

We talked for a time about the vocal competition that night. Mr. Bellenfant seemed to have the impression that we were dating, even going so far as to apologize for neglecting to invite me to their Independence Day party. I wanted to die, but nothing explicit was said, so I didn't mention it as we passed on. I could hear my mother in my head telling me that a young woman did not walk around with a single man at the Cornhusk Festival without inviting talk.

Just then, I saw Mateo in line for a funnel cake. "Be right back," I said. I dashed over.

He smiled when he saw me. "Mississippi!" Bending, he kissed my cheek.

I looked beside him and saw my hairdresser, Paige Prentiss. She was smiling, her hand on his arm. "Hey, Miss," she said.

I looked back at Mateo. "You move very fast."

"It was a good suggestion," he said, looking sheepish. They both looked a little shy but seemed to be bursting with happiness. I was so glad Mateo wasn't mad at me that I didn't even feel bitter. "Well, you're just two of the sweetest people I know," I said, feeling a bit smug in my role as matchmaker. They both grinned. "Okay, I've got to go. Bye, now."

"Bye!" the called in unison as I turned and hurried away.

I almost ran into Joseph. Steadying me, he looked from me across the twinkle light-illuminated darkness to Mateo, a wrinkle on his brow. He looked back down at me. "He's with someone else?"

"Yes." I looked at him for a moment.

Something subtle shifted in his expression. For once, he couldn't seem to think of a word to say. Just then, Melissa and her husband walked up, and we turned to talk to them. The pageant was over, and it was almost time for the vocal competition—the main event of the night.

And Joseph, as I knew he would, showed excellent vocal skills, handily beating out the public defender, and actually becoming a finalist. And if he mouthed "I hate you" in my direction more than once, we would assume he was joking.

Chapter Twenty-Two

Joseph and I were working on trial scheduling when Mary paged us. Frantically, she said, "Joseph, we have Pearl Fitts on Line One. She says the police are refusing to talk to her, and she is *determined* to raise a fuss and a holler!"

"What is she upset about?" he asked.

"I can't make any *sense* of it. Something to do with obscenity."

Joseph's lips twitched slightly. "All right. Thanks." Keeping it on speaker phone, he pressed the first line and said, "General Cane-Steinem."

"Well, thank heavens. That girl was acting squirrely, and I was afraid she was about to give me the run-around. Let me tell you, this town has gone to pot. When the police won't even respond to a legitimate concern of public indecency—"

"What is your concern, Mrs. Fitts?" Joseph asked.

Keeping my hands on the desk, I leaned in to listen.

"There is a mannequin at the boutique. A *male* mannequin, right there in the window, and it is *pants-less*!"

Joseph's eyes flew to mine. I started coughing, covering a gasp. Joseph pressed the back of his hand to his mouth, obviously not trusting himself.

"Who was that? Is the Whitson girl with you? I hope you are keeping the door to your office properly open."

Our door was firmly closed, and just let Pearl Fitts try to get scheduling accomplished during a full moon week with it open, I say! I was hot under the collar, but Joseph, voice quivering, said, "Of course, Mrs. Fitts. I will call the boutique and express your very valid concerns."

Mollified, the lady said, "Well, it is nice to know there is *someone* in this town with a sense of morality!"

Signing off, Joseph's eyes found mine, his own glimmering wildly.

"Do you... Do you need me to find the number for the boutique?" I asked, voice trembling.

"I'm not calling the boutique," he responded.

The investigation into the murder was back on track, and the police asked Joseph and me to meet them at the empty shirt factory. This was the structure from which Mr. St. John had properly identified the shots to have been fired. The building was a late nineteenth century architectural wonder, but it had been sitting empty for about thirty years.

Our office had a great relationship with the police. However, they never lost a protect-and-serve attitude of respect for us, taking care that we were never endangered when we went out on drug busts and, today, pointing out where we were to safely stand on the old floors while taking the greater risk on themselves.

"I don't know if you can see here, General, but this is where we found the fingerprints I was telling you about last night. I couldn't believe they were still there, or that we missed them the first time. But we came in the afternoon this time, and the light was slanting through the windows differently. We're sending them off to the State, and we'll know soon if they find a match."

I looked at Joseph. Fingerprints. Very 1920s British whodunnit. But this was huge. Or at least, it could be.

"I think," Joseph said, "that it will be imperative that this development is not released to the press. It will need to be kept quiet as long as possible."

The officer nodded. "Any lingering evidence will start to disappear really quickly. This whole building could be burned to the ground."

"Let us know if they find a match," Joseph said, holding the officer's eyes and nodding.

The *Hammondsville Herold* had the story by the next morning.

"Apparently, they had a reporter on the street while the place was being re-swabbed and dusted," Joseph said that evening, entering his living room with two cups of hot chai, one of which he gave to me.

I shook my head, although it *was* a little humorous. "You might *think* you could keep something private in a small town, General Cane-Steinem..." I said reprovingly.

He laughed, sitting down on the sofa in front of the fireplace. We were both still in our dress clothes from work, although Joseph's tie had long since been discarded, as had my heels. The room (and the whole house) was now stunning and cozy. The walls around us were a deep olive, the bookshelves wooden and lined with Joseph's books and Southern art and figurines plucked from around the house. Joseph had lit the wood-burning fireplace since there was a chill but not enough to justify using the heater.

"Who would you place your money on, if you were betting?" he asked, looking at me.

I narrowed my eyes in thought. "Someone who is a crack shot, with deadly aim," I said. "I wouldn't have thought Tony could have gotten a shot off that clean. He was raised in town, after all. But he could have been going to the shooting range."

"We have Virgil Baker's word that he's not caught up in it," Joseph said. "And Britta Buford says he's not violent. My money is on Jake Dillon."

"We shall see, sir," I said. "We shall see."

We got to talking, and I asked him whether he had agreed to do the *Vogue* interview. "I've decided against it," he answered. "I don't want to open a can of worms. Sometimes it's just easier to move on."

I narrowed my eyes at him. "Joseph. You clearly adored your mother. What's the hang-up? What can of worms? The legal battles over her images?"

He was quiet for a moment, as if debating whether to confide, rather like he had done when he had first come to town. Only this time, he didn't hesitate as long. "It's my dad," he confessed.

I lifted my brows. "He wouldn't want you to do the interview?"

He shrugged, sighing. "It's really dark, but... Sometimes I wonder if my mom screwed my dad up."

I lifted my brows. He'd sung nothing but her praises, so this surprised me.

Joseph held my eyes. I wasn't going to ask him to reveal anything personal. I did want him to know that I was capable of keeping his stories to myself, though. I must have conveyed that with my eyes. "When my mom died," he said, "my dad was kind of a wreck, and he'd had a little too much to drink. He said that she had wanted a baby, and so she had decided to do it with someone who would never interfere. Someone too young, with a career planned in New York..." He took a drink of his chai, not meeting my eyes. "He apologized profusely the next morning, telling me that it wasn't true, that I had been unplanned but they had both wanted me. That he had adored her, and always had."

I swallowed. The seed of doubt had clearly never left, however.

He looked at me. "Even though my mom and I had a special bond, my dad finished my raising. We don't live in each other's pockets, but he's always been there for me. My loyalty isn't just to my mom anymore. And if I go worldwide, talking about how much I loved her, how special she was... I don't know, I just don't want him to feel like I have some sort of nostalgia."

"There's nothing wrong with nostalgia," I said. "Your dad said he loved her. Have you talked to him about it? He might tell you to go for it."

He looked at me like this was an unexpected and novel idea. Men. Hopeless. Or maybe he and his dad were just particularly dysfunctional.

"Look, whatever your origin story," I said, smiling with reference to "That Summer," "clearly, your mom wanted you. Clearly, she loved you." I thought of the Gucci shoot. You couldn't fake the adoration the photographer had caught in her eyes.

He nodded. "I know. There was never any doubt of that." He looked at me. "Surely this stuff is easier if your parents were married, right?"

"I don't know..." I said, putting my empty glass aside. "My dad was my person. Same wavelength, and everything. My mom and I had some stuff to work through. We still are."

He looked at me sympathetically. "You miss him. Every day—I know."

"Acutely? The sting fades, I guess," I said philosophically. "It sounds crazy, but the Fourth of July is hard for me. And the Christmas cantata. Every year, I go and sit alone. And all I can think about is how much he loved it at our church when I was growing up."

He nodded, eyes flickering over my face. "And the little stuff, too."

"Yes!" I exclaimed, glad he understood. "Just...not being able to *talk* to him. A hundred times a day when something comes up that I would normally *have* to talk to him about, something funny, something only he would be able to understand. There was a lack of a *person* in my life, someone who got it." *Until...* My spirit seemed to whisper the word to me. I swallowed, setting my chai cup aside and standing. Drawing a hand through my hair, I stood. "I really should be going. It's late. I shouldn't have stayed so long."

He stood, and I could feel his attention on me.

I went over to the ottoman by the long windows, where I had kicked off my heels. Sitting, I began putting them on.

A penetrating sound of glass suddenly invaded the quiet room, deafening.

"Mississippi!" Joseph yelled, reaching for me and dragging me into the floor. In seconds, he was completely covering me. The sound happened again, another window breaking with earsplitting volume.

We heard soft voices and then people running.

"What... Was that a gun?" I asked, voice trembling.

Joseph got off me and then reached to help me up. "I didn't hear a report. Stay back." He walked to the window, where he looked out. "Flashlights disappearing over the hill," he related.

I looked at the shattered glass all over the floor and then a few feet out from the windows, where I saw two rocks wrapped in paper. Pulling a tissue from a canister, I removed the rubber band on one and read. *Back Off.* Swallowing, I moved to the other. *I will kill you.*

Joseph got down beside me. I showed him. "Well," he said, "it would seem we have stepped into a hornet's nest."

I could have slapped him for his calm dispassion. However, this trait of his would prove to be an asset over the course of the night and next day. The sheriff's department was soon swarming Cane House. The first order of business was having paramedics check us, but we hadn't been hit, so we just submitted and waited for the next step. The night was endless. My mother, on the phone, was hysterical. Joseph reassured her while I sat on the library table, kind of shell-shocked. In this conversation, he proved invaluable and surprisingly effective. He even told me that my mother would not be driving out to the house, which proved he was a magician.

"You okay?" he asked.

I nodded. "Yeah. Yeah."

They were wanting to take us into custody for protection, but Joseph didn't want that. He considered the options and the details with them at some distance from where I sat. At some point, I would have to evaluate that he had been willing to die to protect me. That my name as he had yelled it had appeared to be torn from somewhere deep down. But we were friends, and men, like women, had strong protective instincts. Certainly, nothing over the course of the night indicated that he had an interest beyond friendship. He was kind, he checked on me a lot, but he didn't haul me up and kiss me within an inch of my life as the urgency of the situation or the relief of being unharmed would seem to call for. Therefore, best *not* to evaluate it, I decided.

At some point, his sunny mood cracked, and his temper wore a little thin. He was faultlessly polite, but only I saw how difficult it was for him to be so. The sheriff suggested I (and the German shepherds) move temporarily into Cane House. It would be easier to secure the property that way, they said, for the officers who were going to be dispatched to watch over us. This, of all things, seemed to improve Joseph's mood.

"Pearl Fitts is going to kill us," I said.

The officers, who knew Pearl well, laughed with us and promised that they would assure the lady that an officer would be present at all times.

Our protection officer escorted us into town the next morning. Joseph and I got into the white Tahoe for the short ride. All of us were quiet, our minds obviously reeling with the import of what had happened. The deputy mumbled something about there being no need for protection officers with Freida on the premises.

Yes, it had been a near thing when she had walked out of my acquisitioned bedroom to find a man she had never met in Joseph's kitchen. But I had apologized, and *no one* had been injured. A little nip was not the same thing as a bite. If Freida had really been intent on showing her feelings, we would have had to have called an ambulance. So I expected no more moaning.

It was hard to get back to business as usual, but I did find filing somewhat soothing. Mary, Melissa, and Paul were worried, but, while solicitous, they did not force the issue on talking about it, seeming to understand that there was comfort in routines.

But by noon that day, it was confirmed that we *had* stepped into a hornet's nest. Joseph came out of his office, having just gotten off the phone. We all waited, looking at him. "Jake Dillon's fingerprints were a match at the shirt factory."

Warrants were quickly obtained, and Joseph and I were out at Jake Dillon's small farm when the arrest was made. As his chickens squawked and ran at random in the yard, Jake yelled that they had *nothing* on him. His wife, a once-pretty woman, screamed too, yelling that anyone could have gone into that old building at any time, and that Jake had been looking for reclaimed lumber. A likely story.

I didn't have any doubt that Jake had killed Reynolds Buford. But I did have doubt that he was at the bottom of the whole thing. There was a leader at the head of this organization, and it wasn't Jake. He was too poor and too addicted to be the one.

I also didn't doubt now that Jake's wife had also succumbed to an addiction. Her eyes appeared huge in her head, her arms bone-thin, her teeth gone, her skin covered with sores. A glance inside the house, which the police had a warrant to search, revealed even more horrors.

The five beautiful children were living in utter squalor and filth. Needles and drug paraphernalia covered the counter, the kitchen and living room hadn't been cleaned in...I couldn't even guess. The children were thin and dirty, and they looked like if they had just one more uncertainty in their lives they would crack.

It was too much. Too pitiful. Too horrible. I felt traumatized by their plight. It put a lot of things into perspective really quickly. Blinking away tears, I stepped away from the house, crossing my arms as if to hug myself. Joseph, however, didn't lose his composure even for a minute. He just picked up his phone, called Mary, and said, "Hey. We need to get DCS out here."

By the time the children were taken away, headed for foster care for the near future, I felt just about flattened. The sound of their mother screaming as they were driven away would haunt my dreams. And in that moment, I *hated* heroin.

Joseph was like a rock, making plans here, signing there, fielding calls... I don't know how he did it, because I was just at my wits' end.

Blinking away tears that wouldn't seem to go away, I accepted our officer's offer to be driven out to Cane House to check on Fritz and Frieda. I changed clothes and leashed the dogs. I had to go back into town, since I had left my purse and laptop at the office. And I wanted my babies with me. The officer, who saw this kind of thing every day, seemed to take pity on me and agreed even to allow his persecutor (Frieda) to go.

We were into October now, and evening shadows were just beginning to fall as I went into the office, the dogs walking circumspectly beside me. Joseph was still here, I knew, because I had seen an officer outside waiting on him. I picked up my purse and walked back to his office.

He was sitting on the floor against the wall, his coat off, his eyes staring into the distance, his cheeks wet with tears. My heart twisted. He looked up, seeing me, and turned his face away, wiping his cheeks.

I walked over to him, getting down beside him. We sat silently in a spirit of painful reverence. "Do you know," he said after a time, "the case worker said it's not even that uncommon."

I swallowed. We had both known this, of course. Seeing it was different. I didn't know what to say. He didn't know what to say. And so we just sat.

The dogs had been making a sweep of the premises, but Freida stopped at the door, her head tilting when she saw Joseph. Then she walked forward. I sat up, on the alert. "Freida!" I said when she walked right toward him. But soon, she was licking his face, as if he were her pup and she was making him better.

Joseph's lips parted. "Oh, Freida," he said, looking completely moved. He rubbed her scruff. He rasped, "Good girl. Yes, you're such a good girl."

I smiled through my tears. Trust the dogs to turn a fragile situation into something completely heartwarming. And I was so proud, I beamed like a pageant mom. But there *were* tears. My girl had accepted Joseph. There would be no going back for her now. And that would make it all the more possible for me to leave at the appointed time.

Chapter Twenty-Three

You may be thinking that I should have quit at this juncture. You would probably be right. I mean, how much was one person really supposed to take? Only so much could be expected in the line of duty. But, despite a few metaphorical bruises, my mental health was sound, my physical health was untouched, and the same gritty ancestry that had made it possible for me to take Hetty Gibson out if necessary made me dig in my heels and declare that I would be damned if I abandoned ship now.

Of course, my mother instantly jumped on me for cussing, and at the Sunday dinner table, no less. My womenfolk, naturally, were concerned, but I reminded them that with Halloween just around the corner, I only had two months left to go. I might stay over just a little past that if necessary to get to the bottom of the whole situation. After all, I would have until the following summer to apply for colleges and decide what to do.

Jake Dillon's house had been searched, and there were some red and black paint cans found as well as a drawing where he had practiced the charming mural left on the District Attorney's office wall. So...that was solved. Idiot.

He was definitely someone's puppet, and tightly in their clutches. The only plausible reason for this was that he was desperate for drugs to feed his addiction, and he had no money. But the fact remained that there was something big enough going on that people were willing to threaten us, to paint nasty things on buildings, to kill.

My mom got up and went into the kitchen to finish up the pie for our dessert. My grandma patted my wrist. "Grandma, I've got too many irons in the fire," I said.

"Well now, let's talk about those irons," she replied. "One would be the psychos on the loose trying to kill you and the people you work with."

I nodded. "It's...scary. Enough to give you a severe case of paranoia." I swallowed. "And...I'm worried about starting my life over again after I leave."

"You were destined for great things," she said confidently. "You're going to have to take the risk and go to fashion school. Or at least get a really good internship."

I smiled, loving her dark blue eyes, her rounded face and perfectly curled hair. There was wisdom in those eyes—hard-won wisdom. But my smile went a bit misty.

"You're afraid you're falling behind," she said.

I bit my lip, striving to keep my eyes from filling with tears. "Everyone my age, and even many significantly younger, is in a relationship. Most have kids. I want kids.

But it hasn't happened for me. And I'm not sure it ever will." Grandma patted my hand, and I wiped a tear that spilled over. "The thing about someone unmarried at my age wanting kids...I don't get sympathy for it. I get blame. *That's your life choices! Selfishness!*"

"You're young," Grandma said soothingly. "Plenty of time. And since when have you cared what people said?"

"I know. It's just...all the missed opportunities. I will never be a mom in my twenties. The narrowing window."

"Do you regret it?"

"I mean—"

"No, no, no," Grandma said, suddenly lit up with fire. "Do you regret it? Becoming the woman you have become? Taking the time you have taken? At the end of the day, would you go back and change it?"

I sat for a long moment. "No. I wouldn't."

"Well, then. I think that says it all, sugar lump. It's other women's story. But it's not yours. And there's no use crying over having been who you are. You couldn't change that even if you tried, and I don't know why you would want to. Not everything in life is a plot point leading up to your romance story, you know. There's a whole lot more to life than that, and if somebody's told you any different, they're flat lying."

My lip trembling, I nodded. As a tear spilled over, running down my face, my grandma stroked it away. "It's going to be just fine. *Everything* will be just fine. God has *promised* me this, Mississippi. Do you think He's going to leave an old woman wondering about the only granddaughter she has? No! *Blessed is she who has believed that the Lord would fulfill his promises to her!*" she quoted. "And I need all the blessings I can get, so I don't have any choice *but* to believe."

I laughed, wiping my eyes and reaching for a hug. "Thank you," I whispered. "Thank you. But greatness will have to wait. Right now, we've got to get through this storm."

Taking a breath, she paused for a moment, obviously feeling the weight of my responsibilities, too. Patting my back, she said sagely, "How do you eat a whale?"

I choked on a laugh and repeated the childhood phrase with her: "One bite at a time."

I got out of the officer's Tahoe at Cane House and told him I was going to take a walk. He said this would be fine as long as I didn't leave the property. I had changed out of my Sunday clothes before going over to my mom's for lunch, and my boots crunched over the grass, which was turning brown with the inevitable change of seasons.

Crossing my arms and snuggling into my cream, cable-knit sweater, I headed out toward the Cane family cemetery. It had been a year since Henry's death. My mom had been in charge of laying flowers on her church's vestibule this Sunday, so she had given me some beautiful autumnal blooms from her extras to lay on his grave.

I missed him. There was no getting around that. I probably always would. And I couldn't believe he had been gone a year. I felt guilty that time marched on so ruthlessly. That we had managed so well without him. But we hadn't really. He had left a hole that couldn't be filled. It was just that we had been competent without him. And Henry definitely would have wanted that.

I looked up and saw Joseph standing over the grave. His people were buried here, even his mother. That was why I couldn't imagine him ever selling the place.

I opened the heavy iron gate, and it made a heavy scrape. Slipping through, I went to stand by him. He looked at me, and then back at the stone. *Beloved Husband. Father. Grandfather. Friend.* Joseph had included the last for me, I was certain. I'm not sure why I had ever thought he could be a prick.

Kneeling, I laid my flowers beside Joseph's.

"They say the first year is the hardest," I said. "And I know this one was especially hard." *Losing this last member of the Cane family besides you,* I thought. Losing his girlfriend. Moving. Everything.

"Ah, Mississippi. You know that a good portion of grief is guilt," he said with ruthless honesty. "I had always meant to be here for him."

I bit my lip. "You were right where he wanted you to be: living your life."

He looked down at me, giving me a small, sad smile. As his eyes lingered, he did appear touched. We looked back at the headstone, letting the moment soak over us, marking a milestone. *Goodbye, Henry.*

Jake Dillon refused to talk. This may have been upon the sound advice of his lawyer. It was also likely because Joseph couldn't offer him a very good plea deal given that he had, you know, *killed a man*. The Feds were considering charging Jake with a hate crime for the painting as well. If they did, Joseph would have to conflict out from the whole thing since he was the victim.

"I'm thinking about doing it anyway," he said on Monday morning. "There's just so much evidence against him that he's the one making the threats against us that I think I probably need to step aside."

I agreed that it would be best. "Do what you have to do, and get a different prosecutor on it, then."

He nodded, turning to his computer for the necessary forms.

"But I don't want you to hand over this drug thing," I said. "I mean...is it a conflict?"

He shook his head. "No one has been charged, and there's nothing substantive to link Jake to any larger ring yet."

I nodded once. "Good. Because we're going to bust them."

This seemed to startle Joseph, but I took off to go take care of some business with the clerks' offices. I was gone for a while and returned right as Jepp Lewis swung by. Just my luck.

"You remember when I said there was more than one way to skin a cat?" Jepp asked, settled into the chair across from Joseph's desk.

"I do," Joseph said, eyes alight. "I very much do."

"Well, I've been thinking that we can get Howell for parking his camper in his driveway. You might not think it, being out in the country like we are, but we're under restrictive covenants."

"Jepp, again, that is a property law matter. Out of curiosity, why *won't* you sue Mr. Howell? You could take care of the sewage lines and the camper all in one," Joseph said.

"Well, the thing is, I want him to go to jail," Mr. Lewis said simply.

Joseph looked highly charmed, but I wanted to toss the man out on his rear. "We can't just lock people up, Jepp!" I exploded.

"Aw, I know. But a man like that *needs* to be in jail. Piece of shit. Not doing anybody any good. His moonshining has really gotten into my legal operation. And I *do* run a legal operation—"

I watched the growing wonder, amazement, and wrath on Joseph's face. "Jepp!" he exclaimed. "Do you mean to tell me Dan Howell is a *moonshiner*?"

"Well, yes."

"You've been in my office a dozen times in under a year, begging me to have the man arrested, and you never thought to tell me that he was *illegally manufacturing alcohol*?"

Jepp, too, looked struck. "Well, no."

Joseph looked too astounded to speak. So I spoke for him. "Mr. Cane-Steinem will need you to go down to the sheriff's office and give a statement. They will decide whether to take it from there."

Jepp, lips downturned, nodded. "All right. Yep. All right. This could work. It will, Lord willing and the creeks don't rise."

As soon as he was out the door, Joseph buried his head in his hands, shoulders shaking when no other emotion would suffice. "Mississippi! Why do you think he never told us?"

"I *told* you that the day you started: it's because Jepp's moonshine operation is anything *but* legal. He finally admitted it today: it's not so much the *easement* encroaching, as Dan's *operation* encroaching on Jepp's! *That's* why he's wanted the man arrested right from the beginning!"

Chapter Twenty-Four

We plunged straight toward Thanksgiving. Pearl Fitts called the police over her neighbor's blow-up turkey, but other than that, we brushed through the run-up to the holiday season fairly easily. The search for Jake Dillon's alleged motive was still underway, so in the meantime we just did our jobs.

Our protection officers had been dispensed with, and I was back home at the cottage. Not much had changed while I was there. I had been too busy to notice I was technically living at Cane House. But at least everything was a lot more convenient now I was home. I could drive myself and I didn't have to make endless trips to the cottage to get stuff I had forgotten.

Imani had invited me over the day after Thanksgiving for "Friendsgiving," and I, proving there was something of a housewife in me after all, pulled a delicious-smelling pumpkin pie from my oven.

Removing my apron, I sat down to pull my Ralph Lauren boots over my jeans. Slipping on my quilted riding jacket, I blew a kiss to Fritz and Freida and headed out.

Imani had made it sound as though she would be having numerous people over to her house. I thought about it as I pulled in. She had also, on another occasion, made it sound as though I would be the only guest. Still confused on that score, I reached for my pie and got out.

I knocked, and Marcus answered. I swooped him up, kissed his cheek, and took him into Imani's huge and gorgeous kitchen. And saw Joseph Cane-Steinem. He held my eyes for a moment, looking equally surprised.

I looked around. We were literally the only two people there besides the Reeds.

While Mitchell and Joseph were talking about the merits of pumpkin pie over sweet potato pie, I hissed to Imani over by the stove, "What is going on here?"

"I need to observe," she said.

"What—?"

"We never got to thank Joseph for helping out when Grandpa DeShawn had his heart attack," Imani said for the benefit of the room, silencing me.

I gave her the stink eye, certain she was up to something.

"How *is* your dad?" I asked Mitchell.

"Almost completely recovered," he answered, smiling. Well, that was something to be truly thankful for today, then. Mitchell did give thanks as he said the blessing, for that and for our safety throughout the investigation.

"So Joseph, are you going home for Hanukkah?" Imani asked, eyeing him as she took a bite of her greens.

He shook his head. "I can't go anywhere until... Well, we have some stuff to wrap up at the office." I knew he was talking about the investigation, but of course, no one outside the office could know how big the problem we thought we were dealing with was. "I missed Yom Kippur, in September, too."

"I told you we could have held down the fort then," I scolded gently.

Beside me, Joseph said, "I know. I'll make it next year." He gave me a smile. I met it, until I saw Imani looking at me, lifting a significant brow.

Mitchell asked for more clarification on Yom Kippur, the holiest day of the year for Jews. I was glad he did so, because my knowledge was rudimentary, and I never got to see Joseph talk about his faith. He explained the rituals of purification and forgiveness, fasting and prayer, very eloquently.

Imani then asked Joseph to explain Hanukkah to the boys, which he did. I was pleased with her for giving him the opportunity. To my knowledge, there weren't any other Jewish people in Hammondsville, and I would imagine that felt lonely.

DeShawn, who was just old enough to know this was all very different, said, "You didn't have Santa Claus?"

Joseph smiled. "Yes, I did. Don't worry. He came to Paris."

Joseph met my smile across the table.

"Oh, my gosh," Imani said. "I completely forgot you grew up in Paris. Okay. We're planning a trip. Give me the details..."

We settled in for a nice talk on all things France, and Joseph became very relaxed and animated, the life of the party, although not in a domineering way. He encouraged me to talk about my love of all things British, enquired more deeply into mine and Imani's obsession with the Royal Family, and asked for our takes on the latest drama. And believe me, we had takes. We could talk for *days.* Mitchell groaned, foreseeing ahead his evening's doom, but we ignored him and dove happily in.

After my pie was devoured, we went into the living room, where Mitchell and the boys showed Joseph the ins and outs of an intricate, manly boardgame they had been playing.

"Well, aren't you an excellent hostess," I said as Imani and I settled across the room.

"I am," she agreed. The Corgis nestled in beside us, and with the fire going, it was a toasty, snug Thanksgiving scene.

"Now, *what* are you doing?" I whispered.

Imani glanced at me. "I'm not sure I'm taking questions," she answered.

"Imani!" I hissed. "You are not the Queen! You cannot refuse to take questions!"

"I am queen of this house," she countered.

I sent her a withering look. She looked from Joseph to me, and back again. "I have my purposes," she said. "And that is all I am willing to say."

"Honey, I'm going to need you to invite the Cane-Steinem boy to Christmas at Grandma's."

My mom, of course, didn't say *hello* as I answered the phone on the Saturday after Thanksgiving. "Mom. I'm still in a turkey coma. Can you give me some time to—"

"There is no time. Christmas is upon us. Thanksgiving is behind us. The planning begins today." It was too early for dramatic language, but my mom hadn't gotten the memo. "Honey, I'm just saying, I heard Pearl Fitts say something about inviting him. Do you want him to have to spend Christmas at that morgue?"

I sighed.

"Or maybe you would prefer Hetty Gibson to have him over now that she's kicked Jason out?"

"No," I said, sitting up in bed. "Fine, I'll invite him."

"Good. And don't worry about the menu. We're all kosher, all the way, baby. And I don't think he's *opposed* to Christmas, do you? What I mean is, I don't need to trim back the Christmas explosion, do I?"

Asking my mom to tone down Christmas would be like asking a bird to clip its wings. "I don't think so. If he feels uncomfortable, he just won't accept the invitation."

"Right. Just get to him *fast*."

As it happened, the opportunity presented itself soon. I had just gotten dressed when he knocked on the cottage door.

He smiled, his eyes bright, his grin boyish. "Just dropping by to advance my cause with Frieda. Do you think she would like to take a walk?"

"You're not getting out of here without taking Fritz too, just to warn you," I said. Fritz was already standing in the kitchen with his leash in his mouth.

Freida was persuaded, after wavering, to join them. I watched Joseph set off with the dogs he technically owned and felt a pang.

I was still their favorite person, but they would be okay. My child support check had been included with my paycheck for the month. Would that be the last one? Did we need to go ahead and smooth the transition for them over to Cane House? Or, if the investigation spilled over into January, would he let them stay with me one more month?

I swallowed, wiping away tears. This was silly. *I* was being silly. There was no way I could afford two massive dogs, much less take care of them, if I was going to school. I would be fine. I just had to convince my heart, and all would be well.

Crap! I forgot to tell Joseph about Christmas. If Pearl got to him on his cellphone out there before I could, my mom would kill me. I looked out the window and, seeing a promising game of Stick underway, I slipped on my boots and walked to them.

It had been raining a lot recently, and I made a mental note to be careful going down the hill...which I promptly forgot. Hitting a patch of mud, I slid, squeaking, and finally came to a halt on my rump. But that was only after I had slid a good three feet.

"Mississippi!" Joseph was at my side. "Are you hurt?"

He looked me over, trying to help me up, but my hands, covered in mud, kept slipping out of his. "Only my dignity," I said austerely. His eyes were dancing by now. "What?" I demanded.

He suppressed a laugh. "You have a very long name to yell in alarm."

"Well, that," I said, "is not my fault!"

His laughter bubbled over as he tried, and failed, to help me up again.

Sending him a reproachful look, I said, "You would laugh at me!? The mother of your German shepherds!"

"Very bad," he agreed, foregoing my hands and hauling me up by my waist. "There!"

I rolled my eyes, trying to wipe my hands against each other to clean them, a hopeless endeavor. "And here I was coming to invite you to *Christmas*," I said bitterly.

His eyes twinkled. "I find falls humorous. I can't help it. I *did* ask if you were okay! Am I uninvited?" He looked like a little boy again, caught for being naughty but sufficiently convinced of his charms to be sure he could get out of it.

"Yes, you are uninvited!" I said. "Or you would be, if the invitation came from me. Unfortunately, it comes from my mother." I cracked and gave a smile. "And she won't take no for an answer."

He met my smile. "Well, then, with compliments to your mother, I accept."

I nodded, trying to suppress my smile. "Good. But you're taking care of those heathens the rest of the day as punishment for laughing."

Holding up his hands, he agreed to it hastily. And when he brought the dogs back to me that night, he did ask with earnest eyes whether I had any injuries. So I decided to forgive him.

Chapter Twenty-Five

Joseph kept the dogs on Sunday so I could go to church. When I returned, I walked over as soon as I parked my car and knocked on the door. He let me in, putting a finger over his lips, like one might if a baby was asleep. However, it was two German shepherds snuggled up on the rug in front of the fireplace. Their proud father looked on with self-satisfaction. We had come a long way, indeed.

Going into the library, he said, "About Christmas... I just got word this morning that one of my friends is going to be able to come down for a visit. He has a few days off work. I know it's short notice to add someone else to the list for the dinner, so we will probably need to back out."

"Oh, no! No, no, my mom and grandma make enough food to feed an army!"

"Are you sure?"

"Yes, of course. It'll be nothing just to add another chair to the table," I answered.

He nodded. "We'll come, then. He's Muslim," he said. "Just thought that might be relevant information."

I nodded slowly. Then nodded again, foreseeing multiple potential family disasters ahead in the future. "Okay." I drew a breath. "Okay." I nodded. "I need to begin a series of *very specific* conversations with my mother and grandmother," I said, in emergency mode. I nodded shortly. "Today. This begins today."

Joseph looked like he was suppressing a laugh. "They're fine."

"Today," I reiterated, firmly. "Fritz, Freida, come with me," I commanded, snapping my fingers.

Joseph's dancing eyes followed me out as I departed.

"Honey, I'm out shopping for groceries. What do you need?"

Oh, sure, the *one* time I instigated a phone call with my mother I was inconveniencing her. "Mom, Joseph is bringing a friend."

"A *lady* friend?" she demanded.

"A gentleman friend. From New York."

"Oh, how nice. I'm putting an extra box of macaroni in the buggy now."

"Mom, he's Muslim."

She said, "Okay, so we'll need to go halal as well as kosher." Without missing a beat.

I blinked. "Um...yeah. Yeah."

"I work for an airline, Miss. Did you think you were going to throw me?" I heard satisfaction in her voice.

In fairness, I tended to forget the broad exposure to various cultures she received in her job. I had never had any doubt she would be anything but respectful to anyone who sat down at her dinner table, however. "No. No. But, Mom, I'm going to need you to tell Grandma to choose her words *very* wisely."

"That is probably a good thought. Let's buzz her in."

And just like that, I was on a three-way call, listening to my mother and grandmother argue over what was acceptable for Muslims to eat. Which, of course, was the crux of the matter for any Southern hostess; serving anything offensive would be the ultimate embarrassment. "Is anyone listening to me?" I demanded.

"No," my grandma admitted.

"Well, listen up. I've had another thought: Grandma, I think there's no need for Joseph to know the name of your cat."

"Otto Frank Smith?" she demanded.

"Yes," I said firmly.

"Well, why on earth? He was the sole survivor of his litter, just like Otto Frank was the sole survivor—"

"Of the Frank family," I agreed. "Yes."

"It is an honor! That cat is a member of this family!"

"Is anyone following me here?" I asked, a little hysterically.

"Well, I can't say that I am," my grandma answered tartly. "You know *The Diary of a Young Girl* is my favorite book of all time."

"No one can see that it might be a little... For someone who actually had family members...?"

My grandma sighed. "Well, I guess I can see that. What the heck are we supposed to call him, though? Joe?"

"Yes, Mama, everyone's going to believe your cat's named Joe," my mother said sarcastically.

"We'll call him Kitty and tell everyone you have no imagination," I said flatly. "That's sorted. Okay. Does anyone have anything they need to say?"

"Honey, you called me," my grandmother said.

I pressed my lips together and closed my eyes. "Good. See y'all at Christmas." If we made it there.

"Dan Howell is about to be arrested." I dropped this news on the office with the smug satisfaction of being the first to know. I removed my gloves, but nevertheless had to blow on my fingers to warm them up after the short walk from the courthouse.

"They have enough on him?" Paul asked, looking up from his desk and pushing his glasses up.

"Yep, they've confirmed moonshining based on some sales they had tracked down. Jepp Lewis will be rubbing his hands together in glee," I said.

"Do they have a search warrant for his place? I would be interested in seeing the operation," Joseph said.

"They're working on it. They said they would call us," I answered, sitting down at my desk. "They think they'll make the arrest in the next few days."

I finished up everything that needed addressing before the holidays and left work at five o'clock. It was already dark then, and that really was the pits, since it had been dark when

I had left for work, too. I was like a bat who never saw daylight these days.

On the way home, my mom called me. “Honey, I need to finalize the menu. You’re bringing the coconut cake?”

“Yes. Getting the ingredients tomorrow.”

“Okay. Well, I had thought I might email that Muslim girl from that British baking show that you made me watch—that show I thought I would hate because it looked boring, but it wasn’t?”

“Mom, you can’t email Nadiya Hussain,” I said.

“Why on earth not?”

“Because she’s *famous*!” I exclaimed.

“Honestly, the timidity of your generation. Bunch of chickens.”

“Just don’t email her, okay?”

“Well, I already did,” she said. “*And* she emailed me back. I always thought she was a nice girl.”

My jaw dropped. I was utterly speechless.

“She gave me some recipes for keeping things halal *and* kosher, and she was just the sweetest thing, telling me she would like to try my Southern cooking sometime!”

I blinked. Pictured the BBC cameras out at my mom’s bungalow. A cooking match made in heaven that started a worldwide obsession. You may think I’m crazy, but you don’t know my mother. It could happen.

There was nothing she would not do, no length to which she would not go, to ensure guests walked away from her table declaring the meal to be the best one they had ever had. And if that led her to be crazy, and to make me crazy, from time to time, that was just a cross I was going to have to bear.

It was a week before Christmas, and it was freezing outside. I got out of my car and made my way toward the church. Snowflakes were randomly falling, and the downtown looked surprisingly...charming. New lampposts lined the streets with wreaths on them, the sidewalks were in decent shape, and the storefronts, which had gotten a fresh coat of paint, seemed to be mostly occupied. When had that happened?

The bells were peeling, announcing our candlelight service and joint cantata with the African Methodist Episcopal Church, and it was delightful. Families were walking together. Couples holding hands, moms tucking kids into their sides...

I did feel a pinch of loneliness, I'm not going to lie. It was very rare, but here it was.

I waved at some of Imani's friends from her church as I entered the foyer. They were in choir robes which matched our church's, and both choirs were lining up. My pastor and Pastor St. John took my hand as I crossed the threshold. One of our ushers gave me a candle and a program, and I thanked him.

Slipping into the sanctuary, I went to my usual pew and opened the door. It squeaked and clicked shut, and I flipped through the program. It was going to be great. My dad would have loved it. I bit my lip, trying to see through suddenly moist eyelashes.

The choir walked down the aisle toward the front. Just in time. I brought my head up and watched them, settling in as their pure, sweet voices began to sing of Jesus's birth. "O Little Town of Bethlehem" had never sounded so angelic.

They had been up there about five minutes when I heard something and looked beside me. Joseph stood outside the pew, smiling at me. Lips parting, I met his eyes, held them, then opened the door and slid in for him to take a seat.

An usher brought him a candle, and he took it, nodding his thanks. I smiled at him, standing as it was time for the congregation to sing along. We joined in song, and I looked back at the choir, still smiling.

"Okay, kids, I'm going to need you not to destroy anything," I said the next day, looking at the German shepherds with firmness. "I have to go to the grocery store, and I am going to leave you out in the house. Do not make me regret my choice." After looking them both in the eye, I left, going out to my car.

As I passed Cane House, I saw Joseph's Jeep and his friend's rental SUV. I had seen them go to and from the cars a few times, but we hadn't been introduced. My impression was of a tall, handsome person who seemed to be very at ease with Joseph. I was glad he had someone here. He had made a lot of friends in Hammondsville, and the effort was less and less, but everyone needed some people with whom absolutely no effort was necessary.

The ride into town was marked by an occasional truck with deer antlers, trailer parks with blow-up Santas, and the odd car with a live Christmas tree strapped on top.

I got everything I needed (although I almost had to fight a woman over the last coconut), and took my buggy out to the car. While I was loading everything in the trunk, I looked a few cars down and saw Tony Tonneau next to his Range Rover on the phone. He had stopped and was listening intensely to whoever was on the other end.

I regarded him, this ex-boyfriend of Britta Buford, this apparently upstanding citizen that even Virgil Baker was willing to go to bat for, this incredibly handsome, popular kid of my youth.

The man who had Britta's email, who had handed Jake Dillon a note at the Cornhusk Festival, who had been caught with drugs last year. Something still didn't add up for me. I looked at his vehicle. Expensive. His clothes. Expensive. But then, that was nothing new.

"Are you serious?" I heard him say under his breath, almost in a whisper.

Changing course, he decided against going into the store, and swung back into the Range Rover. And then he tore out of there, as my grandma would say, like a bat out of Georgia.

I debated a minute, and then, closing my trunk, I dialed Joseph.

He answered. "Mississippi? Is everything okay?"

"Is there anything new on Jake Dillon, Joseph? Has he spilled the beans on his fellow criminals, or something?"

"Not to my knowledge. Why?"

"I'm pretty sure Tony Tonneau just got bad news that lit a fire under him."

"Where are you?"

"At the grocery store, in the parking lot."

"I know you're not standing outside your car talking to me about this where anyone might overhear you. Because that would be endangering yourself, which you promised me—"

"Relax, there's no one around. They're all in there fighting over the honey glazed hams." Which we would certainly *not* be having.

"I'm feeling paranoid now. Get in your car and come home. If something's shaking up, I don't want anyone to think you're suspicious. We've already been targeted, Mississippi. This is no time to let our guard down." He was being bossy, but I heard genuine concern, maybe with an edge to it, in his voice.

"All right. But he *could* have just gotten bad news about a family member or something."

"That's the way it always is with him," he agreed.

I shut my car door, drawing a deep breath. "Well, sorry to bother you—"

"You're not."

A long pause.

"I'll see you and Ahmad at Grandma's."

I could feel the smile return to his voice. "See you then."

Chapter Twenty-Six

I was a nervous wreck as our festivities got underway. This was not helped by the fact that Joseph and his friend had barely walked through the door when my mother pronounced them both to be "lookers" and our household to be blessed by their handsome faces. Joseph's eyes had twinkled, and he had kissed my mom's cheeks charmingly in the French way, but it was enough to make me consider finding my mom's cooking wine and guzzling it.

I had a feeling I would need all of my faculties, however. "Miss, what on earth?" my mom hissed at me as she came in the kitchen. "You're a ball of tension!"

"Mom, Grandma just asked Ahmad where his people were from!"

"And now they're having a nice conversation about Jordan," she said. *She* was in an excellent mood, looking like Mrs. Claus in a red apron.

I pressed my lips together. "I accidentally told Ahmad the cat's name is Joe."

My mom gave me an astonished look. "You are spiraling! Take a breath and drink some tea." She dusted off her hands. "That Joseph! Such a charmer!" Without clarifying, she swept out, a bowl of something I had never seen her cook before (but which looked delicious) in her hands, destined for the table.

In fact, the whole spread was *magnificent*. So colorful, flavorful, and, apparently, appropriate, that Joseph and his friend gave exclamations of delight throughout the entire meal and went back for seconds. No hostess could ask for more, and my mother's good mood was sealed for the night.

"Where is Joe?" Ahmad asked. He was an animal lover. He had a female Yorkie which had come all the way on the plane with him and of whom Frieda was not fond. He had already showed my grandma pictures. "He is a beautiful cat."

"Um, I'm not sure," I said, leaning out. Drat the cat, if he didn't mosey into the kitchen just then.

"Joe!" Ahmad called.

Joe, obviously, did not come to us, having never heard the name before. After a brief cruise around the counter, he departed. "Shy," I said.

"Ah, yes." Ahmad smiled at me. "The famous Mississippi Whitson."

I lifted my eyebrows. What were we talking about? As his words settled in, I felt myself flush. "Famous?"

Not replying to that, he said, "You wish to be a designer. This makes Joseph very happy."

Now I flushed deeper. Had...Joseph talked to his friend about me? "We...talk about his mother sometimes. I think that is very welcome to him."

Ahmad would only smile enigmatically.

"The vases?" I heard my grandma say, looking across the open floor plan to the mantle in the living room. Ahmad and I joined back into this conversation. "Yes, they *are* Dutch! Antiques out of New York, I mean. Cost my husband an arm and a leg. He bought them for our first anniversary."

Grandma got to talking about my grandfather, which Joseph encouraged her to do. I was glad. It was hard, but we always tried to mention my dad and grandpa at Christmas, to keep their memory alive.

"Crazy man," my grandma said fondly, dabbing her eyes. "I always told him we could have afforded another child if he hadn't bought those vases!"

I smiled. "But then I might not be your one and only granddaughter, Grandma," I said, reaching for her hand.

"Well, that is true." She squeezed my hand and released it. "Now, Ahmad, tell us about your family. No, tell us how you and Joseph became friends, and then tell us about your family."

He smiled. "In college," he answered. "Intramural sports, and later roommates." And then he set about answering his second directive.

He was patient and kind, and he looked touched when my grandma handed both him and Joseph their own stockings full of delightful stuffers. We went around opening each of ours. Christmas music played on my grandma's old record player.

Ahmad and I happened to be sitting on the couch across from everyone. We watched my mom show Joseph how to spin an old-fashioned top he had gotten. I was beginning to question whether I had been replaced altogether.

"She was a disaster," Ahmad said in a philosophical spirit. I looked at him. He had the habit of starting a conversation in the middle of a conversation. "Well, there was nothing wrong with Rachel. They were a disaster *together.* Not at first. Just on the end. I am friends with both. I was nearly made insane."

I opened my mouth to speak, but he continued, "And you, Mississippi? You are going to college, I believe?"

"Yes, next year." I tried to keep up. I told him about my plans, and he told me about his job in finance. He worked in a skyscraper that would probably give me a nosebleed just by looking at it. I told him I had never made it to New York yet, and he filled me in on all that I should do if I got to go.

My mom and grandma looked truly happy. They were laughing more freely than I had heard since my dad had died, and they were *utterly* charming. Even my coconut cake was perfect, the precise combination of sweet and buttery.

Otto was the only distraction, occasionally chewing the lights, causing my grandma to have to swat him away so we didn't have a *Christmas Vacation* moment. I swear she nearly said his name a dozen times.

And then, out of the corner of my eye, I caught the cat climbing the mantle. Whipping my head around, I saw him eyeing the sacred anniversary vases. I said, "No!" He stopped walking, glancing at us furtively. My mom, grandma, and I were all frozen where we sat, trying not to move, lest the cat do so. And then, the little turd lifted his paw and extended it right toward one of the porcelain vases.

We all three jumped up, extending our hands and screaming, "Otto Frank!"

He stopped, responding to his name as he always did. I covered my mouth, stifling a gasp. We were all silent for a second.

"Well, I didn't *think* his name was Joe!" Joseph said genially, as if he were delighted to have a mystery solved.

Mortified, with my pride hanging by the veriest threads, I nonetheless gathered myself to make evening farewells in my grandma's little foyer. I could hear my mom and grandma explaining to Ahmad how to make sweet tea, which he, having tried, now feared he could not live without. Which, obviously, was a legitimate problem.

Joseph's eyes smiling, he looked from them down at me. "Will you thank them for me? I did, but tell them how grateful I am. I can't imagine the hours that went into the meal. It was perfect."

"It was their pleasure. There really is nothing they would prefer to making people happy at their tables." I looked over at them. "But it's not really about the food, at bottom. It's the love."

His smile was warm and reminiscent. "My mom was the same way. You can take the woman out of the South, but..."

I met his smile.

He handed me a box, which I quickly realized was a present. "You didn't have to do that," I said, slipping the bow off.

He watched me. It was heavy, and I opened it to find coasters with Buckingham Palace soldiers on them. I gasped. "Oh my gosh! I love them!"

"I saw them in Nashville during the County Attorneys' Conference. Couldn't resist."

I gave a little laugh, feeling warm inside. I looked up, meeting his blue eyes. "Thank you."

"You're welcome," he said gently.

Ahmad was ready by then, and I stepped back, letting them pass. Closing the door behind them, I saw snowflakes in the glow of the exterior light. I bit my lip, holding my coasters against my chest. I have to say, it was a good evening, and it had gone quite successfully, our kosher, halal Christmas.

Chapter Twenty-Seven

"Hey, Mississippi, did you hear that arrest was made—Dan Howell?" Melissa asked on our first day back.

"When?" I questioned, handing her the copies I had made for her.

"Two days before Christmas," she said.

"Ah. I was fighting people for a coconut in the grocery store. That would explain how I missed it."

"Calling me a half-lawyer," she muttered, shaking her head. "Serves him right. They had enough to do it without executing the search warrant, but they have one if y'all want to go out there. The police said they're going to later but just have too much on their plate for the next couple of days."

"I'll see what Joseph wants to do," I said, taking one of the files from her desk and going to mine to notarize a couple of documents I had watched her sign earlier.

When Joseph got out of his meeting, I asked if he was still interested in going out to look at the moonshine operation.

"Sure, why not?" he said. "Anyone else want to go?"

Paul shook his head without looking up from his computer, Melissa said something about getting the kids from basketball practice, and Mary wrinkled her nose. "No, thank you," she said.

So, changed into our jeans and rubber boots, we set out to observe. When we saw Tommy Bonner's zebra behind a fence, I knew we were close. "There's Jepp's truck, so it'll be the next one," I said. We drove on down to the closest farm.

The driveway was rough, but the Jeep took it easily. We got out at the farm, appearing to be the only ones on the property. Sure enough, in the barn right behind the house was all of the moonshining equipment. It was like the Baldwin sisters on *The Waltons*, only more high-tech. I would bet my bottom dollar Jepp had something very similar in his barn, the stinker.

I wondered if there was really any money in moonshining this day and age. Was it really so hard to get a license? Maybe it was the thrill of getting away with something.

"Cold?" Joseph asked.

I shrugged. "Not too bad." I had on my coat and gloves, and the sun was still fairly warm.

"I would like to walk back on the farm. It seems like the property is pretty extensive?"

"Yeah, these farms are pretty big," I agreed. We weren't too far from my grandma's house, so I knew the territory somewhat.

We walked along a fence line in a long, flat field that would probably be thick with corn next summer. We seemed to go for a mile, maybe a two. "I didn't realize it was *this* big," I said.

Joseph squinted in the distance. "I'm just wondering...why would there be eighteen wheelers back here? I think that's what I'm seeing."

"Some of the farmers have them," I answered. "Hauling grain to the mills and such."

"But back here, in the winter?" He shrugged. "It just seems odd to have them so far from the house."

I narrowed my eyes as we neared. "They don't look like grain hoppers, to be honest. Those are cargo containers, intermodal freight like they take to the ports in New Orleans or Savannah, and put on barges."

Joseph looked at me for a minute, but he wasn't really seeing me. His wheels were spinning. "Does our search warrant cover them?"

"Yep. Anything on the property."

We went over to them, but they were all locked up tight. Joseph looked around for a minute. I'm not sure I was on the same wavelength, but he was definitely thinking a mile a minute. His eyes scanned the horizon. There was a pretty nice shed that appeared to be empty, and a huge old barn just about to fall down. No one would approach it. It probably had all kinds of creepy-crawlies, and a strong wind would blow it over. Imagine the shacklety places they get reclaimed wood on HGTV shows, and you have a pretty good idea.

From the trailers to the barn, there was a lot of residue: a piece of plastic here, a broken pallet there, black plastic straps littering the way... And there were footprints; the grass was so worn it looked like a cow path from the barn outward. Only there were no cows here.

Joseph started walking toward the barn, and I followed him. He reached for one of the doors that looked like it was about to collapse and dragged it open. I tried to do the same with the other, but it was too heavy, and he came to do it for me.

We stood in the wide-open doorway. The first thing I noticed was that there were brand new support beams on the inside, cleverly crafted to bend with the falling angle of the barn. The second thing I noticed was pallets and crates. They went on and on, as I could see in the light of the sunbeams which reached the back of the barn.

In them were plastic bags of what appeared to be pure heroin.

My stomach dropped. I had read enough about heroin busts to know that we were looking at a *massive* supply. Worth *buckets* of money. Enough to supply addicts of entire small countries. Talk about a hornet's nest.

Joseph's eyes scanned in front of us. I felt his hand grab the back of my shirt. "Mississippi... We need to get out here. *Now.*"

I swallowed, the hair on the back of my neck standing.

We started running.

Joseph was clearly in better shape than I, but he dragged me along, clearing the way through brambles and brush as we came to a small wood near Jepp's property.

I looked over my shoulder. And I could have sworn that near where we had been standing examining the trailers a white Range Rover had just pulled up.

"Joseph... Tony!"

"Are you sure?"

I swallowed. "No."

"Whoever it is, if they've seen us..." Joseph didn't finish the sentence. We just kept running, praying, and running. Could we have gotten out just seconds before they showed up? I *never* imagined this. We hadn't even brought a gun, much less an officer!

I put two and two together. Tony on the phone at the grocery store, getting news that Dan had been arrested for moonshining, of all things. Knowing the property was about to be searched. A mad dash to load everything on container trucks and move them. But geez, how many people were involved? Reynolds Buford, their money launderer, was dead after threatening to get out. Jake Dillon, the hitman and vandalizer, was in jail, as was Dan Howell, whose property was headquarters. But there had been *a lot* of people out here on the farm over Christmas, if the worn grass was any indication.

We sprinted for so long.

"Joseph..." I was getting exhausted.

"You're fine, keep going," he said encouragingly. I knew he was right. I knew we were dead if we were seen. I just wasn't sure how much longer I could hold out. I couldn't even see Jepp's house yet.

I stumbled. "Please, I..."

Joseph grabbed my arms. "They had to have seen the Jeep, Mississippi," he said, looking into my eyes, willing me to understand. "When they came in."

My skin tingled. Why hadn't I thought of that? They *knew* we were here. They just didn't know *where*. With renewed energy borne of desperation, I nodded, and we set off again.

I had never been so happy as when I saw Jepp's farmhouse rise in the distance. Joseph pounded on the door, and when Mrs. Lewis answered, he told her quickly what was going on and asked her to bar the door and close the blinds. He took me to a chair. Hands on my shoulders, he looked at me. "Are you okay?"

I nodded, unable to speak. Each heartbeat seemed to propel the next, my throat burned, and I could scarcely breathe.

"Honey, do you need water?" Merla asked.

"Yes, please," Joseph answered for me. He took out his phone. There had been no cell service anywhere out on the farm, and it would appear that this inconvenience remained true here. Calmly, he added, "And we're going to need you to call the police, ma'am."

"Six hundred pounds of heroin," my mother read the next morning at Joseph's kitchen table. We were again corralled here with police guards. Joseph had called my mom to come and stay with me the night before. I *had* been pretty shaken up. She snored, but I had been glad to have her with me. I joked it was my fault for not letting Imani get me into shape. But the truth was, I was recovered from exhaustion. The trauma of having to run for your life... Well, that would take a little longer.

My mother stared, wide-eyed, at the newspaper. "The largest drug bust in the State of Tennessee, says the TBI. Well, well, well, haven't you been busy at work, young lady?"

she said. "And no additional arrests yet. How can that be?" she demanded.

If Tony Tonneau wasn't at the middle, directing the whole ring, with who-knew-how-many people involved, my name wasn't Mississippi Marie Whitson. I couldn't say that *here*, of course, given confidentiality rules. I had told the TBI about the Range Rover, and about how rare that brand of cars was in Hammondsville. But they had said it wasn't enough. Would anything ever be enough to nail Tony Tonneau?

My grandma, sipping Joseph's coffee (to which she had helped herself after swinging by) said, "You know they're saying the Tonneau boy may be involved. The handsome one." Honestly, it was like the woman read my mind sometimes.

"The one that was in Mississippi's class?" my mom asked.

I didn't participate. They knew I couldn't talk about stuff, and they never pushed me.

My mind wandered. There was a lot more questioning to be done. Joseph had offered to go in first so that I could sleep later, even though the strain in his eyes was pronounced. To be honest, I wondered how much more he could take. He looked like he was on his last thread.

"Didn't they always say Virgil Baker was his real daddy?"

I tuned back in. Who were we even talking about? The rumor mill in this town... If our elegant estate attorney wasn't immune from gossip, who was? "Who?" I demanded.

"Tony Tonneau," my grandma answered, shrugging. "That's who we were talking about."

My brain seemed to halt.

My mom nodded darkly, "Remember when all the rich people had those houses up on the river, and they got to swinging?" Seeing my stunned expression, my mother said, "Well, I'm sure they all regretted it very much, but never let me hear of you behaving in such a manner, Mississippi Whitson!"

It was useless to ask how this had turned around on me. It always did. I touched the table. My mom obviously thought we were just having an idle gossip, but my heart was hammering. "Wait. Tony Tonneau...is Virgil Baker's biological son?"

"That's what they say," my mom said, nodding like one in possession of a deep secret. Which, to be fair, it was. "Well, he looks just like him, if you think about it," she continued, unaware of my wheels spinning. "Handsome as all get out. Siddie Baker couldn't have kids, and it would have killed her if he'd left her for Priscilla Tonneau. And Roy Tonneau had been caught up in all that mess, too, so he just decided to look the other way. And there you have it." My mom sat back with satisfaction.

My memory started suggesting images to me. Virgil remembering I was in Tony's graduating class. Virgil remembering I was the *valedictorian* of that class. Virgil telling us he would vouch for Tony under any circumstances. Virgil trying to throw the dust in our eyes by mentioning Reynolds and Tilda Buford's bad divorce.

He knew. He was a good man at his core, and an attorney to boot. He had sworn an oath not to obstruct justice, to uphold the law and the Constitution. I would bet it was about to kill him. What would he have done if we had actually started *investigating* Tilda? The violation of personal ethics was monumental. Protecting his son had come at the highest cost for Mr. Baker, and no one could expect him to have gone this far. I was almost certain that if we told him the game was up, he would talk.

And if we got Tony Tonneau, we got the whole ring.

I stood, picking up my phone.

"Well, don't leave mad!" I heard my mom say.

I slipped into the library and dialed Joseph.

He answered on the second ring. "Hey." He didn't even sound like himself.

I swallowed. "Joseph... They need to get Virgil Baker in for questioning."

Chapter Twenty-Eight

Well, trust Southern gossip to bring down an entire interstate drug ring. Virgil Baker talked. Tony Tonneau was found halfway to Texas. I could only assume he had reasoned the whole thing was over and decided to leave the country. He hadn't counted on my mother remembering every juicy tidbit she had ever heard in her life.

Over the month of January, arrest after arrest was made, and the whole ring came crumbling down. It was all over but the shouting now. I wish I could have felt confident it would solve the drug problem in the area. I knew it wouldn't. But it was a start. And maybe no one else would die, the way Reynolds Buford had died.

As for me, my spirits were low. I had boxed up a lot of my stuff at the cottage. I couldn't stay here any longer. The truth was, I was no longer Joseph's employee. Saying farewells to everyone at the office had been difficult. I was completely wrecked, to be honest, when I broke away and made it to my car.

Joseph had vehemently denied that there was any need for me to leave the cottage, especially until I had another place lined up. I felt a pain in the pit of my stomach, but I had to move out. I wouldn't be a hanger on, relying on his goodwill. And I would *not* be dependent on a man. I would, you know, Jane Eyre-style, starve to death in a barren field first. And so I was (regretfully, you understand) going to stay with my mom until I figured out where to go.

As a long shot, I had sent some of my work to a swanky fashion design firm in Nashville simultaneously with filling out college applications. At the beginning of February as I was packaging up my Tupperware, I received an email from the firm offering me an internship. An internship that, if I wasn't mistaken, could turn into a job. My heart had jumped.

My mother would kill me if I didn't go to college. But I was wavering. It seemed like it could be a really good job. As it was, I was glad I had been saving my money. I had the nest egg I needed to get me through this new, uncharted phase.

I told this to Joseph in my yard on Leap Day. I stood on the cottage porch looking down at him. "It would probably be easier to move to Nashville than to commute."

He was quiet for a time, his eyes traveling over the planes of my face. "You're leaving Hammondsville?"

"All I've ever wanted is out." I felt false even as I said it. I could have an entirely new life in Nashville. But I could also take the internship and commute, at least for now. I wasn't sure what was motivating me anymore. Or what I wanted. All I knew was that my throat burned.

"You're...sure?" he asked softly.

"*Yes*," I said, with firmness.

He held my eyes for a long moment. He opened his lips to speak, closed them. "You know, Mississippi, Hammondsville... Well, you warned me about it frequently when I first moved here." He paused, seeming to consider. "But you're not indifferent to these people. You would take a bullet for them—literally."

I bit my lip. If I bit it hard enough, maybe the prickle in my nose wouldn't develop into anything.

"I don't know," he said. "Maybe it's some childish illusion I'm clinging to. But it always felt like home." He shook his head. He studied me, seemingly yearning, almost, to hold onto that child's belief in a place he had belonged.

"You didn't have to grow up here," I countered, passing this off. "You've been out in the world."

"When you hear John Denver's 'Take Me Home, Country Roads,' can you ever listen, and not think of Hammondsville and tear up?" He asked, almost as a challenge. "I never could."

I teared up just thinking about the song. But I didn't contradict him. "It's my one chance, Joseph," I whispered.

There was a long pause. At last, he nodded, holding my eyes. "And you deserve it, Mississippi," he said finally. Then he looked away. He was silent for a long moment.

He was still low, too. The stress had gotten to him. He had been under death threats for months, work had been otherwise trying, and it had all culminated in a harrowing escape.

I suddenly wondered if he was considering moving. Not like I had speculated before, but really this time. He had been through a lot. Going home had to be more than appealing.

I bit my lip.

Turning his head back toward me, he said, "Would it inconvenience you very much to stay at the cottage through the beginning of April?" He swallowed. "I need...some time off. If you could keep Fritz and Freida until..."

To be honest, it was stubborn pride that had made me declare I would move out before I found an apartment. We both knew it would be more convenient for me to stay. And I would do pretty much anything at this point for more time with Fritz and Freida. "Sure. Of course. Were you thinking to hang around and rest up?"

His striking eyes scanned over my face. I wasn't sure I had ever seen him look more vulnerable. "I was thinking of getting away."

My heart seized. I wasn't wrong. He was considering moving. Oh, he would stay to make the transition smooth for Paul, Melissa, and Mary. He wouldn't abandon the German shepherds at this point. But I knew him well enough by now to know that he was contemplating changing jobs.

And probably moving to New York.

I walked to my mailbox on the first day that felt the slightest bit like spring. Some buttercups were peeking up here and there, feeling a little bold and risky. Fritz and Frieda were snoozing inside, so I walked alone.

Looking up at the big house, it looked vacant, closed up, and missing life. Joseph was away on his vacation and had been for a week. Things—the whole property—felt different. Hammondsville even felt different. I mean, for crying out loud, you couldn't even drive through the downtown without seeing a hundred different projects the man had touched.

If he was leaving... I didn't know.

I opened my mailbox and pulled out my bills and the March issue of *Vogue Magazine*. Tucking all of it under my arm, I made the walk back down the driveway to the cottage. I closed the door behind me, wiping my feet.

Grabbing a glass of sweet tea, I went to sit down on my couch, putting my feet up on the coffee table and removing the magazine from its plastic wrapper. Pungent smells of perfume samples greeted me. I opened the cover, my eyes scanning over the initial fashion ads sharply. They rolled like beautiful credits, and I, of course, arrogantly considered how I could do better.

Then I flipped to the main life story. They were always wonderfully told, luring you in and sticking with you. But *this* one made me suck in a breath and sit up straight.

"Lillette Cane: In Her Son's Words, Twenty Years After Her Death."

I felt a little short of breath.

He gave the interview.

My hungry eyes lapped the words up. He talked about his mom and him, her career, and her lasting legacy. Just the things that mattered. Stories I had never heard, which made me have to stop to wipe a tear several times. It was beautiful. He had obviously put a lot of thought into what he wanted to say. He talked about where she had grown up. About their years together and the bond they had shared. About his reticence to give the interview. And about the friend who had encouraged him to do it...

Fumbling for my phone, I furiously dialed. I'm not even sure I looked at the phone. It was answered on the second ring.

"Hello?"

I swallowed. "Melissa..." I paused a long moment, taking two breaths. "Is Joseph in love with me?"

"Um...*yes*." My heart nearly stopped.

I swallowed, my heart rate suddenly kicking into high gear now. "Does everyone at the office know?"

"Yes," she said. "Everyone except you."

I covered my mouth.

"How'd you figure it out?" she asked.

"Well, I *thought* when... But I could never be sure. But he gave this interview that he really didn't want to give, and...oh I can't explain it. Melissa, I've got to go!"

She laughed. "Okay. Bye."

I flagged Imani down on her run, jogging up to her. She, of course, took my unprecedented exercise to mean that something was drastically wrong, probably that someone had died. Ignoring this slight, I panted, saying, "We need to talk! Can we talk?"

Taking my arm, she said, "Come sit down. What is it?" She sat beside me, looking at me in concern. "Are you crying? Is this about your applications?"

I shook my head. "I'm going to take the internship. That wasn't what I..." I swallowed, meeting her eyes. "I am in love with Joseph," I said, in a rush, tears spilling over.

"I know."

I met her eyes.

"I've been talking to Ahmad, and—"

"What?" I demanded.

"Your mama got his number for me. That isn't important. We've observed the facts: you two making that mind connection, him looking at you like you're *all* of his joy... The thing is: we're all agreed. The two of you have to be together."

"But I don't know if he wants that!" I exclaimed.

She examined me. Even she, who was always so certain, couldn't deny that there was a possibility she was mistaken here, given that he had never said anything. She squeezed my hand. "Well, I guess you better go and find out."

I wiped some tears. "He isn't here." My lip trembled. "I think he might be leaving, and—"

"Slow down, don't panic," she said. "Where is he?"

"In the Hamptons with his dad."

"Okay...plane tickets. We need plane tickets," she said, pulling out her phone.

"I can't..." She winced. We both knew such a purchase would put a significant dent in my nest egg. One I couldn't afford. I looked out across the road, desperate, heart pounding, fear rising. If I didn't see him, didn't tell him...

Imani similarly seemed to be considering. "What am I thinking? I'm rich," she said. "I'll write you a check."

"Imani—"

"Mississippi, if I can't fund my best friend's crazy attempt to bag the love of her life, what's the purpose of life?" she said, laughing, gripping my upper arms. "*Go!*"

Chapter Twenty-Nine

There were several things which occurred to me as soon as I touched down at La Guardia.

One: It was colder here than I had expected.

Two: It was a little creepy to show up at Joseph's dad's mansion. Technically, it was a violation of privacy and stalkerish.

Three: I had absolutely no hard proof Joseph had any interest in me. Melissa was notoriously...unrelational. She could be wrong. He had never made a move. I could think of reasons why he wouldn't, but still... I could be wrong.

Teeth chattering, I buttoned my all-too-flimsy coat and found my rental SUV (courtesy of Imani). Traffic was terrible. There was nothing like arriving right during morning rush hour in *New York City*.

Irritated, harassed, and pretty sure I looked like a bedraggled cat, I accepted that I would be lucky if I made it to the Hamptons by noon. And the Hamptons... The houses, the luxury, the *wealth*. Doubts crept up. Even if he did have feelings, surely he would come to his senses here. After all, he was a New York Ten, and I was a Tennessee Seven. Well, let's just go ahead and say Eight.

I swallowed, stopping the car in front of the right house. Its weathered shingles were deceptive. Everything was luxe, from the enormous bay windows to the grass. I would bet there was marble inside. Lots of it. My heart was pounding.

No one answered when I knocked.

Furthering my crimes, I went around back. In moments, I found myself in a formal garden. I shaded my eyes and looked out across the horizon.

What a view: the ocean in the backyard, sailboats dotting the vista... I didn't see anyone, but I did perceive birds swooping in to fish off the surface of the water. There were some kids far down the beach and evidence that a boat had been taken out recently. Maybe they weren't home.

Suddenly, I heard a noise, like footsteps on cobblestones. I turned.

"Mississippi?" I heard utter, whispered disbelief.

Joseph had come out of the boathouse. He looked *good.* Our eyes met.

He dropped whatever he was holding. "Why are you here?" His eyes, as blue as ever, examined my face. He walked toward me, taking my upper arms in his hands. He surveyed me, searching, intent.

"Nothing's wrong." I swallowed. "The thing is..." I paused. Then I met his eyes again. "You do belong, Joseph. In Hammondsville, I mean. It *is* your home. You're one of us. I'm not going anywhere. And I don't think you sho—"

One moment I was talking; the next— He swept me up right into his arms and kissed me within an inch of my life like he had been wanting to do that more than he had ever wanted anything in his whole life.

Trying to catch my breath after, I looked into his eyes with complete wonder. I was trembling. Breathless. Shaken. All the things they said would happen.

I swallowed. "Joseph..." I croaked. Where were those words I had prepared? I scarcely remembered my own name, let alone the thoughts I had torturously typed out on the plane. "I felt like you understood me. Like I didn't have to *explain* to you. It felt right and comfortable, and exciting and real, and I'm not sure what happened, but I—"

"Mississippi." He shook his head. His eyes held mine, and then he put it much more simply: "We fell in love."

My heart skipped a beat. "It's happened to me before," he added, "or some poor comparison of it, but I don't think it will happen again." That was kind of a serious statement, if you think about it. I knew he had been in love before. But I'm pretty sure he was trying to tell me that I was the love of his life.

My eyes welled up. "Why didn't you say...?" I whispered.

His fingers had been exploring my jawline, his eyes on my lips, but at that he looked up, almost put out. "Mississippi!" he exclaimed, eyes wide, although he obviously was trying to contain himself. "Half the time, I wasn't even sure you *liked* me!"

That was...fair. I bit my lip on a smile. His eyes danced. He looked better now. He was himself again, full of life and vitality.

"Whereas *I*," he pressed, "would have felt like I was cheating on you if I had even *looked* at another woman from about the second time we met!"

I took his face in my hands and kissed *him*, although it soon became entirely reciprocal. It was deeper this time. Let's just say he was a good kisser. It was as if he created an impression where the world blurred. We were so focused on each other that I couldn't have told you where we were, what I was wearing, or what state we were in.

We explored pleasurably until we found our music together, and it didn't take long at all. The give and take flowed as rhythmically as a Tennessee stream.

At *long* last, we finished the kiss, my legs weak. He said softly, face close to mine, "I love you, Mississippi. And I'm not leaving Hammondsville." He rested his forehead against mine.

I could feel him smiling, admitting that he had almost considered it, acknowledging the town's craziness and his for staying, along with his tender love for the place. And for me.

He studied me, blue eyes shining in their joyful, completely loving way. "Thank God for you, Mississippi," he said. I shook my head self-deprecatingly. "No, I *do*! Where would I be without you?" he demanded, gratitude and awe in his voice.

I bit my lip, staving off tears. "Well, probably straight off a cliff, to be honest," I said.

His eyes twinkled. I twinkled back.

"Come," he said, taking my hand in his. "Meet my dad."

I looked at him questioningly, a little nervously.

"I think you should," he said, smiling with a pointed look.

I smiled, joy spreading through me. And Reader, I think you know what this meant. I was getting a Jewish wedding.

THE END

Author's Note

Dear Readers,

Cue "Two Doors Down." I hope you enjoyed Mississippi's story as much as I came to do over the course of writing it! Just a couple of notes on the story...

I wanted to mention that Joseph *technically*, without the work-arounds mentioned, wouldn't meet state residency requirements for holding his particular office. I also know none of you care. This is purely informational and for the benefit of my attorney friends who might catch it!

I strove for accuracy, but you shouldn't take the book as the last word on the way the justice system works. While I am a practicing attorney, I am not a criminal attorney, and it is possible that there are mistakes. In addition, the story is fictional. There were some adjustments for the sake of the storyline or pacing.

Thanks for taking a wild ride to Tennessee with me!

Many Thanks...

To Kaiser and Lukas, between whom and Fritz and Frieda any resemblance is *purely* coincidental. Kaiser graced ages two through fifteen of my life—the most loyal, protective, and intelligent dog. Lukas graced ages sixteen through twenty-eight—the most fun-loving, affectionate, and *funny* dog. We lost Lukas while I was writing this book, and it was very cathartic to write Fritz and Frieda as characters. We laughed and loved so much as a family over the years because of our two German shepherds, and I wanted to give Fritz and Frieda a special place in Mississippi's heart.

To my mom, dad, and sister, all of whom read the book and offered valuable suggestions. To my beta readers, Rian Rowland and Beverly Crouch, for your much-appreciated feedback and support!

To my sister-in-law, an even bigger Dolly fan than Mississippi. Thanks for taking my author photo!

To my brother, in the legal depths with me every day. It's an honor to work with you.

To all of the law enforcement (police, attorneys, judges, court officers, probation officers, clerks, legal secretaries, paralegals, investigators, and more) who drink from a fire-hose every day out trying to sort out criminal matters for the community—you have my tremendous respect.

To all of the Southerners I consulted to determine whether there was any irreverence in the title I chose for this book, all of whom assured me that if we are *thanking* God, it is not the same as using it in an oath.

To my friends, family, acquaintances, and more for giving me endless delightful Southern fodder for the story. Don't worry; you're all safe. No character was based on any person. Only events, lines, actions, and circumstances were plucked from here and there—and *most* everything that happens *is* based on true stories. But I'll never tell.

And, as always, to my God. Thank You for having a sense of humor, and for reminding me not to take myself too seriously. Humor is such a gift, and all good things come from You.

TARA

Books by Tara Cowan

About the Author

TARA COWAN is the author of the *Torn Asunder Series*. A huge lover of all things history, she loves to travel, watch British dramas, read good fiction, and spend time with her family. An attorney, Tara lives in Tennessee and is busy writing her next novel.

Tara holds a Bachelor of Science Degree in Political Science with minors in English and History from Tennessee Tech University and a Doctor of Jurisprudence from the University of Tennessee College of Law.

To connect with Tara, visit her blog at www.TeaAndRebellion.com, follow her on Instagram, or find her on Facebook or Twitter.

Made in the USA
Coppell, TX
13 October 2022